Whisper of Love

The Bradens
at Peaceful Harbor

Love in Bloom Series

Melissa Foster

ISBN-10: 1941480586
ISBN-13: 9781941480588

Cover Design: Elizabeth Mackey
Cover Photographer: Sara Eirew

WORLD LITERARY PRESS
PRINTED IN THE UNITED STATES OF AMERICA

A Note to Readers

I've had Nash and Phillip in my heart for more than a year, and have been eagerly awaiting bringing them together with Tempest. They're each incredibly special. I hope you fall as hard for them as I have.

Sign up for my newsletter to keep up to date with new releases and to receive an exclusive short story.
www.melissafoster.com/News

The Bradens are just one of the series in the Love in Bloom big-family romance collection. Characters from each series make appearances in future books so you never miss an engagement, wedding, or birth. A complete list of all series titles is included at the end of this book, along with previews of upcoming publications.

Visit Melissa's Reader Goodies page for…

– Complete Love in Bloom series list
– FREE Love in Bloom ebooks
– FREE downloadable reading order, series checklists, and more

Love in Bloom Subseries Order
Snow Sisters
The Bradens
The Remingtons
Seaside Summers
The Ryders
Billionaires After Dark
Harborside Nights

Standalone Romance Titles
Tru Blue
Truly, Madly, Whiskey

For my mother

Chapter One

"THERE ARE TWO types of people in this world, Tempe." Jillian Braden moved across the kitchen floor in her sky-high heels with a glass of Diet Pepsi in one hand and a purple scarf in the other. "There are people like me, whose brains never sleep, and there are people like you, whose brains need to sleep." She wound the soft purple fabric around Tempest's neck and fluffed Tempest's long blond hair. She'd made the scarf for Tempest's six-year-old client who was undergoing chemotherapy. "I could never hate you for being who you are. I love who you are."

"I just don't want you to think I'm ungrateful." Tempest set her guitar case on the floor and hugged her petite cousin with whom she'd lived for the past three weeks. "Thank you for making this. She's going to love it." She admired the scarf, then put it in her bag for her visit with Mary later that morning.

After moving her children's music therapy business to Pleasant Hill, an hour and a half drive with traffic from her home in Peaceful Harbor, Tempest had needed a place to stay, and Jillian had been gracious enough to offer her a room. She and her cousin were as different as night and day. Jillian, a fashion designer and owner of a high-end, slightly outlandish dress shop, worked all night, slept odd hours, and still somehow managed to function like the Energizer Bunny all day long, while Tempest required a solid seven or eight hours of sleep, lots of coffee, and tranquility.

Jillian gulped her Diet Pepsi and set the empty glass in the sink. It was seven thirty in the morning, and she'd been up all night working on a new design. Unfortunately, her studio was above the guest room where Tempest was staying, and Jillian had a penchant for dancing while she worked. They'd lived together for three weeks, and if Tempest didn't get some sleep soon, she just might begin writing angry rock songs instead of the serene melodies her music therapy clients needed.

"So what's your plan?" Jillian fluffed Tempest's hair again.

She had a way of touching those around her, making them feel special and loved without appearing too handsy. Tempe had always been a little jealous of that ability. She wasn't cold by any means, but she was *careful*. Careful in life, careful with her emotions, and careful with herself. *Too* careful. At closer to thirty than twenty, she was feeling hemmed in by her small hometown and, she had to admit, by her own careful nature. Moving to Pleasant Hill offered a fresh start for the direction of her business, and maybe, *just maybe*, the new town would expand her social life, too. That is, if she ever got enough rest to actually enjoy going out and meeting people.

"I'll look for a room to rent someplace quiet until I see how my business grows and I can afford a place of my own. Or not, I guess," she said, feeling disheartened. "There's no need to sign a year lease until I'm sure I can make a go of things here." She worked part-time at the hospital playing music for the pediatrics ward and ran a children's musical playgroup two days a week at the community center, with the hope of one day taking the playgroup full-time. She was also still traveling back to Peaceful

Harbor every weekend to work with a client until her therapy program had run its course.

"Oh, please. Once the moms around here meet you, they'll be clamoring to sign their kids up. When you're at Emmaline's, check out her posting board. It's always covered with ads. I bet you can find a cheap room for rent there." Jillian looked at her reflection in the door of the microwave, using one finger to brush her wispy brown-slash-burgundy bangs from her forehead.

Emmaline O'Connor and Jillian had grown up together. She owned a café, appropriately named Emmaline's, in the center of town. It was one of Tempest's favorite cafés because the people were so friendly, it reminded her of home.

"That's a great idea. I'm so focused on coffee or breakfast when I go there, I forgot she even has an ad board. Good luck with your designs." Tempest picked up her guitar and pulled the strap of her bag across her body.

"No designing today. I'm going to sleep for two hours, and then I've got a group of girls coming into the shop for fittings." Jillian headed for the stairs. "I don't want you going to strange houses alone, so call me if you find someplace you want to check out. If I can't go, we'll grab one of my brothers."

Tempe laughed as Jillian's voice faded at the top of the stairs. She'd never escape her cousins' overprotective nature. It was in their blood. *Just like being careful is in mine.* She buried that thought deep, because part of her worried she was fighting a losing battle by trying to break out of her cautious ways. But as a trained therapist she knew how her own insecurities could stifle her ability to grow and expand her horizons. She'd convinced her younger sister, Shannon, to spread her wings and move to Colorado, and now Shannon was madly in love and living with the man of her dreams, Steve Johnson. If only Tempe could convince herself to take a few risks, she just might get lucky, too.

"Tempe!" Jillian yelled from upstairs.

"Yeah?"

"Don't forget, we're meeting Jax and Nick for drinks tomorrow around five at Tully's Tavern."

"I work until five, so I'll meet you shortly after."

"Fine. But don't blow us off!"

She cringed. She'd blown off Jillian's invitations to happy hour pretty often over the past three weeks in lieu of taking advantage of the peace and quiet at home. But she loved seeing her cousins, and she hadn't seen Nick in months. She hollered upstairs, "I won't. Gotta run!"

It was early September. Soon the leaves would take on beautiful fall colors, and she'd pull out her sweaters and knit caps. She faced the oncoming breeze as she walked to her car, reveling in the reprieve from Maryland's scorching late-summer temperatures. She placed her guitar in the trunk and settled into the driver's seat, humming the tune of the song she was writing for her client who was in a coma, and drove toward the center of town.

While Peaceful Harbor was anchored by long stretches of beach, Pleasant Hill was defined by rolling hills and sprawling pastures. The town of Pleasant Hill was busier than the harbor, although it wasn't much larger. Brick buildings and upscale shops lined wide, brick-paved sidewalks along the main streets. Flowering dogwood trees were planted along grassy areas on each corner, providing shade above wooden benches.

Tempe rounded a beautifully landscaped cul-de-sac in the center of town and parked in the lot behind the café. Surrounded by a sea of high-end cars, she noted the difference from home, where most of the vehicles were pickup trucks, Jeeps, or convertibles, with a requisite amount of sand in the bumpers. She missed her quiet apartment overlooking the water, where she could sit outside and smell the ocean while she played her guitar. She was sure the change in scenery would be even more inspiring once she had a chance to enjoy it. She had a notebook full of ideas for song lyrics, but she desperately needed peace and quiet to put them together.

She followed a couple into the café, inhaling the invigorating scent of fresh roasted coffee and warm, baked breads. A gigantic chalkboard boasted today's coffee specials in bright pink and breakfast specials in green, interspersed with happy sayings written in blue like, "Find your happy place," and "Create your life!" Sunny yellow walls featured beautiful paintings from local artists, round tables lined the walls of the narrow café, and in the rear, a spiral staircase led to a loft with more seating. If the café weren't so busy, she'd try to write there.

"Morning, Tempe," Emmaline, a vivacious brunette, called from behind the counter, where she was filling a to-go cup. "Jilly just texted. The ad board's over there." She pointed to an overflowing corkboard on the far side of the register.

"Thanks." Shaking her head at her overzealous cousin, she weaved around an elderly couple and a group of women to get a better look at the board. Help-wanted ads, ads for maid services, rooms for rent, and what seemed like a hundred miscellaneous items for sale were stuck to the board by colorful pushpins. A flyer announcing a children's art boutique opening caught her eye, and she tore off one of the dangling strips of paper with the time, date, and place of the event and tucked it into her purse, making a mental note to ask the owner if she could play her guitar at the opening. She had a business to grow, and networking was everything. In fact, she realized, the café was the perfect place to catch the attention of busy moms who might need a break during the week. She made another mental note to make flyers for her children's group and put them up around town.

Turning back to the board, she ripped off another tab from a flyer announcing a fall concert. There would be plenty of places to network *and* things to do if she could just find a place to sleep. A piece of white paper with crayon markings on the edges peeked out from between an ad for a car for sale and a blood drive. Drawn in by the cute childlike markings, she moved the other ads to the side, revealing an ad written in messy handwriting. *Single room for rent. Quiet setting. No college kids. No partiers.*

Now, that seemed perfect.

"Jilly said you're looking for a place to rent," Emmaline said as she handed her a to-go cup.

Tempest didn't have to taste it to know it was her favorite, a caramel French vanilla latte. "Hopefully an affordable, *quiet* place."

"If you want affordable," Emmaline said, "avoid anything near the center of town. Did you get tired of Jilly's crazy hours? I swear that girl hasn't slept a wink since sixth grade."

Tempest laughed. "She's a bundle of energy. Unfortunately, I need quiet, so…" She pointed to the ad she was interested in. "This one looks like it might be perfect."

Emmaline made a *tsk* sound. "I know most of the people who put up these ads, but I don't know much about the guy who put up that one. He's real quiet. Has the cutest little boy, but…I don't know."

"Do you think he's a bad guy?"

"No, not necessarily." She leaned closer and said, "He's an *artist*," as if that explained her concerns. "He lives on the outskirts of town, keeps to himself. That's about all I know. He's just…I don't know. Maybe I'm being overly critical. He's mysterious. *Yes, that's the right word for him.*"

Tempest breathed easier. "A reclusive, mysterious artist with a cute kid? He just might be the perfect housemate." After chatting for a few more minutes and promising to pass along a hug to Jillian, Tempest headed out to her car and called the number from the ad.

"Hello?" A deep voice came gruffly through the phone.

"Hi." Caught off guard by his harsh tone, she forced herself not to be judgmental. "I'm calling about the room for rent."

"It's a single room. Four fifty a month. You're not a college kid, are you?"

"No. You're not a serial killer, are you?"

He was quiet for a moment, and she held her breath. *No joking with Mr. Serious.*

"Not today I'm not."

His voice was so powerful, so serious, she thought about Jillian's offer to accompany her. *The guy put up a flyer in a public place, and according to Emmaline, he has a son. Surely he isn't collecting bodies on the outskirts of town.* She thought of her cousin Nick, one of Jillian's older brothers, who could be just as gruff as this guy sounded, but he wouldn't hurt a fly. Unless they hurt his family. Then all bets were off.

"You want to see the room?" he asked.

"Sure." Her heart hammered against her chest. They agreed to meet after she was done at the hospital, exchanged names, and she wrote down the address. "Great. I'll see you this evening." After the call she immediately pulled up the Internet and searched *artist Nash Morgan*.

The few articles she found were dated more than four years ago, focusing on his artwork being sold in galleries along the East Coast. The accompanying pictures of his intricate wood and metal sculptures took her breath away. She searched back in time, seeking a picture of the gruff man behind the talent, but the only photograph was dated more than ten years ago. He was sitting on the hood of a truck wearing a pair of faded jeans and a gray T-shirt. Several leather bracelets circled one wrist, and a silver ring shone on his right ring finger. Dirty-blond hair stuck out from beneath a red Washington Nationals baseball cap. He had a small, beautiful mouth that curved up at the edges and a hint of a five o'clock shadow. His smallish dark eyes were fringed with lashes so thick they looked fake.

Handsome and artsy, an irresistible combination.

She set her phone on the passenger seat, telling herself she shouldn't be thinking that way about the man who might become her landlord. As she drove toward the hospital, his image lingered in her mind. She struggled to reconcile the unguarded man in the photograph with the gruff one with whom she had just spoken.

NASH MORGAN SHIFTED his three-year-old son, Phillip, onto his hip and reached behind him to shut the gate. The chickens scurried away amid cackles and mad wing flaps. He set Phillip on the ground, and his son shook his head, shrugging like he'd been doing this for twenty years and couldn't believe the chickens still ran from them. He ruffled his boy's springy dark curls, drawing a serious, expectant look and an out-stretched hand from Phillip. Nash loved his little man's eagerness to get started on their evening chores. He handed him a smaller bucket from inside his larger one and nodded toward the coop.

Phillip returned the nod and clomped his booted feet into the coop to collect the eggs. Nash adjusted his baseball cap, listening as Phillip counted off each egg with an "Mm-hm."

He drew in a deep breath, hoping, for the millionth time, that he was doing enough for his son. He was the only parent Phillip had. Or rather, the only one who wanted him, a fact that never failed to grate on him like nails dragging along a chalk-board. His cell phone rang and Larry Robert's number flashed on the screen. Nash uttered a curse. Larry owned a gallery in North Carolina, and he'd given Nash his first big break. A break that could have carried him to a lifetime of success. But after Phillip was born he'd been unable to keep up with the demands of custom orders. Larry was opening another gallery in Virginia, and he wanted to feature Nash's work. Nash had turned him down, but Larry was persistent.

Swallowing the acidic taste of disappointment, he let the call go to voicemail and looked across the yard at the barn, which served as his workshop for the furniture he made and sold in town. He'd long ago locked up his metalworking and wood-sculpting workshop and stored his unfinished work. Gallery-worthy pieces, if he ever had the time to finish them. *Pipe dreams.* He'd had them, even made them a reality for a while. But that was a long time ago, and there was no sense thinking about something that could never be—at least not until Phillip was much older.

He ducked into the coop and checked the chickens' food

and water. Scanning the nesting beds, he snatched up the few eggs Phillip had missed. Phillip leaned against Nash's leg and yawned. Nash couldn't imagine anyone not loving their child with all their heart, but Phillip's mother, Alaina, had taken off three months after their son was born, and other than receiving official documents releasing her from her parental rights, he hadn't heard from her since. Not a day passed that he didn't worry about the long-term effects her leaving would have on his son.

"Good job, Phillip." He said his son's name so fast it came out sounding like "Flip." He set down his bucket, wrapped his arms around his boy, and whispered in his ear, "I love you, little dude." He kissed his cheek and scooped him up, earning the sweetest giggle known to man.

Nash grabbed the buckets and headed for the goat pen. Big and Little, the two goats, trailed behind them as Phillip followed Nash through the process of checking their food and water and sweeping out the goat house, as he did every night. Phillip wiggled the nozzle of the water pipe, just as Nash had, mimicking his "Hm." Nash tossed a cup of oats in the food bin and waited while Phillip did the same. Big nibbled on Phillip's shirt, and Phillip leaned down and kissed his head.

"C'mon, buddy." Nash had grown up in rural Virginia. Most of his friends had lived on farms, and he had no doubt that caring for animals would help Phillip learn responsibility. Not to mention that his son adored all types of animals, from squirrels to goats to worms. That was just fine with Nash. In his experience, animals were a lot more trustworthy than people.

The sound of tires on gravel drew his attention. He scooped Phillip into his arms, locked the goat pen, and grabbed the buckets.

"Visitor," he said, carrying Phillip toward the house and eyeing the Prius parking behind his old Ford pickup truck. His truck was a gas guzzler, but as much as he hated that, he needed the bed of the truck to haul the furniture he made into town. He hoped Tempest Braden, the woman coming to see the room he was renting out, wasn't a preachy tree hugger. Hell, he hoped she would turn out to be the silent type so he could pretend she didn't live in their house.

Phillip's brows knitted, his hands firmly planted around Nash's neck. He wasn't used to visitors. The last several people who had come to see the room they had for rent hadn't been the kind of people Nash wanted around his son. They'd rubbed him the wrong way—too aggressive, too loud, too shady, too flighty. He just needed a stable, responsible person to rent the room so he could afford to upgrade a few of his tools and start saving for Phillip's future. He tightened his grip on his son and headed up to meet the tall blonde stepping from the car.

Her wispy skirt fluttered around her knees. Large pink roses with muted green leaves looked as if they'd been thrown onto the flimsy white material haphazardly. A fringe of lace lined the edges. On anyone else the flouncy, floral skirt might look immature. But her legs went on forever, and coupled with her tight, curve-hugging tank top, she looked like Sweet and Sexy collided at the corner of Sinful Temptation.

She turned as he approached, and Nash stopped in his tracks, standing still as a stone. The setting sun caught her hair, highlighting several different shades of blond in long, cascading layers that hung to the middle of her back. Her nose was slightly upturned, and she had a cute, rounded chin. He'd never seen such natural beauty.

She smiled and tilted her head. "Nash?"

Shaking his head to clear his thoughts, he forced his legs to carry him forward. "Yes. Tempest?"

She met him halfway up the hill. "Thanks for seeing me so quickly." She peered into the buckets. "I hope I'm not interrupting."

"Evening routine. Did you have any trouble finding us?" She was even more beautiful up close. Her hair was tousled, as if she hadn't brushed it all day, and her eyes were so light blue, they had starbursts of white around the pupils, sparkling like diamonds. It had been a long time since any woman had caught Nash's interest, and he reminded himself to rein in that attraction. The last thing he needed were complications in Phillip's life. Even for a girl with the most spectacular blue eyes he'd ever seen.

"No. Your directions were perfect." She smiled at Phillip, and when she spoke again her voice was soft as a summer's breeze. "What's your name, cutie pie?"

Phillip's fingers dug into his neck. Nash nodded his approval.

"Flip," Phillip said.

Tempest's eyes widened with amusement. "Flip? That's a unique name." That beautiful smile lit up her face again. "I'm Tempest, but everyone calls me Tempe. It's nice to meet you both."

When she turned that smile on Nash, his entire body heated up. As a sea lover, he knew the word *tempest* meant a violent storm. It was obvious what type of unexpected storm this sweet-natured, soft-spoken beauty could cause, and he couldn't afford to be caught in a squall.

"My son's name is Phillip." He said it faster than he'd meant to, and realized his son's name came out sounding like

Flip. He'd also said it harsher than he'd intended. Reeling in his attraction was going to make him look like an asshole.

"Then Flip it is."

The way she said it sounded so damn cute, he wasn't about to correct her.

"Flip," Phillip repeated.

"Come on, I'll show you the room." He caught a whiff of her floral perfume on the way inside. It had been a long time since he'd smelled anything so feminine. Maybe this housemate thing wasn't such a good idea after all.

Chapter Two

EYES THAT HAD gone slightly hard *and* a father? At least Tempest was safe from fantasizing *too* much about the six-four-or-so stud leading her through his front door. He was strikingly handsome, with thick Viking-like legs and shoulders made for carrying the weight of the world, but she wasn't into married men, and tension rolled off this guy like a heat wave.

He led her through a rustic living room with stunning, hand-carved wooden furniture. The scuffed wood floors had seen better days, and the walls were painfully bare. A fireplace, dark with ashes, was tucked between two bookshelves on the far wall, each packed from top to bottom with books and toys. A leather couch sat before a coffee table littered with toys. A soft-looking child's blanket lay across the arm of the couch, and the sunken end cushion revealed Nash's favorite spot to sit. She imagined him and Flip curled up on the couch. Spicy scents of wood and *man* hung in the air.

"Hold up," he said, and disappeared into the kitchen to the left of the foyer. She heard running water and assumed he was washing their hands. He returned a minute later without the buckets and motioned for her to follow him upstairs.

The muscles in his back rippled beneath his white T-shirt.

Flip peered over his father's shoulder. His skin was the color of chestnuts, and he hadn't lost that sweet toddler chubbiness yet. A shock of dark curls hung over his eyes and brushed along his collar. He and his father could both use a trim, but the longish hair made Flip even cuter—and softened some of his father's rough edges, the way it peeked out from beneath his red baseball cap. She wondered if that was the same hat he'd had on in the picture she'd seen online.

"I read that you were a sculpture artist. Did you make the furniture in the living room?" She stepped onto the landing of a barren, narrow hallway. He obviously didn't believe in decorating.

His lips parted in surprise. "You checked up on me?"

"Single girl going to a stranger's house. I call it being safe." She had wondered about there being no recent articles about him, but it was clear that he was protective of his son and their privacy.

"Probably a smart move. Yes, I made it." He motioned toward the bedroom at the end of the hall.

She glanced into another bedroom as she passed. A child-size bed with an intricately carved headboard sat against the wall. A lamp sat atop a tall dresser beside the window. In the center of the room, plastic tools lay beside a heap of plastic and wooden animals on a plush navy rug. She took that all in quickly, her attention drawn to the left side of the room, where intricately carved squirrels perched along branches of tall, sculpted trees. They looked as if they'd grown right out of the floor. Nearly life-size wooden carvings of raccoons, bears, birds, and deer in various stages of play also decorated the wall, making the entire room feel like a veritable forest. The hours it must have taken to create the scene were nothing compared to the love Nash had obviously poured into them. She stole a glance at the big, brooding father, who was completely focused on his son, silent messages she couldn't read passing between them.

She continued down the hall, thinking about the mysterious man following her. His demeanor, and his size, made him appear hard, but she'd glimpsed moments of softness in the way he held and looked at his son.

She pushed those thoughts away as she entered a cozy, L-shaped bedroom. The walls were painted a dull wine color, which might feel oppressive if not for two sets of French doors that led to a small deck off the back of the house. Cream-colored drapes framed the glass doors. A bed, dresser, and nightstand took up the space to the left, and a gorgeous claw-footed bathtub sat beneath a set of windows in a nook to the right. The tub faced one set of French doors, providing a gorgeous view of the yard. She imagined relaxing in the tub at the end of a long day. The room had old-fashioned charm, and the bathtub made it feel luxurious despite its small size.

"Does the bathtub work?" She moved across the hardwood to check out the tub. It was sparkling clean, save for an old and rusted faucet.

"No." He hiked his thumb over his shoulder. "The bathroom is down the hall."

She tried to hide her disappointment. "Have you lived here long?"

He ran a gentle hand down Flip's back. "About four years."

Her mind spun with questions. Had he rented the room out before? Had his wife moved out, taking half of their family's earnings with her and leaving him short on cash? Did he share custody of Flip? Why had he named his son *Flip*? Was it a family name? A nickname? She decided to focus on the room itself, and not the reasons it was available, the adorable child's name, or his baby mama. *One thing at a time.*

It was slightly dark, rather small, and she'd prefer a private bathroom, but despite all of that, the room, and the house, had a homey feeling. As if it had somehow soaked up the love Nash had for his son. She looked over as he brushed a kiss to Flip's forehead. Sharing a house with a quiet guy like him would definitely provide hours of uninterrupted time for writing songs and making plans for the Girl Power group she helped her sister-in-law run.

"May I?" She motioned to the French doors.

His heavily muscled body moved swiftly past her, his large hand swallowing the handle as he unlatched the lock and held the door open for her. An act of chivalry or control, she couldn't be sure. That perfect mouth of his was set in such a serious line, she felt a challenge growing inside her to make it curve up in the smile she'd been thinking about since she'd seen his picture. If not for the dirty-blond hair, silver ring on his right hand, and leather bracelets around his wrist, she might think he was a different man from the one she'd seen online.

She stepped outside, feeling his presence like a powerful guard dog behind her. His authoritative demeanor relayed a sense of safety despite his brusqueness. Maybe she was just used to that from growing up around overprotective brothers.

"The property follows the tree line," he said a little more kindly.

The pastoral views took her breath away. A lush forest buffered the property from the rest of the world. Not that there were neighbors close by. His house was on the edge of town, about fifteen minutes from any other residential areas, which suited her perfectly. Colorful wildflowers grew in patches along the tree line and throughout the yard. A picnic table sat a few feet away from the house with an upside-down bucket in the center of it, and a short distance away there was a bonfire pit that looked as though it had been recently used. The land sloped gently to the left, leading to a chicken coop and another animal pen of some sort. At the base of the hill, a large, weathered barn faced the road. The deck ran the length of the house, with a built-in bench on either end. On the other side of the house she spotted another, smaller barn, a pond she hadn't seen from the road, and a large vegetable garden. Her heart skipped a beat at how calming the setting would be after a long day of work. It wasn't the beach, but it was definitely the next best thing.

"Do you keep animals other than chickens?" she asked.

"Goats, a few barn cats."

"And what's in the barns?"

He pointed to the weathered barn by the animal pens. "My workshop's there." Motioning toward the barn by the pond, his expression grew darker. "Supplies for work. It stays locked."

That answer might make her nervous if it weren't for his adorable son. But it made her even more curious. Flip rested his head on Nash's shoulder with a sleepy sigh. He looked tiny against his father's broad chest and brawny arms. Nash kissed his forehead, gently stroking his back. *You might be gruff, but you love your boy.*

She followed the deck to the other side of the house, passing the window to Flip's bedroom and finding another set of French doors at the far end. The curtains were open, the master bedroom in full view. Toys and a child's fluffy, animal-print blanket lay on the center of an unmade bed. A dark wooden dresser took up residence opposite the bed. There were no pictures on the walls or decorations of any kind in there either, which struck her as odd, although it was clear that he'd put a lot of effort into decorating his son's room.

"Will I have a chance to meet your wife?" She wasn't above fishing for information.

He brushed a hand protectively over Flip's head, and when he met her gaze again, it was with a slightly warmer expression. "It's just us, but I can assure you I'm not the kind of guy who would try to take advantage of you."

"Oh, I didn't mean…I don't think you'd do that. I was just curious who else lived in the house." She hurried back to the bedroom, feeling awkward for making him think she was worried about that, and tried to focus on her surroundings, rather than the urge to flee from embarrassment. She could picture herself sitting on the deck playing her guitar and writing songs, taking a moonlight walk in the yard, maybe working in the garden if he'd allow it.

"How would this work?" she asked. "I've never rented a room from someone I didn't know before. Would I put my groceries in the kitchen with yours?"

He motioned toward the hall, and she followed him downstairs to the kitchen, which was as rustic as the rest of the house. Dark wooden cabinets with nondescript countertops lined the right side of the room. A red plastic bucket sat beside the sink, along with another plastic hammer. The little boy must love tools. A farmhouse-style table took up most of the left side of the room. A pile of crayons and paper lay in the center. A pretty iron light hung above the table. The kitchen felt lived in and inviting. It would be simple to brighten up the place. *A few vases of wildflowers, a fresh coat of paint.* But she wasn't there to decorate. She was there to find a quiet, safe place to live, and this might just work perfectly.

Nash opened a door that led to a walk-in pantry, which was full of canned foods, water bottles, and a few essential children's staples like oatmeal, cold cereal, and macaroni and cheese. He kissed Flip's forehead as he moved to the refrigerator and pulled it open, revealing the buckets of eggs he'd been carrying earlier along with a few grocery items.

He tilted his head to one side, his lips twitching in an *almost* smile. "Plenty of room for your food."

She was glad he was easing up. "Are there house rules I should know about?"

"The safety of my son comes first. So I wouldn't want a stream of men coming in and out of the house."

She stifled a laugh. Obviously he had no idea how lame her social life was. The list of available men in Peaceful Harbor who didn't feel like family was short and littered with too much history to ignore. "That's not a problem."

"Are you a heavy drinker? A smoker? I won't allow drugs in my house."

She crossed her arms, wondering what type of people had tried to rent the room in the past. "Do I seem like a raging alcoholic or a drug user to you?"

"Just looking after my son," he said with absolutely no apology in his voice or his expression.

She admired the seriousness with which he took his parental responsibilities and let that lack of apology slide. Lord knew she'd seen enough parents who weren't nearly as careful.

"Do *you* have any bad or strange habits, or…?" *Late-night visitors?* She bit back the question. He might reek of rugged, brooding maleness, which equated to a hell of a lot of sex appeal, but she doubted he had a revolving bedroom door. He was as closed off as Fort Knox, and he was clearly too protective of his son to let strangers anywhere near him.

His eyes never left hers, and the combination of the silence and his piercing stare was like a slow-burning fire. A flutter of attraction she didn't realize she'd been tamping down bloomed inside her. *Okay, maybe he could have a revolving bedroom door. After his son goes to bed at night.* She inhaled a shaky breath, taking a closer, more assessing look at him. The tension around his mouth made her wonder if the heat she felt was one-sided, which was a good thing since she shouldn't be attracted to her potential landlord. Why was she, anyway? He wasn't exactly warm and welcoming. She told herself his incredible body would *not* look good naked, and his enormous hands would *not* feel heavenly on her skin. She snapped her mouth closed against the barrage of unfamiliar—*and inappropriate!*—racy thoughts.

NASH LINGERED IN the mental space between thinking this was a bad idea and the reality of needing the income from the rented room. And then there was the beautiful blonde with the inquisitive mind, looking at him like she was trying to figure him out. *Good luck with that.* He was still trying to figure himself out. A few years ago he'd thought he had life figured out. Now he was just trying to make it from day to day without fucking up his son.

He realized he hadn't answered her question and said, "No strange habits. You?"

"Strange habits?" She shook her head. "I'm pretty dull, actually. I spend most of my free time either hanging out with family, playing guitar, or writing music for my music therapy clients."

"You play guitar?" He hadn't picked a guitar up in years. There was a time when his guitar was his constant, and only, companion. His brother, PJ, had taught him to play "Something" by George Harrison when he was thirteen. *When you meet a girl who rocks your world, this is the song you'll play.* He'd played it nearly every day after PJ died. He couldn't remember when he'd stopped playing the song, but it was well before he'd met Phillip's mother, and not once had he played it for her.

"Is that a problem?" she asked. "I can play outside. And I don't play angry or offensive music."

He chewed on that for a minute, wondering if seeing her play would stir painful memories, and weighing his options. He needed to rent the damn room, and she seemed responsible, fairly quiet, and trustworthy. Where Phillip was concerned those were the most important things. "It's fine."

She gazed tenderly at Phillip, who'd fallen asleep on his shoulder.

"I better put him to bed," he said. "But I'd like to know a little more about you before we make this decision. Can you wait a few minutes?"

"Sure."

He motioned for her to make herself comfortable in the living room and took the stairs two at a time to put Phillip to bed. Something about Tempest had his gut churning, and he didn't know if it was that she had already asked him more pointed questions than any of the other people who had inquired about the room, or that she'd stirred feelings that had been dead for a very long time. But he *liked* that she was careful, had checked him out before showing up, and asked a million questions. And the rest? Yeah, he liked that, too. He'd buried his emotions for so long, ignoring his attraction was just tossing another log to the pile.

Phillip slept as he changed him into his pajamas and tucked him in bed. The poor guy was whipped every night. Nash didn't know any other kids, but he was sure his boy was the best sleeper around. He would have liked to brush his teeth, but he could skip a night.

He found Tempest looking over the books by the fireplace. She turned as he came into the room, flashing another easy smile that brought his guard down a notch.

"You like stories about the sea."

"Among other things."

"My father used to tell me stories about mermaids hooking fish on the lines of fishermen."

My father used to tell me and PJ stories about a future that would never be.

"Mind if we talk in the kitchen while I clean off those eggs?" Without Phillip, he needed something to do with his hands, and there was always something to be done—laundry, cleaning, caring for the animals. The list was endless.

He waited for her to go into the kitchen before him. *Big mistake.* There was no place to look besides her long, thick hair, which his fingers itched to touch, or her gorgeous ass in that sexy little skirt, which the *rest* of his body wanted a shot at. He hadn't been with a woman since Alaina left, and in all that time, he'd been so focused on Phillip, not one woman had made him think twice about sex. Suddenly Tempest breezed through his front door and he was like a fucking hound dog? He moved past her to distract himself from the lust heating up inside him and grabbed the buckets of eggs from the refrigerator.

"Can I get you a drink?" he asked as he set the buckets beside the sink. "We've got iced tea."

"No, that's okay." She leaned against the counter on the other side of the sink, looking comfortable and serious.

And pretty. Very, very pretty.

"How old is Flip?"

"He's three." He shook his head. He should correct her, but hearing her call his son Flip was adorable, and oddly sexy. He began washing the eggs, wanting to take the focus off his son and to get his mind on something other than how cute she was. *Hot. You're definitely hot. Fuck. This isn't helping.* "Why are you looking for a place to live?"

"I'm from Peaceful Harbor and I just moved my business to this area. I've been staying with my cousin, Jillian, but she's a night owl and I'm more of a give-me-sleep-so-I-remain-sane type of person."

He felt a grin tugging at his lips and set the clean egg on a towel beside the sink, grabbing another egg to wash off. "I hear ya there."

"I was beginning to wonder if you ever smiled." She picked up the egg and dried it with the towel.

I don't do it often around strangers. He concentrated on cleaning the eggs, trying not to make too much out of how easy she was to talk to, or that she'd noticed his smile. It'd been a long time since anyone had noticed anything specific about him. Sure, he'd noticed women gawking when he and Phillip went into town for groceries or dropped off furniture at the stores that sold his work. But she wasn't noticing the big guy with the baby. She'd noticed his *smile.*

"When I've got Phillip with me around people we don't know, I'm always a little tense. Sorry."

"I get it. I work with kids all the time, and even though I'm not their parent, I'm protective of them around strangers, too." She took a few paper towels from the roll and spread them on the counter for the eggs.

"Why are you renting out a room?" She set another egg on the paper towel and tucked a lock of hair behind her ear. It immediately sprang free.

"To cover some expenses for my business."

She tucked her hair behind her ear again, and it fell forward. She sighed with a soft laugh that was so melodic he wanted to hear it again.

"Happens to me, too," he teased, earning another sweet laugh.

They finished cleaning the eggs in comfortable silence. He placed them in a bowl and returned them to the refrigerator. "How long are you looking to rent?"

"I haven't really figured that out. I was hoping for a month-to-month lease to start, until I see how my business grows."

He held open the back door and she stepped out to the porch. "Sound won't carry up to my boy's room from out here."

She sat on the steps, and he sat beside her, consciously leaving space between them. Tempest leaned back against the railing post, her long legs dangling down to the second step. He tried not to stare, but she had gorgeous legs, and she was wearing sexy sandals with thin leather straps that wrapped around her ankles. He imagined running his hand along her smooth skin as he unwound those tantalizing little straps.

"What else do you want to know?" she asked, pulling him from his fantasy.

He cleared his throat, shifting his eyes to the grass, the trees, the sky. Anywhere but her legs as he tried to force the lascivious thoughts away and concentrate on evaluating her as a *housemate*. That was, if he could keep his frigging lust in check.

"I've never rented out a room, and because of Phillip, I want to be sure that I cover all the bases. The truth is, I'm not sure what I need to know. The basics, I guess, because inviting you into my house is really inviting you, your family, and your closest friends." He hadn't planned on asking about any of that, but he knew all too well how true the statement was. "Any psycho boyfriends or ex-boyfriends I should know about? Wild friends? Bizarre family members?"

She smiled and a puff of air escaped her lips. Add another sexy, hard-to-ignore thing about Tempest Braden.

"No current boyfriend, psycho, *or* sane exes to worry about. Most of my friends are back in Peaceful Harbor, and as I said, I usually hang out with my family. And they're…" She sighed, and it was one of those happy sighs girls made when they were grasping for the right words to describe something or someone they loved.

Anyone with that much love and clarity in her eyes when she spoke of her family couldn't have anything to hide. There was a time when he'd had the same love and clarity in his own eyes, but that was before his brother had gone and gotten himself killed.

TEMPEST ADORED HER family, but she often felt funny admitting that to strangers. She knew some people didn't have the love and support she'd grown up with, and she thought it might be hurtful to hear of her good fortune. But something about the way Nash was looking at her made her think he needed to know the truth, and the fact that he understood how family dynamics could affect a person was a bonus in her eyes.

"I have a big, close-knit family. Four overprotective, but not overbearing, brothers, and my sister and I are pretty different, but we're close. I think I got lucky in the family department. How about you?"

He was quiet for so long she didn't think he was going to offer any insight into his family, and now that he'd brought up how living under the same roof was like inviting her relatives into his home, she wanted to know about his.

"It was just me and my parents," he finally said. "We were close." He leaned his elbows on his thighs, wringing his hands together.

When he cocked his head to the side, his eyes rolled over her face, lingering long enough around her mouth to make her nerves prickle and her stomach flutter. Every interminable second made her breathe a little harder. Unsure of how to handle the sudden and intense attraction, she shifted her eyes away. She shouldn't even be *thinking* about renting a room from him when the impassioned way he was looking at her made her want to step outside her boundaries and take a walk on the big, gruff, sexy side. She should thank him for his time, walk straight out to her car, and drive away as fast as she could. But she was riveted in place as his expression softened and his eyes warmed.

"Did you grow up around here?" she asked.

"No, in Oak Rivers, Virginia. When I was in tenth grade my parents sold the house, packed up everything, and for the next two years I was homeschooled as we sailed around the world." His solemn tone didn't match the exciting trip he'd described.

"That sounds amazing. I guess your parents are boat people,

too. My dad has a boat, and a few of my brothers do, but then again, almost everyone in Peaceful Harbor does."

"My father loved the sea, but he was a professor, and my mother is an artist."

Loved? She hoped he'd just misspoken. "I guess artistic talent runs in your family. Do they live close by?"

His gaze turned serious. "We lost my father more than a decade ago."

"Oh, Nash." She resisted the urge to reach out and comfort him. If only she had her guitar so she could sing his heartache away. As the pieces of Nash began coming into focus, she realized he wasn't just gruff. He'd been touched by loss, and he was protective of his son. She wondered again about Flip's mother. Had he lost her, too?

"I'm sorry about your father. I can't even begin to imagine how difficult that must be."

He nodded, drew in a deep breath. His chest expanded as he straightened his spine and rolled his shoulders back. All his strength shifted back into place, as if he'd had a lot of practice coming out of the dark place he'd fallen into.

"He was a good man," he said with a thoughtful smile. "But if life offers one guarantee, it's that death is inevitable. All you can do is move forward."

As correct as that statement was, it made her sad that he sounded so accepting of it. "How about your mother? Do you see her often?"

"She's remarried and has a busy life." He cleared his throat. "Tempest," he said in a thick, husky voice. "It seems you have some sort of truth serum in that perfume of yours. I'm supposed to be asking the tough questions."

"Sorry," she said, feeling like she'd gotten a glimpse of the man beneath the armor and wanting to peel away a few more layers. "Go ahead. Ask me anything. I've got nothing to hide."

"No?" His eyes narrowed, and he leaned so close she could see his lashes bend as they brushed the top of his cheeks. "Everyone's got secrets." His lips curved up, but even his perfect smile didn't ease the intensity of his gaze.

He was so big and powerful, but in these last few minutes he seemed vulnerable and unguarded. A bud of attraction rooted itself deep inside her. She felt as if her entire being was holding its breath, waiting for him to reveal more of himself. She wanted to know more of his secrets. The dark kind of secrets that lovers shared in the quiet of night, when their bodies were sated and sweaty and nothing else in the world existed. *Holy cow. I do have a secret.*

"I…" She looked around the yard, as if the words she need-ed to extricate herself from the situation were tucked among the trees. "I should be going."

She pushed to her feet and he rose beside her, tall and stur-dy as a towering oak. She wobbled on the edge of the step.

"Whoa." He steadied her with his hands on her hips, and their eyes caught—and held.

Oh Lord did they hold. Her pulse quickened at the electrici-ty sparking between them. She wasn't prepared for this, much less for the urge to run her hands over the delicious muscles straining against his thin T-shirt.

This is crazy.

Insane.

But he was hot. Super-hot. *Forget-my-boundaries hot.*

She must really be overtired. Exhausted.

Or I'm losing my freaking mind.

"You okay?" His brows drew together, but his lips curved up

again.

Another smile for her to take a mental snapshot of for later. Great. Now she sounded like one of those dreamy-eyed girls who used to chase her brothers around. Standing up straighter, refusing to become *that* type of girl, she met his gaze—and felt herself looking for *more* in it. Would it be rude for her to ask him to go back to being gruff and closed off?

"Yes, fine," she lied, wishing he'd move his hands because she clearly wasn't capable of doing it herself.

His eyes coasted down her body, assessing her as if he wasn't sure he believed her. *Smart man. Smart sexy man.*

Stop!

He released her slowly, the heat of his touch lingering long after his hands moved away.

"So, you'll think about the room?" he asked with a hint of hope in his voice.

Not trusting what might escape her mouth, she nodded.

"Okay." Concern lingered in his eyes. He touched her lower back as they descended the porch steps, removing it when they hit the grass. "I'll walk you out."

"It's okay—"

He gave her a disapproving look. "I have to make sure I locked up the chicken coop anyway."

Yeah, right.

When they reached her car, he said, "You have my number. Call me with any questions."

She nodded. Since when had she become the silent one? This was ridiculous.

"Okay," she finally managed.

"I've got two appointments to show the room lined up for this weekend, but if you're interested, it's yours."

Her mind twisted that into a far more personal invitation.

"Thanks. I'll be in touch." She climbed into the car and he closed the door for her, gave a curt nod, an *almost* smile, and headed for the chicken coop.

Ohmygosh. Had she completely misconstrued *everything* that had just happened? She must truly be exhausted.

Chapter Three

NASH PARKED BEHIND the Country Charm furniture store, one of the retail outlets that carried his work. He unhooked Phillip from his car seat and lifted him into his arms, giving him a quick kiss before setting him on the ground. "Hang on to my pants leg, buddy."

He needn't have said a word. Phillip knew the drill. Nash never made a delivery without him. He retrieved the chair they were delivering from the bed of the truck. Phillip clung to his pants leg as they ascended the concrete steps to the back door of the showroom. He set the chair on the landing and tousled Phillip's hair, then nodded to the doorbell. Phillip pushed the button.

"What do you say we hit the diner when we're done?" The Main Street Diner was a rare treat for them. They had a walk-up ice cream window that opened to a patio and an old-fashioned jukebox, and Phillip loved to push the buttons and hum along to the songs.

A smile lifted Phillip's chubby cheeks as he nodded, sending his mop of dark curls flopping over his forehead.

The showroom door swung open and Mrs. Padgerly, a fiftysomething widow with straight dark hair and a hankering for matchmaking—*Call me Mrs. P; otherwise I feel like you're talking to my mother-in-law*—smiled back at them. "If it isn't my two favorite men." She crouched and tickled Phillip's belly. "Your daddy better watch out. Soon you'll be as big as he is."

Phillip giggled and moved behind Nash's leg.

"Sorry we're so late." Nash carried the chair into the receiving area and set it down. "I lost track of time."

He had worked during Phillip's nap, and then again while Phillip played in the barn. But they'd taken a late-afternoon break, collecting vegetables from the garden and feeding a few to the goats. Phillip had plunked himself down in the middle of the goat pen and had come out stinking to high heaven. His bath had delayed them even longer, but Nash didn't mind. They'd had a fun afternoon, and it was days like today that made him wonder how parents left their kids to go to work each day. He'd lose his mind if he had to go hours without seeing Philip, if he missed out on seeing Phillip's excitement when he found the biggest tomato or hearing his endless giggles as Big and Little nibbled the vegetables right out of his hands. But then again, his unwillingness to miss those things was precisely why he needed to rent out the room, and that presented its own issues. Especially now that he'd met a particular blonde whom he couldn't get out of his mind.

"Maybe one of these days you'll let me introduce you to a nice young woman who can help you stay on track." She raised her brows.

"Thanks, but we have a pretty full life." He lifted Phillip into his arms, thinking about how their lives, or at least their house, were about to become even fuller if Tempest rented the room. Last night he'd spent hours going over their interactions. He didn't think he'd come on to her, but it had been so long since he'd hit on a woman, he honestly couldn't be sure if he'd stared too long or given away his attraction in some other way. She'd scurried off so quickly he also worried he'd shared too much of himself, and he could kick himself for that. But she was right to ask about his family. If he expected answers about hers, she deserved the same from him.

Mrs. P wrote out a receipt and handed it to him. He mentally calculated the commission that would land in his bank in three days. His father had taught him a lot about budgeting and finance during their two years at sea. It had been his way of avoiding dealing with the devastation of their lives after losing PJ. If Nash's nose was in a book, there was no need for words. Nash was a fast learner. He'd not only learned to repress his emotions, but he'd learned to budget and save. From the moment he'd struck out on his own, he'd had a plan for his finances, and he'd stuck to it. When Alaina had gotten pregnant, he'd modified the plan to include a savings account for Phillip's future. Half of each check went toward living expenses and spending money, a quarter went into savings for machinery maintenance, vet bills, and unexpected repairs, and the last quarter went into savings for Phillip's future. There was a time when those savings accounts had grown at a rapid pace, but that was before Alaina had taken off. It had been shortsighted of him to think his ability to keep up with orders, and his plentiful commissions, would last forever.

Mrs. P placed a hand on her rounded hip. "The two of you boys probably do have a full life, but the right woman can make it even better."

His thoughts returned to Tempest. Beyond dissecting their interactions, he'd spent a good part of last night thinking about her in other ways. Like how beautiful she was and how she didn't walk like most people did, intent on reaching their destination. She strolled gracefully, taking in everything around her and showing her enjoyment with a lifting of her lips, a widening of her eyes, or that sweet sigh he wasn't even sure she was aware of making. And her legs? He'd had so many fantasies about them wrapped around his waist, around his shoulders, pressed beneath his thighs that he'd had to take matters into his own hands just to find relief. He was pretty certain he shouldn't even be thinking about letting her rent the room for that reason alone. But every time he told himself that, the *man* inside him rebelled.

Needing to change the subject—and get his mind off Tempest before he ended up sporting wood he couldn't chisel away—he said, "I'm running a few days behind on the other piece you ordered, but I should have it done inside of a week."

Her eyes sparked with mischief again. "As I said, the right—"

"Mrs. P," he interrupted. "I'll have it done by Monday *if* you stop pushing women on me."

"Fine." She ran her hand over the carving of an eagle flying near a range of pine trees on the back of the chair. "Take until Friday if you need it. Your work keeps getting better and better. I just wish we could get more of it."

And therein lay the crux of his trouble. Before Phillip was born, he was able to work as many hours as he needed to keep up with orders *and* keep a few stock items on hand. But the last three years he'd had to adapt to being a single parent, which meant catching a few hours here and there to work, and completely giving up working with the forge. His business had suffered, but there was no way he would skimp where his son was concerned. Most of the time he was grateful for the extra time with Phillip, but his truck had a hundred thousand miles on it, his tools needed replenishing, and if he had any hope of giving Phillip life experiences beyond caring for a few farm animals, something had to give. Renting out the room was a start.

"I'd like to pick up my production schedule eventually. I'm working toward it, and I appreciate you keeping the orders coming in."

They made two more deliveries, and then Nash drove to the diner. Phillip practically leaped from the truck into his arms, knocking his forehead against the bill of Nash's cap.

"Whoa, buddy. You okay?"

Phillip rubbed his forehead.

Nash moved his little hand and kissed his boo-boo. His phone vibrated in his pocket, and he set Phillip down, holding his hand as he pulled out his phone, hoping it was Tempest. Disappointment came with the sight of Larry's name on the screen. He needed to be firm with Larry once and for all, but for now he let the call go to voicemail, adding it to the long list of things he didn't want to think about.

"ONE MORE TIME, Mary. You're doing such a good job. I'm really proud of you." Tempest strummed "You Are My Sunshine," singing the tune slow enough for Mary to sing along as she underwent a chemotherapy treatment. At Pleasant Hill Hospital they used music therapy for patients of all ages, and while Tempest enjoyed working with adults, she preferred working with the children. This was her third time visiting Mary during her treatment, and the music not only served as a great distraction, but Mary's parents, Walter and Caroline, said they'd seen marked improvement in her outlook. She no longer cried before her treatments, and she looked forward to singing with Tempest.

The nurse came in to take out her IV, and Mary continued singing throughout the process, nervously running her fingers over the new purple scarf Jillian had made. Tempest tried to bring a little something special when she worked with children undergoing particularly scary or painful procedures. She knew all the gifts in the world couldn't take away the fear or the pain these children faced, but every bit helped.

After the nurse finished, Mary scooted forward and wrapped her arms around Tempest's neck.

"Will you be here next time, Tempe?" Mary asked.

"You bet I will. Any special requests?"

Mary looked to her mother for help. She'd lost her hair from the treatments, and she wore a pretty white knit cap with red stars on it. Mary's prognosis was good, but Tempest knew that could change at any time.

Caroline brushed her hand over Mary's arm. "How about that One Direction song you love?"

"Oh, yeah, yeah, yeah!" Mary said. "'What Makes You Beautiful'! Do you know that song?"

"I happen to know that song very well. My younger sister, Shannon, is a big One Direction fan."

"I didn't know you had a younger sister," Mary said. "I have a younger sister, but she doesn't come to the hospital with us."

"I bet she misses you."

"I miss her, too, but she's two and she's a pain sometimes."

Tempest set her guitar in the case. "My sister is in her twenties, and she's a pain sometimes, too. But you know what? I bet she thinks I'm also a pain sometimes."

Mary laughed.

Walter pressed a kiss to the top of Mary's head, and like the last two times Tempest had visited, his glassy eyes gave away the emotions he struggled to keep contained. "Thank you, Tempe. We'll see you next week."

"I look forward to it."

As she was leaving the hospital, Dr. Tolson, the head of the Physical Medical and Rehabilitation department caught up to her. Ever the professional, her blond hair was secured in a clip at the base of her neck, the perfect accompaniment for her black pencil skirt and white blouse. "Tempe, I'm glad I ran into you." She pushed the exit door open and held it for Tempest. "We had a staff meeting today, and your name came up quite a few times."

"Should I worry?" She knew she was good at her job, and the doctors and physical therapists seemed to really like her, but there was always that kernel of doubt with a new place of employment.

"Not at all. You're doing such good work with the kids, and the parents rave about you. We're thinking about expanding the music therapy budget. Would you ever be interested in taking on more hours? Maybe doing more work with the adults, too?"

The opportunity would allow her income to grow, but she knew how quickly her days and weekends would fill up with clients at the hospital. "I really appreciate you asking, but I'm still trying to grow my children's music group. Can I think about it?"

Dr. Tolson dug her keys out of her purse. "Of course. How's it coming along?"

"Slow, but good. I spoke to Hattie Rivers, the owner of the Downtown Art Boutique, today. She's holding a grand opening of the new children's section of her boutique in a couple of weeks and I'm going to be playing at it. I think it's a good way to get to know families. Hopefully that will lead to more referrals."

"That's wonderful. You can probably spread the word through the pediatric unit as well. Talk to some of the docs and see if they can pass your name along."

"That wouldn't be considered rude, trying to grow a business elsewhere?"

Dr. Tolson smiled. "We're all interested in making sure the kids are happy and healthy. You're not taking patients away from the hospital; you're doing good for the community." She glanced at her watch. "I've got to go, but think about it. We're hoping to meet with the board next week, and we'd love to see you helping more of the patients."

On the way to her car, Tempest mulled over the opportunity. But she couldn't ignore the voice in the back of her head reminding her why she had come to Pleasant Hill in the first place. Doing the same things she'd done in Peaceful Harbor was hardly a fresh start. She climbed into her car, wishing she could sit beneath the stars and chill, but she had a commitment to keep. She pulled out her phone and texted Jillian, *I'll be there soon. Just leaving the hospital.*

After another sleepless night, this one not caused by her vivacious cousin, but by thoughts of a big, brooding single father, she'd woken up with no clearer answers about her living arrangements than she'd had the night before. She'd been too busy today to spend much time dwelling on Nash, but he'd been there, lingering in the recesses of her mind like forbidden fruit. Maybe her cousins could help her come to a decision.

Twenty minutes later she walked into the crowded tavern,

immediately assaulted by loud music and air too oppressive to breathe. Bars had never been her thing. She preferred quiet cafés, or outdoor venues, where she could actually hear her friends speak.

She moved through the crowd and spotted Jillian dancing with a guy who towered over her by at least a foot. His longish dark hair and tattoos gave him a dangerous vibe, one Tempest would *not* be comfortable with, but Jillian loved edgy bikers. Of course, if Nick and Jax were there, then this guy was probably one of Nick's friends, because there was no way he'd allow Jillian to dance with a guy like that unless he knew him.

A heavy hand on her waist startled her. She turned and found her burly cousin Nick smiling down at her. Tempest had always thought of Nick as being caught somewhere between a country boy and a biker, since he drove a custom-made Silver-Stone motorcycle and trained show horses. He took after the Braden side of the family—tall, dark, and built for a fight—while Jillian took after her mother, petite and feisty.

"Hey, beautiful." Nick leaned down and kissed her cheek, keeping a protective arm around her waist.

"I was just thinking about you. Who's Jilly getting sweaty with?"

"My buddy Jace Stone." He guided her over to a table where Jax was ordering a drink from a pretty blond waitress.

Jax rose and hugged Tempest. "How's my favorite cousin?" He was almost as tall as Nick, but fairer haired and leaner.

"Sleep deprived and in need of advice." Jax was a great sounding board. Of all her cousins, he was the most like her. He was cautious, with an underlying sense of calm that translated into everything he did. She guessed he had to be. As a high-end wedding gown designer, he spent his days trying to please bridezillas.

"I ordered you a glass of wine." He pulled out a chair for her and said, "Sit down and tell me all your problems."

Nick sat across from them. "Need me to kick someone's ass?"

"Maybe my own? I'm not sure yet." She reached across the table and took a sip of Nick's beer. She wasn't a big drinker, but tonight she needed something to calm her thoughts.

"Uh-oh." Jax eyed Nick's beer. "What is going on with you?"

"You know how Jilly likes to stay up all night?"

"You knew this when you were six," Nick said. "Remember the sleepovers?"

"Yes. I always ended up sleeping on the floor in one of your bedrooms." They had three other brothers, Zev, Graham, and Beau, and she'd spent more nights on their floors than she had in Jillian's room. "But I thought she'd outgrown it. I mean, look at her."

Jace and Jillian were dancing like they owned the dance floor, bumping and grinding so sexily they put the *Dirty Dancing* crew to shame. Tempest was a little jealous of her cousin's ability to let loose like that. "She's got more energy than ten women. I'm exhausted just watching her."

"Everyone's exhausted watching her," Jax said. "Jilly said you were looking for another place to live. You know you can stay with me if you'd like."

"I'm sure she'd appreciate finding a different woman wandering around nude every other week." Nick winked at Tempest. "I've got your back. You don't want to live with one of the Braden boys."

Boy, wasn't that the truth. "Thanks, you guys, but I think I found a place to live. I just…There's this thing standing in my way."

"Yay! You made it!" Jillian said as she and Jace returned to the table. She sat beside Nick. "Whew. That was fun."

Jace gave Tempest a hungry once-over as he sank down to the chair at the end of the table.

Nick put a hand at the base of Jace's neck, laying a death stare on him. "Buddy, this is my *cousin*, Tempest."

Why did she think explaining to her two male cousins that she was trying to figure out if she was too attracted to a guy to rent a room in his house was a good idea? They'd try to forbid her from ever stepping foot in that house again. They were Bradens, after all.

Jace swore under his breath. "Dude, you're related to every gorgeous woman in this town." He flashed a killer smile at Tempest. "Jace Stone. Nice to meet you."

"It's nice to meet you, too. You're a really good dancer."

The waitress brought Tempest's wine, and Tempest took a long sip.

"Yeah, he is," Jillian said, earning a harsh glare from Nick. "Back off, big brother. I said he was a good dancer. I didn't invite him into my bedroom."

"Did I hear 'bedroom'?" Jace waggled his brows.

They all laughed, except Nick, who scowled.

"I swear it's like being out with my family before my brothers had their hearts stolen." Tempe thought about that as she sipped her wine, remembering the lightning-fast rush of excitement that Nash had stirred. What if *he* was *her* heart stealer?

"Speaking of having hearts stolen, you came in awfully late last night," Jillian pointed out. "Did you meet someone special?"

Maybe? "I went to see a room for rent. It's on the outskirts of town. A farmette with a pond and a garden."

"Sounds like it's right up your alley," Jax said. "What's the issue?"

She took another gulp of liquid courage. "I don't know if there is an issue, but the guy renting it out is a single father. He's got an adorable little boy, and…" *He's smoking hot and an artist, and—*

"A man with a child is a total aphrodisiac," Jace said. "At least that's what my sisters tell me."

Jillian leaned across the table with a glimmer of mischief in her eyes. "It's more than that, isn't it? There was chemistry between you two. He made your belly tumble. I see it in your eyes."

She looked away. "*Pfft.* Hardly."

"Oh yeah. I nailed it. Look at those cheeks. She's blushing." Jillian reached across the table and squeezed Tempest's hand. "Face it, Tempe. You're hot for this guy."

"Who is he?" Nick demanded.

"His name is Nash Morgan, and I'm not hot for him." She looked away again, knowing they'd see right through her.

"You've always been a sucky liar," Jax said for her ears only.

Tell me something I don't know.

"Let me guess," Jace said. "You're worried you'll end up hooking up if you rent the room."

"Dude," Nick snapped.

"Ohmygod," Tempest said under her breath.

"If you're hot for him, and he's hot for you, then where you live will make no difference," Jillian pointed out. "You'll hook up anyway at some point."

"Enough, Jilly," Nick said sharply. "I want to meet this guy. His name is familiar, but I can't place him. Your brothers would kill me if I let you move into some guy's house without one of us checking him out."

Tempest rolled her eyes. "I don't need your permission or theirs."

"No, you don't," Jax said. "But there's no harm in our meeting him, letting him know you've got us watching your back."

"Do I have a choice in this matter?" she mumbled.

"No," Nick, Jax, and Jace said in unison.

"You don't even know me," she said to Jace.

"I do now." Jace flashed a cocky grin. "Besides, you're related to Nick. That makes me your honorary big brother."

"Like I need any more of those." She pushed from the table and grabbed her bag. "I think I need some air. I'll be right back."

"I'm coming with you." Jillian caught up with her and wrapped her hand around Tempest's arm. "They're just watching out for you."

"I know. It's just that I'm confused enough as it is." She pushed through the doors and walked outside, taking a deep cleansing breath of the cool evening air.

"Was his place that great, or was it him?" Jillian asked. Leave it to her to get straight to the point.

They walked around to the side of the building and sat on a bench.

"I don't know how to answer that. It's not like the house is anything special, but at the same time, the whole place felt like it was *waiting* to be special."

"Um...? You've lost me."

"His house needs work, and he hasn't done a lick of decorating, except in his son's room. But you know how you walk into some places and it feels like home? Not just a house? I don't think most people would feel it when they walked into his place, but when you're there *with* them, you can feel their love, you know? It's like decorations don't matter. And there's no one around, so it's peaceful and they have goats and chickens. I feel like it's *all* calling to me. You know what I mean? And he...*he*..." She inhaled deeply and blew it out slowly. "He's quiet but strong, and he's so dedicated to his son, it practically oozes out of him. He's as protective as our brothers are toward us. Maybe more so."

"Wow. That's saying a lot."

"Right?" Tempest's heart warmed with the memory of Nash's hand running over Flip's head and down his back. "He looked at his little boy like he was the only thing that mattered on earth, and then there was the soulful way he spoke about his family. When he wasn't being gruff."

"Gruff?" Jillian's face grew serious. "That doesn't sound great."

"Well, he was only that way at first, when he was carrying Flip around—"

"Flip?" Jillian laughed. "Like...Flip Wilson? Who would name their kid Flip? Flip. Flip. Flip. Actually, it's kind of cute. Like, really cute."

"Jilly!"

"Sorry. Go ahead. I'll behave."

"Anyway, after he put Flip to bed he was a lot less gruff. I think he has two personas, the one that protects his son with all his might and the *man*. You know what I mean?"

"Do I ever."

"It's like there's this part of him that is trying so hard to be what his son needs, and that's so sexy, right? And then there's this other part of him that's maybe not used to being let out to play. It's hard to explain, but I could feel him sort of coming out of his shell, then pulling back."

"You explained it perfectly." Jillian squeezed her hand. "I can see why you're drawn to him. It sounds like he's mysterious, and a farmette? That's so *you*."

"There's more." Her chest tightened at what she was about to reveal, but talking about Nash was helping her to see him more clearly. "He lost his father, and I have no idea where Flip's mom is, but I get the sense that there's a painful story there. I just wish there was a sign, or something I could draw on, to know if renting from him is the right thing to do, or a big mistake."

"Let's do pros and cons." Jillian reached for Tempest's bag and dug around in it, pulling out one of her notebooks and a pen.

Tempest laughed. "Help yourself."

"I did." Jillian drew a line down the center of the paper. "Okay, pros?"

"The location is perfect." She watched Jillian write, *Perfect location*, then *He's hot*. "Jilly."

"What? That's a pro, regardless of what my brothers say."

"Whatever. Pros…" Tempest smiled at a young family walking by. From where they sat on the bench, she could see the shops on Main Street and the ones around the corner. She liked watching people going about their evening, and she wondered what Nash and Flip were doing. Were they collecting eggs? Was Nash reading him a story? She hadn't seen a television, which was a big plus, because she'd always felt that televisions were distractions from getting out and living life. Then again, everyone watched shows on their phones these days. She tried to picture Nash watching some mindless show on his phone, and she couldn't do it. His bookshelves were packed with classics, and titles like *In the Heart of the Sea.*

"Earth to Tempe." Jillian waved her hand in front of Tempest's face.

"Sorry. *Pros.* The rent is reasonable. I think we'd get along well, and he said he doesn't have any strange habits."

"Says the *man.* Just remember, what we think is strange *he* might think is perfectly normal."

"True." Tempest watched a couple walk out of the diner across the street holding hands. The man spun the woman in his arms and kissed her. Tempest looked away, feeling like a voyeur.

Jillian leaned closer and lowered her voice. "Can you imagine *that?*"

"Imagine it? I *hope* for it." Tempest laughed. "I've dated plenty of guys and never felt that wanted. But you have."

"Nah." Jillian waved a hand dismissively. "Wanted yes, but not like that. That's *in-love* wanted. I'm more of a let's-get-crazy-for-a-while girl. Although don't get the wrong impression—I don't sleep around."

"I know that." Tempest didn't want to talk about sexy times with men. That would just make her think of getting hot and bothered with Nash, and that would not help at all. She turned her attention back to her dilemma and said, "*Pros.* His son is incredibly cute, and quiet, like Nash." She loved the way his name rolled off her tongue.

Jillian stopped writing. "This isn't even a question, is it? You've got that look in your eyes that I get when I've made up my mind about something."

"No, I don't. I can't. I'm too worried about moving in and wanting to attack my landlord."

"Now we're talking." Jillian pressed pen to paper, writing as she spoke. "Pros. *Nash is attackable.*"

"Cross that out!" She reached for the pen and Jillian pulled it out of reach. "Seriously, Jilly. I've never wanted to attack anyone in my life. I roll my eyes when girls say that. I can't even believe *I* said it."

"That's because you're all universe-oriented and hippie-girl cool. You float through life on a serious cloud of helping others and enjoying the simple things in life, like gentle breezes and butterflies."

If anyone else had said that to her, it would have sounded sarcastic, or off-putting, but despite how different they were, Jillian understood those parts of Tempest that others sometimes found odd or boring.

Jillian put her arm around her and said, "You always put yourself last, so it makes sense that you've missed out on this kind of fun, sexy stuff. You don't look for it the way some of us do."

"I wasn't looking for it last night, either." She really hadn't been. After their phone call she'd been ready to face a stoic, grumpy guy.

"That's why I think you should stop worrying so much and let yourself enjoy it. If your connection is that strong, and you truly wanted to attack Nash, it has to mean something." She tapped the paper with her pen. "But I know you're all about making careful choices. So let's go over the cons."

"Nash is attackable," Tempest said with a heavy sigh.

Jillian laughed. "*Attackable*, pro *and* con. You've got that right. And…?"

"That's all I've got," she admitted. "The room is small, but there's a claw-foot tub—which doesn't work, but it still looks cool—and a fantastic deck off of the bedroom where I can play my guitar, and it has the most amazing views."

"Oh, my sweet cousin. You've got *no* cons? The only thing holding you back is that you're attracted to him?"

Tempest nodded. "My brain says it's not a good idea to move in, but…" She shrugged, not wanting to describe what parts of her were telling her not to walk away.

"I know you're a big believer in signs and all things cosmic, but sometimes you just have to go with your gut. Take my business, for instance…"

As Jillian talked about the risks involved with starting her business, Tempest thought about Nash's expression when he told her about losing his father, and the way he'd looked at Flip throughout their visit. And the way he'd looked at her. Or at least the way she *thought* he'd looked at her.

Jillian grabbed her arm. "Oh my God," she whispered. "Talk about hot."

Tempest followed her gaze across the street. Her heart stumbled at the sight of Nash lifting Flip up. His biceps strained against his short sleeves as he kissed Flip on the nose, then lifted him higher, turning him around and settling the little boy on his shoulders. He reached up with one hand and circled the boy's lower back, while the other held his ankle. Flip giggled and patted the top of Nash's ball cap as they approached the walk-up ice cream window.

"I'm suddenly hungry for ice cream." Jillian rose to her feet, and Tempest absently reached for her hand. "What?" Jillian asked.

"That's him." *There's no bigger sign than seeing the man I've been thinking about since last night.*

"That's Nash?" Jillian whispered. She wrenched her arm free and started across the street.

Oh no. No, no, no. Lord only knew what type of inquisition Jillian would give him. Tempest hurried after her.

"Tempest!"

Nash turned at the sound of Nick's deep voice calling her name, his eyes slammed into her, landing like a bolt of adrenaline to her already rapid pulse. His lips curved up. Nick called her name again, and Nash's eyes shifted over her shoulder. His chin tipped down, his eyes became hooded, and his smile turned to stone.

Chapter Four

NASH HADN'T FELT the muscle-clenching determination of competition in years, but as three large men converged on Tempest and her friend, all those instincts flared to life. He drew his shoulders back and stepped closer to the woman he had no claim on, meeting each of the men with what he knew would come across as a fierce and protective glare.

The heavily muscled, dark-haired guy who had called Tempest's name came to her side, giving Nash a serious once-over, then turning his attention to Tempest and her friend. "Y'all ditched us?"

"No, we didn't." The petite dark-haired woman who had crossed the street ahead of Tempest was visually devouring Nash one inch at a time as the other two guys stepped up beside them.

The tallest of the three was rough-looking, tatted up, and eyeing Nash and Phillip. Nash tightened his arm around his son, weighing the situation. The third man was fairer haired and appeared more curious than threatening.

Nash lifted his chin in acknowledgment to them.

Tempest's eyes flicked up to him. She had worry written all over her face, making him feel even more protective of her.

Stepping closer, he said, "Everything okay?"

A tentative smile spread across her lips. "Hi. I was just thinking about you. I mean, your place. The room you have for rent." She spoke so fast her words ran together.

An amused expression washed over the lighter-haired guy's face as words spilled in fast succession from Tempest's beautiful, full mouth.

"These are my cousins. This is Jillian." She motioned toward each of the men, "My cousins Nick and Jax, and Jace, Nick's friend." Pointing to Nash, she said, "This is Nash Morgan, and his son, Flip."

Damn, he loved hearing her say his name like that, breathless and nervous, but from the look on the other guys' faces, they had noticed, too, and hadn't liked it nearly as much.

Jace stood up taller and crossed his arms. The dude was seriously ripped and had a few inches on him—*and no child on his shoulders*. Nash inhaled deeply, standing tall and proud against their scrutiny.

"Nice to meet you," Nash said, offering his hand to Nick first.

"You, too. Cute boy." Nick's tone was serious, but Nash appreciated his acknowledgment of Phillip.

"Thanks." He shook Jax's hand. "Jax." Then he held a hand out to Jace, whose threatening gaze held his a beat too long. "Jace," he said with a touch of humor in his voice. Nash had never been easily intimidated.

Jace shook his hand, his eyes flicking up to Phillip. "Good-looking little man you've got there."

Thank God he wasn't a prick. "Thanks."

"Are we done ruffling our feathers?" Jillian patted Jace's shoulder. "Down, boy." She looked up at Nash. "Sorry. We're a bit too closely knit sometimes, but at least you're getting a full dose of it before you two share a house. You know we have to ask you all the requisite questions since Tempest is thinking about renting a room from you."

"I am," Tempest said. The confidence he'd seen last night returned in the squaring of her shoulders and the determined set of her jaw.

Nash raised his brows. "You are...?"

"Renting a room from you. I mean, if the offer is still good."

"It is. That's great." Would it be rude of him to do a fist pump?

"You are?" Jillian couldn't hide the surprise in her voice.

You hadn't decided until just now?

Nick shot a half-smile, half-warning look at Nash. "Guess we should start those questions now."

"Back off, Nick. The guy's got his kid on his shoulders." Jax sighed. "Don't hurt her, screw with her head, or otherwise do anything offensive to her. Got it?"

"Jax!" Tempest groaned. "Sorry, Nash. I failed to mention that in addition to overprotective brothers, I also have a few overprotective cousins."

He didn't like having to defend himself to strangers, but he was glad Tempest had strong family ties and people who would look out for her without hesitation. He admired that, although he could see it mortified Tempest.

"No worries." His eyes slid over each of the men. "I'm just a single dad trying to grow my business. I'll treat her with the same respect I'd hope each of you would treat a woman living under your roof."

Jillian and Tempest exchanged a look of approval.

"All right, then," Jax said. "How about some ice cream?"

Nash glanced at Tempest, who lifted one shoulder in the cutest shrug he'd ever seen. He would rather spend time alone with her and Phillip, getting to know her better, but this would have to do. A twinge of guilt followed that thought, because it had nothing to do with his aversion to hanging out with three guys he didn't know and everything to do with the awareness coursing through him as he compared Tempest's nervous smile to the easier ones from last night and the way her clear blue eyes were moving between him and Phillip, then shifting away when he caught her watching them.

The next few minutes were uncomfortable as they ordered ice cream and settled in around a table on the patio to eat. Within a few minutes the conversation moved from scrutinizing him as a potential housemate for Tempest to lighter topics, which was a damn good thing. Nash was nervous enough wondering if the electricity buzzing between him and Tempest was as palpable to the others as it was to him. Phillip sat happily on his lap, devouring his ice cream while they talked. They made cute remarks to Phillip and generally proved they weren't the assholes he'd thought they were when they had chased Tempest across the street. Jillian jumped in and out of the conversation between texting. And Tempest…Tempest was as sweet and alluring as she'd been last night.

"So you all live around here?" Nash asked no one in particular. It'd been a long time since he'd sat around a table with anyone other than Phillip, and he had to work hard to quiet the untrusting voices in his head. Part of him was itching to leave. But another part of him, the part he had tried, and failed, not to think about for the last twenty-four hours, was in no rush to leave Tempest.

"I travel quite a bit," Nick said. "But this is home base for me. Family, you know."

Family. Yeah, he remembered what it was like to have a family. He kissed the back of Phillip's head. Phillip was his family now. There was a time when Nash had lived a bohemian lifestyle. Moving from state to state, going wherever he could to sell his artwork. It seemed like a lifetime ago.

"Jax and I live here, too," Jillian said as she finished her ice cream and her phone vibrated again.

Tempest was watching Phillip with a soft gaze and a genuine smile. It did something funky to his stomach to see her admiring his boy like that. Trying to distract himself, he turned his attention to Jace. "How about you? Are you from around here, too?"

Jace shook his head. "I move around a lot with my business. I design motorcycles and have a number of shops throughout the United States. But speaking of moving around, I've got to cut out. I'm heading out of town to see my sister, Mia, in New York." He pushed from the table.

Nash stood, bringing Phillip up with him as he extended a hand to Jace. "It was nice to meet you."

"Thanks, man." Jace cracked a smile at Phillip. "See ya around, little man."

Phillip buried his face in Nash's chest.

"I'd better go, too. Lots of designing to do. Right, *Jax*?" Jillian gave Jax and Nick a very obvious, let's-leave-them-alone look, and they both took the hint. She hugged Tempest and smiled at Nash and Phillip. "I'm so glad we had a chance to meet. I'm sure we'll see you soon."

"Sorry for the abrupt introduction," Jax said, and patted Nash on the back as if they were old friends.

Nash tried not to bristle, but the habit came too fast. "It's all good. You can't be too careful these days." He said goodbye to Nick, and as he sat beside Tempest again, her cheeks flushed. "They seem nice," he said, hoping to ease her discomfort, and maybe his own.

"I'm so sorry." She looked tenderly at Phillip. "I didn't expect to see you, much less intrude on your time with Flip."

He opened his mouth to correct her, but she was embarrassed enough. He didn't need to make her feel funny about mishearing his son's name. "I'm glad you did" came out before he had a chance to think it over, and her cheeks burned redder. "Look, there's no pressure for you to rent the room. Take your time and think it over."

"I have. I want to rent it. That is, unless…Oh my gosh. They scared you off. I don't blame y—"

"No, they didn't." Their eyes connected, and for a minute, the world around him silenced.

"Are you sure?"

Sure? Oh, right. "Positive." He placed his hand on Phillip to keep from reaching out to brush a lock of hair from in front of her eyes. "They're just looking out for you. You're lucky to have them." *Luckier than you might know.*

She blessed him with one of her stunning smiles, and it struck him that if she moved in, he'd have the pleasure of seeing that gorgeous smile every day.

"Thanks. But as you can see, they can be a little over the top. My brothers are less in-your-face than Nick and Jace, but I think Nick feels a sense of responsibility in their absence."

Phillip yawned and rested his head on Nash's shoulder.

"He's so quiet," Tempest said. "I hope they didn't scare him."

"He's always quiet." He wanted to stay right there, with the leaves rustling in the breeze and Tempest's full attention on him, but the dad in him spoke louder than any other voice in his head. "I hate to cut this short, but I'd better get him home. He's up at the crack of dawn regardless of when he goes to sleep."

"Okay. Do you want references or something?"

He shook his head as they left the patio and reached the sidewalk. "I don't need them. When would you like to move in?"

"Right now," she said with a tease in her eyes. "So I can finally get some sleep."

"That works for me."

She laughed. "I was kidding."

"I wasn't." Her expression turned serious, and he silently berated himself for letting that slip. "Where are you parked?"

"Behind Tully's."

They walked across the street and toward the parking lot. Every step was like wading through a lightning storm. Every time their arms brushed, or their eyes met, sparks ignited.

"Seriously, though," she said when they reached her car. "How soon are you looking to rent the room?"

"As soon as you're ready to move in," he said as she dug her keys from her bag. Phillip's body sagged against his shoulder. His eyes were barely open. He was in that gray space between awake and sleeping.

"Really?" She wrinkled her nose. "I don't want to push myself on you."

Push, Tempe. Please push. She was too cute, too sexy, and he could tell that she wasn't acting that way on purpose. This was who she was, and he found her devastatingly enticing. "Really. You can move in tonight, tomorrow, next week. Whenever works best for you."

She trapped her lower lip between her teeth and hope filled her eyes. "Tomorrow I'm teaching my children's class, but then I'm off for the weekend. Would tomorrow evening be too soon?"

"Do you always ask multiple times before accepting an answer?"

"Only when I'm nervous."

The air between them thickened. He stepped closer. He shouldn't have, but she was *that* compelling. "Why are you nervous?"

The look in her eyes told him she felt their connection just as strongly as he did. She was too real, too likable and honest. That made her dangerous. *Not just to me. To Phillip.* On that thought he leaned back, feeling a rush of cooler air fill the space between them. She unlocked her car and he opened the door for her, telling himself to back off and get a grip.

"No reason," she said shakily, averting her eyes as she climbed into the driver's seat. "Just the idea of moving again."

He waited for her to look at him, and when she did, it was all right there, clear as day. *You feel it too, and you're not running scared. You can't walk away from us either, can you?* He knew he was skating on thin ice. He knew he couldn't get involved with her, especially if she moved in. But for the first time in forever, he wanted to be selfish. Or at least selfish enough to allow himself to walk that tightrope, giving himself time to experience being with her, even if only as friends. Because as much as he wanted to be truly selfish, he wouldn't—*couldn't*—allow that selfishness to take over and risk the stability he'd created for his son.

"I'm nervous, too," he said honestly. "That's probably a good thing."

Chapter Five

TEMPEST'S STOMACH HAD been twisting into knots one minute and all fluttery the next since she'd made the split-second decision to rent the room in Nash's house. Last night she hadn't left the bar just because she felt suffocated by her cousins. She didn't want to be at a crowded bar. She wanted to unwind, to center herself after a long, emotional day. She hadn't realized how frustrated she was until Jillian had said something about her always putting others first. That's exactly what she had been doing forever. She went to bars because other people wanted to and because that's what people her age did. She could only find so many friends who didn't mind hanging out in a quiet café or sitting outside talking without the extra stimulation of crowds or cell phones. When she'd seen Nash and Phillip enjoying a serene moment, focused on nothing more than each other, her fears and emotions coalesced, and she knew she wanted to spend more time with them. *Around* them, in the quiet world Nash had created.

Now, as she pulled into his driveway, fear clawed up her spine and perched on her shoulders. Was she putting herself into a position in which she'd have no control? Was this a mistake? Moving to Pleasant Hill had been a big change in and of itself. Was she pushing herself too far?

She curled her fingers around the steering wheel, trying to calm her racing heart, and caught movement out of her peripheral vision. Flip was running around the goat pen with Nash on his heels. She rolled down her window, hearing the distant sound of little-boy giggles and Nash's stronger, raspier laughter as he hauled the boy over his shoulder. She laughed, and at the same time, reveled in how carefree he was with his son compared to everyone else. He maneuvered Flip into his arms and hugged him tight. Her heart warmed, and for the millionth time today, she rationalized her decision. *What's wrong with wanting to be in a low-key family-oriented environment? That's what I know. It is what I'm used to.* Yes, she was attracted to Nash, but she wasn't someone who couldn't control her impulses. All she had to do was take a stroll down her very limited sexual-partner lane to prove that point. Guys were all about combustible energy. Most reeked of it. She could practically see them plotting out their moves, deciding exactly how long it would take to get her into bed on their very *first* date. And she'd had enough first dates that she'd never allowed to lead to seconds to know.

Breathing deeply, she cut the engine. *I can handle the heat.* And if she couldn't, she wasn't too proud to get out of the kitchen. *Or the house.*

Nash turned with a wide, unguarded smile, looking ridiculously sexy as he set Flip on the ground. She stepped from the car and his eyes found her. His smile took a different, darker turn, and the atmosphere heated about fifty degrees. He followed Flip up to the edge of the driveway, where his son stopped and looked up at his father. Nash nodded and held a hand for him to take. He wrapped his little fist around two of

Nash's fingers, and together they crossed the gravel, stopping a few feet from Tempest. Nash slipped his free hand in the front pocket of his jeans. Flip, watching his father closely, pushed a hand into his own pocket. They were quite a pair, these two quiet, new boys in her life.

"How's it going?" Nash's typical bravado seemed less brusque, reminding her of what he'd said last night. *I'm nervous too. That's probably a good thing.*

"Good." *I'm freaking out a little.* "Are you still sure this is all right? It's okay if you've changed your mind."

He looked down at her sandals, shaking his head, and lifted only his eyes, looking up at her from beneath the bill of his ball cap. He looked hot and sweet and manly all at once, sending her heart into a flurry of nervous beats.

"If I changed my mind I would have called you before you went to all this trouble."

She nodded, wondering if he could see how paralyzed she felt. Needing to do *something*, she pushed the button for her trunk on her key fob and went to collect her things.

"I'll help with that." He reached into the trunk and grabbed her biggest suitcase before she could protest. Surveying the few items in the trunk, he said, "Is this all you've got?"

"Mm-hm. I'm still in the beginning stages of growing my business in this area. I have no idea how my client load will pan out, or if I'll need to go back to my business in Peaceful Harbor full-time, so I left most of my stuff in my apartment."

The muscles in Nash's jaw twitched. Flip curled his fingers around the edges of the trunk and went up on his tiptoes, trying to peer inside. He was much too little, and squinted curiously up at Nash.

"Do you mind if I let him carry something?" he asked.

"No, of course not." She grabbed a small, locked, leather jewelry box her mother had given her and crouched beside him. "Think you can handle this?"

He gave her a confident nod with an expression so earnest she had to laugh.

She grabbed a cardboard box of books from the trunk, and Nash took it from her with one hand. "I can carry it," she protested.

"So can I. I left you the heavy load." He glanced at Flip. "Come on, buddy."

Flip carried the jewelry box like it was made of glass. Nash waited for her to grab the laundry basket full of linens and towels before starting toward the door.

"I carried all of this to my car by myself," she advised him proudly.

"And I'm carrying it into the house."

His smirk was entirely too sexy. How was she supposed to argue with a sexy smirk?

"Please tell me I'm not moving in with an overprotective Braden-like landlord. I love my family, but there's a reason I moved out from under their noses."

Flip pushed the door open, and Nash used his elbow to hold it as she stepped inside. "*Helpful* is a better term. Or maybe I just don't want you to hurt yourself on my property and sue me." He looked at her out of the corner of his eyes with a hint of a smile on his lips.

"Yeah, I'm sure that's it," she teased. It felt strange to walk into his house and know she would be sleeping there for the foreseeable future. It wasn't like staying at a hotel where everyone was a guest, or with family, where she could flop on a couch in her sweats with a bowl of peaches and whipped cream and eat to her heart's content. *Oh gosh, can I flop around in sweats?* She could just hear Jillian and Shannon answering her. *No, you definitely cannot. No sweats, unless it's after a sexy romp in the hay.* Now she was even chastising herself with dirty thoughts. That wasn't good.

She followed Flip up the stairs at a snail's pace. Nash leaned over her shoulder, bringing with him the musky, masculine scent of a hard day's work.

"Still nervous?" he asked in a low voice.

"A little more so, now that I'm here," she admitted.

He didn't say a word, making her even more nervous.

When they reached the landing, Flip looked at him and Nash nodded toward the room at the end of the hall. "That's Tempe's room from now on, remember?"

The cutie nodded and toddled down the hall.

"Wow, that sounds strange," she said softly.

"Does it?" Nash asked as they entered her room. "I think it sounds nice."

Nice. She even liked his choice of words. Most guys she knew used words like *cool* or *awesome. Nice* sounded welcoming. Inviting. Like she wanted to be surrounded by it.

"Shouldn't I sign the lease?" she asked.

"We'll take care of it after you're settled in."

The bedroom looked different. Brighter, more lived in. She realized he'd added brighter lightbulbs to the overhead light fixture. There was a stack of fresh towels and sheets on the comforter, which looked freshly washed. He'd set a stack of books by the bed, too. Her heart swelled at that, even though he'd probably do it for anyone. She glanced up at him as he set her box of books on a cute table with a chair that had hand-carved legs and an intricate mountain scene on the back, neither of which had been there when she'd seen the room. He set her suitcase by the closet. "I guess you don't need the linens and towels."

Flip placed her jewelry box on the table next to the box of books, and when Nash slid a hand into his front pocket again, he did the same.

She set her things on the bed. "Thank you. That was really thoughtful, and I love the table and chair. They're perfect." She noticed a heap of price tags in the trash bin beside the bed. "I can pay you for the towels and linens if you'd like."

He scoffed. "Don't be ridiculous."

Flip scoffed and shook his head.

Tempest felt herself smiling. She had a feeling that with these two around, she would be doing a lot more of that. They made another trip down to her car and carried up the rest of her things.

Nash put a hand on the back of his son's head. "I guess we'll leave you to unpack. Have you eaten dinner?"

She loved how he included Flip in everything he did, and that he was always touching him, as if his son were a physical extension of himself. "No. I packed up right after work, but I can run out after I unpack and pick something up. I need to stock up on groceries anyway."

He glanced out the window, his jaw tensing. "We're having stir-fry if you want to join us, and pick up groceries tomorrow."

"Thanks. I'd like that. I'll unpack quickly and help you make it."

He grabbed the extra towels and sheets and nudged Flip out the door. "We've got it. We're old pros." He stopped outside her bedroom door and glanced back at her. "But if you want to help, you're welcome to."

He pulled the door partly closed, leaving her alone to ponder thoughts of the man who'd gone to quite a bit of trouble to make her comfortable.

NASH HADN'T BEEN this nervous since the first time he'd held his son, and suddenly he was anxious in his own house, preparing a meal he'd made hundreds of times? It was one thing to make dinner for him and Phillip, who he knew liked his cooking. But what if Tempest didn't like it? He looked over the red, orange, and yellow peppers and other vegetables they'd picked from the garden, and the thin slices of chicken he'd prepared—*not* from their own stock. It would be fairly hard to screw this up. He tried to concentrate on the country song playing on the radio instead of the way his gut was churning, but it was like trying to ignore an oncoming tsunami.

Phillip sat on the counter tearing lettuce into shreds and putting it into a salad bowl.

"What do you think, buddy?"

Phillip looked up and sang, "Playin' with fire"—he mumbled a few words—"tangled up."

Nash laughed. *Maybe I'm overthinking this.* He tossed the vegetables into the wok with a dash of olive oil, and Nash joined his son in singing the country song. He added seasonings and the sauce Phillip liked, turned the heat down to simmer, and swept his boy off the counter, spinning as they sang. Phillip loved when he danced with him, and it never failed to remind Nash of the life he'd left behind. He didn't harbor resentment for having to grow up. But there were times he missed traveling to art festivals, sculpting for hours each day, and pulling out his guitar whenever it suited him. But that was a long time ago. He kissed Phillip's forehead, gaining even more enjoyment from dancing with his boy than he did from his traveling days.

"You can sing, too?" Tempest stood in the doorway carrying a mug that said *music soothes the soul*. She'd changed into a pair of hip-hugging jeans and an off-white tank top with lace around the neckline. Her feet were bare, save for a tiny silver toe ring, exuding the perfect combination of sexy and innocence again, which was rapidly becoming his favorite look.

"Hardly." Jesus, could he make a bigger fool of himself? He set Phillip on a stool by the counter, where he went back to tearing lettuce and humming to the song. Nash busied himself stirring their dinner.

She held up her mug. "Mind if I put this in the cabinet? I use it every morning."

"One mug?" He cocked his head. "I don't know. That's a real space sucker."

She smiled and touched Phillip's leg. "Your daddy is quite the jokester."

He gave her a quizzical look and offered her a piece of lettuce.

"His hands are clean," Nash said, taking the mug from her as she accepted the lettuce from Phillip. He opened the cabinet, set the mug on a shelf, and said, "Mugs and glasses." He opened another cabinet. "Plates and bowls." He continued through each cabinet and drawer. When he opened the lower cabinet beside the refrigerator, containing pots and pans, he and Phillip said, "Drums," at the same time.

"I think I'm going to like living here." She opened the drawers until she found a peeler and snatched it up, grabbed a carrot, and put herself to work.

She peeled and sliced the carrots, giving Phillip pieces as she added them to the salad bowl, and something inside Nash unfurled. She picked up a cucumber, singing softly into it like a microphone. Phillip laughed, but Nash couldn't take his eyes off her. Her hair was mussed, like she'd gone through her day without primping the way most women spent way too much time doing, and she wore barely any makeup, which he liked. Her smile was enough to make her naturally beautiful face even more radiant.

She washed the cucumber and sliced it on the cutting board beside Phillip. He snatched a piece of cucumber and gobbled it down.

"I'm surprised you like vegetables," she said to him, then to Nash, "Most kids snub them."

"Not my boy. He's always loved adult foods over kid foods." He grabbed three plates from the cabinet. *Three.* He recalled the day after Alaina had left, when he'd gone from taking two plates out of the cabinet to one. The memories didn't come often, and they no longer hit with the force of a plane crash but with the impact of a bee sting, sharp and anger inducing. He grabbed forks and napkins and placed them in the plastic bucket Phillip liked to use to carry them outside. Pushing the uncomfortable thoughts aside, he dished the stir-fry onto their plates.

"And mac and cheese," Tempest said.

"Hm?"

"He must like mac and cheese along with adult food."

"Nope. That's kid food. He hates it." He set Phillip on the floor and handed him the bucket with the utensils. Picking up their plates, he motioned toward the back door, and Phillip pushed it open.

"Thanks, buddy. Tempe, would you mind grabbing the

salad bowl?"

"I'll get glasses, too." She followed them outside and set the glasses and salad bowl on the picnic table. "I assumed he liked mac and cheese because I saw the boxes of it in the pantry."

Nash set the plates on the table. "Those would be mine."

She laughed. "That's cute. I can't imagine a big guy like you eating macaroni and cheese from a box. Those noodles are *tiny*. You can probably eat a box in three bites."

He straightened the bill of his ball cap, amused by her assessment, and said, "It just so happens that I like those tiny noodles. And yeah, maybe I eat three boxes at once. Four sometimes. But I'll bet you've got your own comfort foods." He lifted the upside-down bucket off the candles he lit during dinner each night, pulled a lighter from his pocket, and lit them. "I'm guessing a pint of ice cream, or maybe cake. Chocolate cake."

"You're pretty far off." She pointed to the house. "I'll get drinks. What do you usually have with dinner?"

"I've got it." He took the porch steps two at a time. "What would you like?"

"Anything. I'm not picky."

He went inside and returned a few minutes later with a pitcher of iced tea, two bottles of apple juice, and a bottle of water.

"Thirsty?" she teased.

He poured juice for Phillip and set a napkin beside him. "I wasn't sure what you liked."

"Iced tea is fine, thanks." She sat across from them as he filled her glass.

"Are you going to keep your comfort food a secret?" he asked.

"Maybe," she said coyly. "You'll think it's weird."

"I'm sure it's no weirder than Phillip preferring steak to mac and cheese." He put his arm around Phillip and pulled him closer on the bench. "Right, buddy?"

Phillip smiled around a mouthful of stir-fry.

"Sliced peaches and whipped cream," she said. "But not just any peaches. Fresh-picked, with the kind of whipped cream that comes from a can. You know, the fake stuff."

The thought of Tempest and whipped cream together took his mind straight to the gutter. "And you think the idea of me eating mac and cheese is cute?" he teased. "You don't strike me as the kind of girl who likes anything fake."

She looked down at her plate. "How can you know that after knowing me two days?"

He was wondering that himself. "I don't know. You just seem very *real*."

She met his gaze. An ocean of deep thoughts swam in her eyes. He wanted to dive in and learn all her secrets. But he was acutely aware of his son sitting beside him, listening to every word out of his mouth. He dropped his gaze to his plate, breaking their sizzling connection.

"What happens in the winter when you need comfort food?" He tried to ask it casually, but even he heard the thickness in his tone.

"This is *so* good," she said far too dramatically, as if she were trying to jostle the heat from her bones, too. "I can't believe I got lucky enough to find a landlord who can sing *and* cook."

He didn't know how to respond to that other than saying he couldn't believe he was lucky enough to find a gorgeous housemate who breezed into his life and swept the dust off all the long-ago buried parts of himself. So he said nothing at all and gave her a curious glance, urging her to answer his question.

"Winter comfort food? Ice cream." She paused and lowered her voice. "Usually on top of chocolate cake."

They both laughed.

"I want cake," Phillip said with a toothy grin, giving Nash the perfect excuse to spend more time with Tempest.

"It's late, buddy, and it takes a while for cake to bake. How about if we make it together? Then we'll bake it while you sleep and you can eat a piece for breakfast?"

"With fwosting?" Phillip still had trouble with his r's.

"Of course with frosting."

Phillip looked hopefully at Tempe.

"What do you say, Tempe?" Nash asked. "Are you up for a little baking?"

She looked at Phillip for a long moment, each second ticking by in slow motion.

Say yes. Just frigging say yes.

She finally said, "I think I'd like that."

FLIP STOOD ON a stool between Tempest and Nash, helping to stir the ingredients. He was a quiet child, but his facial expressions were priceless as he hummed along to the radio.

"Careful, Phillip." Nash showed him how to use the side of the spatula to scoop the ingredients toward the center. A big skill for such a little boy.

Her ears perked up. Did he say *Phillip*? She watched the two of them intently, hoping to *see* Nash say his son's name. Nash's hands covered Flip's, and his broad chest swallowed his son whole, as together they guided the spatula around the edges of the bowl.

"That's it, Phillip," he said slowly.

Phillip. Holy cow, she'd been calling him the wrong name this whole time! He said it so fast it *sounded* like Flip. No wonder Phillip called himself *Flip*.

She moved beside him and whispered, "You let me call him the wrong name?"

Nash's lips tipped up. "It wasn't wrong. And it's cute."

"But it's not his *name*." She moved back to Phillip's other side. "I'm sorry I called you by the wrong name, Phillip."

Phillip's brows knitted.

"I called you *Flip*, but your name is *Phillip*," she said it slowly. Nash said his name so fast she wasn't sure he realized his name was Phillip.

"Flip," he said with the cutest grin she'd ever seen. "Flip Morgan."

That soft "r" killed her.

"At least he comes by it honestly." Chuckling, Nash pressed a kiss to Phillip's temple, then whispered, "You did a perfect job, buddy. It'll be the best cake ever."

Spending time with Nash and Phillip was different than she'd expected it to be. *Better. Much better.* Witnessing such tender, genuine moments reminded her of the way her parents had always been with her. Nash was strikingly different at home than he had been when they'd had ice cream in town. She watched him now, as he let Phillip try to use the spatula on his own and laughing when he flicked chocolate over the edge. Nash scooped the batter off the edge of the bowl and let Phillip lick it off his finger.

"Now we need to add the butter." Nash began mashing the butter with a fork.

"If you warm it, you can whip it."

Nash's eyes blazed down at her, a sinful smile curling his lips. Thunder and lightning collided inside her. She must have looked as light-headed as she felt, because he reached around Phillip and touched her arm.

"I prefer to warm it up slowly," he said with a raspy voice. "No whipping necessary."

His hand slid off her arm, leaving a trail of goose bumps, but his volcanic stare remained trained on her. She mentally ran through what had just happened, trying to decipher how she'd earned that incredibly hot look. That *voice. Your touch.*

"Tempe?"

She blinked repeatedly to try to break the spell she'd fallen under and met his amused expression.

"You must be lost in a really great thought. I had to say your name twice."

Like a smack to the forehead, she realized what she'd said to earn that predatory look. "*Butter.* I meant the *butter.*" *Ugh!* She sounded as flustered as she felt.

"Mm-hm." He pointed to the electric mixer on the counter beside her. "Can you please hand me that? As much as I like to warm things up *slowly,* I'm afraid this needs a little speeding up if Phillip's going to get to bed on time."

The furtive glance he tossed her sent an electrifying shudder straight to her core. She turned and began putting away the ingredients they'd used to escape the nerve-racking sparks before they set the kitchen on fire.

By the time they'd filled the cake pans with batter she was *finally* breathing normally again.

She opened the preheated oven and lifted one cake pan from the counter. "I usually do it on the bottom. Do you like it on top or bottom?"

He stepped around Phillip, his wicked smile more intimate than a kiss as he leaned in close and said, "Careful, Tempe. That's a loaded question."

"Wha—" Her jaw gaped. "The *rack*! Do you like it on top or bottom?" She pushed the cake pan onto the bottom rack.

"Hey, I'll take a rack on top, bottom, sideways…"

She rolled her eyes, and he laughed as he put the other cake pan in the oven.

"How did you grow up with brothers and not learn to watch what you said?" He lifted Phillip from the stool and set him on the floor, then tapped his butt with his hand. "Say good night to Tempe and go on up. I'll be right behind you."

Phillip hugged her around her legs, and she just about melted despite her hammering heart. "Good night, Tempe."

"Good night, sweetheart. Thanks for letting me help you bake." After Phillip left the kitchen, she glared at Nash. "You know I didn't mean *that*."

He stepped closer, his nearness both exciting and agonizing. "You're right. I'm sorry. I don't want to make you uncomfortable."

"You're not," came out way too breathless. "I mean, you are, but not in a bad way."

His eyes filled with heat again. "Is there a good way?"

I'm starting to think there might be. She tried to hold his gaze, but she was too drawn to him, the urge to touch him almost impossible to resist. She glanced at the dirty dishes on the counter and saw her escape. Stepping around him, she turned on the faucet and busied herself scrubbing the measuring cup. "You shouldn't keep Phillip waiting."

"Tempest," he said apologetically.

She feigned a laugh, hoping it sounded casual but fearing it just made her sound a little off-balanced. "Don't think twice about it. You were only reacting to what I said."

He hesitated behind her, rendering her frozen, all thoughts and actions impossible. She desperately wanted to clear the air, and at the same time, she wanted to become invisible. When he finally left the kitchen, she let out a fast breath and grabbed the edge of the sink for stability. His heavy steps ascended the stairs. Tempest spun around, grabbed the bowl with the cake batter remnants, and dove in, scooping out whatever chocolate batter was left. She needed pounds of it. A bathtub full. Who was she kidding? She needed a vat of chocolate to dive into.

Her cell phone rang and she pulled it from her pocket with her left hand. The right was covered in chocolate. *Shannon. Thank goodness.*

"Shan?"

"Hi. What's wrong? And why are you whispering?"

"Because I rented a room from a guy I'm way too attracted to, and he's right upstairs."

Shannon shrieked. Tempest pulled the phone from her ear.

"Shannon!" she whispered harshly. "This is serious." She licked chocolate from her knuckles and then ran them over the bottom of the bowl to soak up more.

"Okay, sorry." Shannon giggled. "Hold on."

She heard her sister tell someone what she'd said; then she heard the sound of kissing.

"You called me when you and Steve were making out?"

"No." Shannon giggled, and another noisy kiss came through the phone. "I called you to tell you we're closer to choosing a wedding date and I want you to be my maid of honor!"

Tempest squealed. Immediately realizing her mistake, she ran onto the back porch. "Oh my gosh! Yes! Thank you," she said quieter. She heard the *thump, thump, thump* of Nash rushing down the stairs. "Shoot. I shouldn't have screamed, Nash is putting his son to be—"

Nash flew out the back door, his eyes darting over the yard as he pushed in front of her, his arm outstretched, keeping her behind him. "What happened? Are you okay?"

"Uh-oh," Shannon said.

Tempest lowered the phone as Nash turned around, his eyes sweeping over her face, her body, and finally, landing on the now empty bowl. "You're okay?"

"I'm sorry," she said quickly. "My sister just asked me to be her maid of honor. I hope I didn't scare Phillip. I'm so sorry. I didn't mean to scream."

"Jesus, you scared the hell out of me." He pulled her against him, squishing her against all his hard muscles. The bowl tumbled from her grip, landing on the porch with a *clank*. He stepped back, a smile creeping across his face. "Phillip's fine."

He reached up and brushed his thumb over her cheek. Eyeing the bowl at their feet, he put his thumb in his mouth. He gave her a look so hot her knees buckled. Holy cow, now she needed more chocolate. *Stat.*

He picked up the bowl, giving her one last long look that nearly melted her panties right off, and disappeared into the house, leaving her reeling.

She breathed deeply, hearing the faint sound of his boots ascending the stairs again. Lifting the phone to her ear, she whispered, "Shan."

"Was that him? What happened? What did he do? All that silence was *so* hot. I think I burned my fingers on my phone."

"Not helpful." Tempest could still feel her heart thundering against her chest. "But, yeah. It was hot. Really hot." Swallowing hard, she said, "I think I'm in over my head."

Chapter Six

COOL AIR BLEW in through the open door to the deck, carrying the sounds of Tempest playing the guitar. Nash paced his bedroom floor, trying to get his head on straight. After putting Phillip to bed and taking the cake out of the oven, he'd stood in a long, cold shower, trying to escape the feel of Tempest in his arms. It was an impossible task. He could still feel her soft curves pressed against him, and on its heels, the fear that had taken hold when he'd heard her scream. He needed to get his head on straight before he did something stupid and scared her off altogether.

He stepped outside, the music coiling around him like a tether, drawing him toward the sound of her voice. Damn she sounded sweet, as ethereal and clear as whispered promises. She sat sideways on the bench, one leg outstretched, the other bent at the knee, her guitar cradled in her lap. Golden waves curtained her face as she strummed out a tune, stopping every few beats to scribble something in a notebook. His pulse ratcheted up with every step, and when she glanced up, her hair hiding one eye, the silence took on a beat all its own.

"Hey," he said.

She smiled, a slight flush coloring her cheeks. "Hi," she said, and looked down at her guitar.

He'd embarrassed her by looking at her like he wanted her, and he hated himself for it. He wanted her to feel comfortable, and he had acted inappropriately. He wasn't an animal. He could control his primal urges. At least he'd sure as hell try.

"Look at that. You do have a nice head of hair."

He ran a hand through his hair, unsure how to respond.

"You wear your hat so often, I wondered if you had a bald spot you were covering up." She glanced up with the tease.

Breathing a little easier, he sat by her feet. "Not yet. That's a nice tune."

"Thanks." She tucked her hair behind her ear and it immediately sprang free. "I'm writing it for a client."

"I'm sure they'll like it."

"He's in a coma." She looked away.

"Oh shit. I'm sorry." *Way to break the ice.*

"Me too. He's only seven."

She spoke so softly, he wanted to move closer just to catch every syllable, but he didn't dare. "I didn't realize you dealt with such heavy stuff. That can't be easy."

"Recovery is never easy. But it's harder for the patients and their loved ones than it is for me. I just try to help ease the pain, and hopefully bring him back from wherever he's gone. I hope one day to do more with my children's music group and less hospital work. It definitely puts me in a better mental place, but it'll take time to build the group up to a sustainable size. So, for now, I'm working more with hospital patients."

"Do they think he'll pull out of it?"

She tucked that stray lock of hair behind her ear again, and when she looked down at her guitar, it sprang free. "Every patient is different. They're optimistic."

He couldn't resist leaning forward and tucking her hair behind her ear. She lifted those clear blue eyes that made his stomach go squirrely and drew in a quiet breath, holding it for a beat before letting it out. It was the sexiest thing he'd ever seen.

"Thanks," she whispered.

There were so many things he wanted to say. *I'm sorry for making you uncomfortable, you're so beautiful,* and *I want to feel your lips on mine* topped the list. But all that came out was, "How do you know what songs will help?"

A sweet, sexy sigh escaped before she answered. "I don't, really. When a family's in pain, they tend to say more than they realize."

Or they don't say anything at all.

After they'd lost PJ and his parents had taken him out of school to live on the boat, they'd stopped talking about his brother. He knew it was too painful for them, and poured his emotions into writing songs. He couldn't sing them around his parents, so he'd eventually learned to repress those, too, until they'd moved back to the mainland and he'd begun traveling. When Phillip was born, lyrics had flowed like a river, and he'd written song after song. But when Alaina left, anger had clouded his every thought, and he'd stopped playing guitar. Now, as he listened to Tempest talk about writing lyrics and helping others, he realized that with the exception of the love he had for Phillip and his mother, after Alaina left, he'd stopped feeling altogether.

"A picture of who the person is comes together," she said, pulling him from his thoughts, "and I put it into lyrics. I never know if I have it right, but I'm not sure there is right or wrong when it comes to reaching a person. I just go with what I feel."

He glanced at the notebook, where she'd written musical notes and lyrics, along with doodles of hearts and swirls. Hell if that didn't seem like *her*. "Can I take a look?"

"Do you read music?" She handed him the notepad.

"A bit."

She set the guitar on the other side of the bench and wrapped her arms around her knees while he looked over her notes, watching him intently and nervously nibbling on her lower lip. He understood the fear of sharing something she'd poured her heart and soul into. He felt that same trepidation every time he sold a piece of furniture—and every time someone new met Phillip.

As he silently read the lyrics, he heard her voice singing them in his head.

They crossed their hearts, swore on stars
Promised to keep you safe, to love you through
Bruised knees, broken hearts, and everything in between
To love and adore you, for forever and a day
You laughed, you played
You filled up their world
With bruised knees, laughter, and everything in between
Your family's waiting
They're right here by your side
They're crossing their hearts, swearing on stars
Can you hear them calling, holding your hand?
Waiting for you
They'll wait forever
Forever and a day

He swallowed past the emotions lodged in his throat. "This is beautiful."

She reached for the notebook, but he held on tight, unable to let the embarrassment rising on her cheeks be all she took from his words. He laid his hand over hers, bringing her eyes up to his.

"Tempest, this is really powerful."

She held his gaze, breathing harder. "Thank you. It's a little sappy, but if you could see his family and the hope in their eyes." Her eyes dampened, and she looked away, lowering her feet to the deck.

Wanting to comfort her, he wrapped an arm around her shoulder and pulled her close. "You're a brave woman. I'm not sure many people could do what you're doing."

"*Pfft.*" She wiped her eyes. "Plenty can and do."

"I don't think so," he said. "It takes a special person to take on someone else's pain."

He loosened his grip and was surprised when she held on to his arm and leaned back against his chest instead of moving away.

"Is this okay?" she asked tentatively.

"Yeah." *More than okay.* "I'm sorry about before. I wasn't trying to make you uncomfortable."

"I know. And I don't want to lead you on now. I just…" She drew in a shaky breath. "When I write like this, it takes a lot out of me."

He rested his cheek on the top of her head. "Then you have the perfect housemate, because I've had a lot taken out of me over the years. And I will try to be here for you without the threat of taking you to bed." *Oh, man.* Did he really say that out loud? Could he keep that promise? He sure as hell would try. He hadn't realized how much he'd missed something as basic as friendship and human touch. "Do you want to talk about it?"

"About you taking me to bed?" she teased.

"I meant your *client*, your *business*. The *music*." Grinding his teeth together, he said, "Just talk about something to get that other image out of my head."

She laughed and looked up at him over her shoulder. "I like you, Nash. You're all kinds of guys wrapped up in one, and a really sweet father."

"I like you, too. Now, stop looking at me." Using his chin, he nudged her face away. "One more second of watching your mouth and I'll make myself a liar."

She laughed, letting out a loud, happy sigh. "I can move over if it's too much."

"Not too much. Just…stay the line."

"Oh, now we have lines."

He held her tighter. "I'm a good guy, not a saint. Compassionate, yes. But never forget, I'm still a red-blooded male."

"I don't think any woman could forget that." She peeked up at him again, studying his expression. "Since we're defining lines, where's the line with asking you personal questions?"

"Where do you want it to be?"

"Gosh, you're easy." She smiled. "Guess your lines are sort of penciled in, not inked."

If he got ahold of an eraser, he was going to be in deep shit. "What are you curious about?"

"Phillip's mom."

THE SECOND TEMPEST said the words, she felt Nash tense up. "We don't have to talk about it. I was just curious."

He didn't respond, and the therapist in her cataloged his

harsher breathing and the tightening of his grip.

"What do you want to know?" he finally asked.

"Do you share custody of Phillip? Are you divorced? I noticed a ring on your right hand, and I assumed…"

She was still leaning back against his chest. He uncurled his fingers, and she sensed him looking at the ring. "It was my father's."

She reached up and touched the beautifully rugged, brushed-silver ring. A strip of darker metal stretched around its circumference, secured with two tiny rivets on either side, leaving a small gap of silver between.

"It's silver and titanium," he said evenly. "I made it for him, back when I worked with metals."

"It's elegant and masculine. Really unique and lovely. You don't work with metal anymore?"

"A lot has changed since Phillip was born. His mother left when he was three months old."

She *left? Why did she leave? Where is she now?* She had dozens of other questions, but the tension in his voice kept her from asking a single one.

"It's too dangerous to work with heat when Phillip is around, and no, I'm not divorced. Alaina and I were never married," he said icily. "She hasn't seen him since the day she left."

She moved beside him, taking in his tight-lipped expression, the narrowing of his eyes. She'd seen similar looks of pained tolerance on the faces of her clients' loved ones.

"I'm sorry. I don't know what to say. I can't imagine a mother leaving her child like that, but it's not my place to judge."

"Sure it is." He pressed his fingers into his thigh muscles, as if he were trying to channel his anger away from his voice. "She left herself open to judgment the minute she walked out on him." He leaned forward, as he had the other night, elbows on knees, face tight, and began wringing his hands together.

"She walked out on you." Who in their right mind would walk out on their family? "That must have hurt. I'm sorry. I shouldn't have pried."

"It's okay." He angled his face toward hers, meeting her gaze head-on. "I don't have anything to hide. Yes, she walked out on both of us, but *I* don't matter. It wasn't like we were high school sweethearts, desperately in love and destined for a happily ever after. We were two traveling artists, following festivals and art competitions up and down the coast, going wherever our art took us. We met, enjoyed each other's company, and hung out for a few weeks. And then she got pregnant." He shrugged. "It happens. People have sex, and sometimes birth control doesn't work. It's a fact of life."

She could tell he'd been over it a million times in his head.

"Neither of us wanted to abort the pregnancy, and like I said, we weren't in love, so there was never talk of marriage or anything like that." He looked up at the stars, shaking his head. "When I found out she was pregnant, I told myself I could learn to love her, but…" He shrugged again. "It just wasn't there for either of us. She was someone I enjoyed being around. We had a lot in common, and we occasionally shared a bed. But I wasn't *in* love with her."

"Was she in love with you?"

He scoffed. "No. She said she didn't know if she was capable of loving anyone. But that didn't matter. As I said, we didn't have that type of connection. We just…We were like friends who sometimes slept together. But from the minute I found out she was pregnant, I loved the baby growing inside of her. I never resented her for the pregnancy, and I don't think she resented me for it, either. Our relationship wasn't like that. We kind of took things as they came. But a child? That's different on so many levels. She wanted to keep traveling and live as a starving artist, but you can't raise a kid on the road, not knowing where you'll be the next day or where your next meal will come from."

He sat up straighter and waved toward the house. "I bought this place using the money my father had left me because I wanted our baby to have a stable home life, like I had when I was a kid, but Alaina had never had that. She'd grown up in a military family, moving every couple years, and she hit the road when she was eighteen and never looked back. It was what she knew, and in the end, it was what she wanted. She handed me the baby one evening, took off with some guy in a van, and never looked back. A month later I got papers in the mail. She'd formally relinquished all parental rights, like Phillip was an old car and she was transferring a title."

Anger rose in his eyes, and she wondered if that was a mask for pain, or if he was truly angry—over the situation, over Alaina's leaving, or even over becoming a father so unexpectedly.

"So, you've raised Phillip alone all this time?"

He nodded, a smile forming on his lips. "We're a team, and I've never regretted a second of it."

"But you *sound* angry."

"I am angry, but not about raising Phillip. I'm angry that she left my little boy without a mother. I'm angry that she's given him a life sentence of trying to understand her inability to be a loving parent. Everyone knows how an absent parent can scar a child. I do everything I can to let him know he's loved, but I'm not his mother."

The *woman* in Tempest was right there with him, upset for the sweet boy sleeping inside the house. But the therapist in her wondered if Alaina had done the right thing. Not all people were meant to be parents, and as much as it sucked for Nash and Phillip, there was something to be said about Alaina knowing herself well enough not to burden others with her shortcomings.

"If that makes me a bad person," Nash said, "then so be it."

"It doesn't make you a bad person. It makes you human."

The tension drained from his face. "Thanks. I do the best I can."

"You're great with Phillip, but you should tell people when they call him the wrong name." She smiled, hoping to lighten the air.

He huffed out a soft laugh. "Thanks. I guess I should slow down when I say his name. But I really did think it was cute, and apparently he thinks of himself as Flip, too, so…" He shrugged, and his face grew serious again. "It means a lot to hear you say that. He's my life, and I'll do whatever it takes to keep him safe and happy. What about you, Tempe? Why are you here in Pleasant Hill, starting over? You said you had no crazy *or* sane boyfriend or exes to worry about. So why is a gorgeous, smart woman like you still starting over, and still single?"

It was her turn to shrug. Her cheeks burned with his praise.

He leaned closer. The tension she'd seen moments earlier was gone, replaced with a softer, and somehow more intense, curiosity. "I just unzipped my baggage and let you rifle through it. You can do better than a shrug."

"I guess I felt trapped in my old life. I wasn't going any-where or meeting new people. I wanted to change the direction of my business. Back home I mostly worked in the hospital, and I wanted to build a child-centric business in a lighter way. But it's hard to reinvent yourself when you've carved out a niche for yourself as a certain type of person, in a certain job. It seemed like a good time to make a fresh start."

"And you're still single because…?"

"I don't know. I work a lot, and I help my sister-in-law, Leesa, run a Girl Power group. I spend time with family."

"And that prohibits you from finding a great guy?"

"No, but when you grow up in a small community, you rarely meet someone you don't know *everything* about, and I knew more than I wanted to about most of the guys my age. It was just time for a change."

"I know all about small towns." A haunted look flashed in his eyes, and just as quickly, they were clear again. She wondered if she'd imagined it. "And what's a Girl Power group? Do you get together with women and bash men? If so, maybe we've discovered the issue."

How could he go from serious to teasing so quickly? "*Please.* Do I seem like a person who bashes guys? We help young girls gain self-esteem through group activities. We meet about every six weeks or so, depending on our schedules. I really enjoy it. It's hard to be a teenage girl. There's a lot of pressure to fit in, dress and act a certain way. Just getting through each day can be traumatic."

"There's a lot of pressure to fit in for guys, too," he said uneasily. "Teenage years are hard."

"I bet you had no trouble fitting in during school."

"Wanna bet? I was gangly and weird, because I was more interested in art than sports." He brushed her hair from in front of her eye with his index finger, and her whole body seemed to flame to life with the intimate touch.

"But you?" he said quietly. "Surely you were popular in high school."

"I had a lot of friends, but I was the nerd girl playing her guitar on the beach in her parents' backyard Friday nights instead of going to parties."

"So, basically you were the mysteriously sexy, artsy, good girl who half the guys in your school probably fantasized about." His low voice was as smooth and warm as velvet. "And now you spend your time helping others. That *really* doesn't explain why you haven't been swept off your feet yet."

"You make me sound so interesting, and I can assure you, I'm not."

"I like talking to you, and I find you very intriguing." His gaze intensified, and his fingers moved over her arm.

Her stomach quivered, and she grasped for a response. "Maybe I'm not easily *sweepable*."

"Maybe you're just careful."

"I am," she admitted, breathing a little harder.

"*Too* careful?"

His fingers moved in slow, mesmerizing circles on her arm, sending shivers of awareness streaming through her.

"Probably." She hoped she said the word aloud, because she was too lost in his feathery touch to be sure she'd actually spoken.

"What are you looking for, Tempe?" he asked, just above a whisper.

She wasn't sure if he was asking what she was looking for in a man or in Pleasant Hill, but she didn't have a solid answer for either. "I'm not sure."

"Sure you are," he said seductively, and if she wasn't too out of her mind to be able to read him clearly, a little nervously, too. "You're the only one who knows what you want."

The breeze, his touch, and the heady sound of his voice blurred together as they gazed into each other's eyes. They both leaned forward, or maybe she imagined it, but his minty breath drifted over her lips. His fingers stilled on her arm, and her mouth went dry.

"Tell me what you want, Tempest," he whispered.

"Right now I want to kiss you." She couldn't believe she'd said it, but she didn't want to take it back, not for anything in the world.

His hand slid to the nape of her neck. Neither one of them blinked. She wasn't sure she was even still breathing as his warm, strong fingers cupped the back of her neck, feeling oh so good. So right. He brushed the tip of his nose along her cheek, and she closed her eyes, anticipating the first taste of his lips.

"I promised not to make you uncomfortable," he whispered.

She opened her eyes, captivated by the raw emotion looking back at her.

"Tempest," he pleaded. "What have you done to me? I haven't kissed a woman since the day Alaina left."

She held her breath, conscious of how hard her heart was beating and trying to think past the desire drawing her mouth closer to his. "It's been a long time for me, too."

His fingers pressed into her skin, his eyes brimming with tenderness and passion. "I really like you. I don't want to screw this up."

"Maybe we shouldn't kiss." She grabbed the front of his shirt, keeping him close, her lips tingling with anticipation. "It's probably a bad idea, but I really want to. Do you w—"

He smothered her words with a press of his lips, pulling her closer as his tongue delved into her mouth. The first taste of him was heavenly, and when he deepened the kiss, her thoughts spun away. He kissed her harder, more demanding, his tongue searching and prodding, as if he wanted to inhabit all of her. Then he was shifting their bodies, lifting her over his legs and onto his lap. One muscular arm circled her waist, holding her so tight she couldn't tell where he ended and she began, and his other hand moved under her hair, cupping the back of her head and angling her mouth so he could intensify the kiss. Oh Lord, did she like that. He was so big, so hard, so gloriously delicious, she wanted to savor every second of their kisses. Her hands moved on their own accord, over his arms, along his shoulders, and into his thick, soft hair. She'd never kissed a man like this before, abandoning all restraint without regard for the message she sent. Her consciousness ebbed and flamed with each stroke of his tongue. Pleasure radiated through her limbs, coursing through her veins, bringing rise to unfamiliar noises—*moans*. She'd only known him three days, and yet she felt like she'd been waiting for this kiss her whole life.

There was no end, no beginning. The kiss went on and on, and when he slowed their pace, he didn't break away, as if he wanted to savor it, too. His hand moved up her back, along her side, his fingertips brushing her breast, sending pulses of heat to places that hadn't pulsed in a very long time. She arched into him, fear and excitement battling for domination. When their mouths parted, she was barely breathing. Or maybe she was panting. She couldn't be sure because his lips found hers again in a series of slow, intoxicating kisses.

"God, Tempe," he whispered.

Their eyes met for a heated second, and then he smothered her lips with demanding mastery, shattering the last of her thoughts. She clawed at his shirt, ate at his mouth, as wanton sounds poured from her lungs. His hips rose beneath her, his arousal pressing against her damp sex, and she was right there with him, grinding with every lift of his hips. She touched his face, wanting to feel more of him. His rough whiskers scratched her palms, and she became aware of the burn they caused on her lips and cheeks as he kissed the edges of her mouth.

"Tempest." His voice was thick with lust. "We're crossing lines."

She brushed her thumb over his lower lip and he trapped it inside his mouth, sucking it slowly. He was sinful, and this was *not* her. She didn't get carried away, didn't cross lines. She didn't let men suck on her thumb, and she didn't straddle them, rocking like a lap dancer. But *oh*, how she *wanted* him. She pulled her thumb from his mouth with a *pop* and captured his lips with hers. Shocked by her own aggressiveness, she knew she needed to rein in her desires. She told herself to stop, but the kiss was too exhilarating, he felt too good, and she succumbed to the forceful domination of her inner woman, giving herself over to their passion.

They kissed until they were *both* moaning. He gripped her hips, holding her firmly as he rocked harder beneath her to the rhythm of their kisses. He never broke their connection as he lowered her to her side, lying on the bench, his thick leg pushing between hers, one arm cushioning her head, the other trapping their bodies together.

"Tell me you won't run scared tomorrow," he said between kisses. "Tell me I'm not fucking this up."

She heard the words in her mind. *Kiss me. I won't run scared. Kiss me. You're not fucking this up. Kiss me.* He needed to hear her say it—she could tell by the frantic beat of his heart—but when she tried to push her voice from her lungs, all that came was another needy sound. She didn't know what was happening, but a force bigger than her, bigger than him, was at work. She could feel it in her bones. She knew he wasn't going to try to take this further, but she was already mourning the moment when their insatiable kisses would end. In five minutes? Ten? At dawn? When Phillip woke up?

"Tempe," he panted out. "I've never kissed like this." Several deep kisses later he said, "I can't stop."

She slid her hand into his back pocket, as if that were enough to keep him from ever moving away, and met his sultry gaze. It took all of her focus to push out the words playing in her mind like a mantra.

"Then don't."

Chapter Seven

TEMPEST LAY IN bed shortly after the sun came up Saturday morning, listening to Nash and Phillip getting ready for their day. They were nearly silent, save for the creaking of the floors and occasional whispers. She listened for Phillip's little feet to run across the floor, but she'd noticed that he didn't run from one thing to the next like most boys his age. He seemed to take his cues from his father, mimicking everything from his mannerisms to his gait. She rolled onto her side, gazing out at the bench where she and Nash had made out last night. She touched her lips, feeling a smile form there. The memory of his mouth pressed against hers was so fresh she could still taste him. They'd talked and kissed for hours, but it felt like they'd done much more. They'd certainly done more kissing and full-body grinding than she ever had so quickly after meeting a man.

She rolled onto her back, thinking about the way he'd held her when she'd told him about her clients. How had he known exactly the kind of comfort she needed? Back home, when she was working on a particularly sad or emotional case, she would go to her parents' microbrewery and hang out with them and whichever siblings happened to show up. That usually made her feel less sad and reminded her of why she was doing what she did. But lately the emotional drain had been getting to her more and more. Nash was right when he said music therapy wasn't for everyone. But the connection she felt strengthening with every moment they spent together went deeper than his knowing to hold her or the way he made her entire body flame with his kisses. She felt like she already knew him better than any guy she'd dated, and they weren't even dating. When they'd finally called it a night, drunk on their kisses, he'd walked her to the French doors that led to her bedroom like he was walking her to the front door at the end of a real date. He'd taken her in his arms for one last good-night kiss, and she felt like it *was* the end of a date. Everything about the night had been perfect, even the embarrassing beginning.

She closed her eyes, exhaling a happy sigh. For the first time since she'd come to Pleasant Hill, she'd actually slept soundly, even if for too few hours. And she'd *dreamed*, which was also rare. Usually she barely remembered a thing about her dreams, but my, oh my, had she dreamed! *Sexy, erotic dreams featuring my landlord.* Geez, she couldn't think like that. *Housemate*, that was easier. Pushing from the bed, she stretched, feeling invigorated despite the few hours she'd slept. She checked the time on her phone, *seven thirty*, and read a text message from Jillian as she padded across the floor. *Did you survive your first night in the same house as Mr. Sexy?*

She opened the French doors, shivering against the brisk air and inhaling the scent of a bright new day, thinking about Jillian's question. She'd done more than *survive*. She'd shocked herself when she'd said she wanted to kiss him. But if she told that to Jillian, her cousin would take her giving in to her desires as a green light and she might try to nudge her to do more. Tempest wasn't ready to be nudged in that direction. She was glad Nash hadn't pushed her, but he was obviously careful, too. *I haven't kissed a woman since the day Alaina left.*

Three years? That was longer than it had been for her.

She typed a response to Jillian. *Survived, slept, and even worked on my songs and baked a cake with him and Phillip. He's the perfect housemate.* She sent the message and sank down to the bench where they'd lain last night. She'd never look at the bench the same again. *Can I ever look at Nash the same again?*

Her phone vibrated with another text from Jillian. *PERFECT as in…?*

Leave it to Jillian to push for more. Tempest looked out over the yard, thinking about how much she wanted to reveal. Worry tiptoed through her. What if he'd woken up feeling differently than she did? What if he thought last night was a mistake?

He didn't kiss me like it was a mistake.

She shook off the thought and decided not to share what they'd done last night with Jillian. Her cousin was used to a faster lifestyle than she was. No matter how she tried to craft it in a text, she knew it would come across as just a make-out session and nothing more, even though it felt like much more. Like they'd each opened a door and dipped their toes into unfamiliar territory.

But can we explore it together?

She grabbed a towel and her toiletries and went down the hall to the bathroom, which smelled even more like Nash than it had last night. She set her toiletries on the counter and found an envelope with her name on it propped against a small glass with handpicked flowers in it. She reached for the envelope with a shaky hand and leaned down to smell the pretty wildflowers. What a surprise Mr. Gruff was turning out to be. Flowers definitely meant he didn't think their kissing was a mistake. She withdrew a handwritten note and read his messy scrawl. *The handwriting of an artist.*

Good morning, beautiful. I hope we weren't too loud this morning. I'm not very good at this stuff and haven't had to face a morning after for years. So if you want to pretend last night never happened, wear a bright red shirt, or something else that's red, and I'll know to steer clear and I'll lick my wounds in private. I thought we were on the same page last night, but as I said, it's been a long time, so what do I know?—Nash

She read the note three times, just to be sure she wasn't overlooking some unwritten message between the lines. He didn't say he was *all in*, but he obviously wasn't regretting it. She showered and changed, too nervous to face him yet, and went to work on the flyer she wanted to hang up at Emmaline's.

A while later her stomach growled, reminding her she hadn't eaten breakfast. She emailed the flyer to FedEx Office to have it printed and went down to the kitchen, where she found a piece of cake covered in plastic wrap, a fork, and another note. Butterflies took flight in her stomach.

Breakfast of champions. N & P

N & P. She loved that. She unwrapped the cake and scooped a forkful of chocolate goodness into her mouth, then picked a crumb from her bright green shirt. *No red lights here.* The idea that she was about to brazenly deliver that message made her stomach go a whole different kind of wild. She really was throwing caution to the wind. *Jillian and Shannon would be so proud.*

As she headed outside, she thought about his first note and laughed to herself over the red-shirt signal. Her big, brooding landlord was all kinds of cute. She could think of many things he could do with his talented mouth, and licking was most certainly involved, but there would be no fresh wounds to tend to. *Unless they come from my teeth.* She'd turned into Jillian overnight. Maybe his kisses were magic and they'd make her riskier and help her break free from her careful ways. They'd done a good job of it so far.

Boundaries, Tempe. Remember your boundaries.

She rolled her eyes at herself as she headed down the hill toward the barn, wishing that part of her would keep its opinions to itself.

NASH LEANED OVER the workbench and blew the wood shavings from the panel he was carving. Phillip blew on the piece of wood on his own miniature workbench Nash had built for him. He squinted up at Nash.

Nash grabbed a fishtail chisel and showed it to Phillip, who scanned his plastic tools and picked up the one that looked most like a fishtail. Nash winked and went to work on the panel, the two of them humming to the song on the radio as they worked. Phillip copied every move his father made, right down to wiping his hands on the back of his jeans. Sometimes the way Phillip looked at him sent painful memories chasing harsher ones. His boy idolized him the way Nash had idolized PJ. PJ was two years older and a whole lot smarter than Nash, or at least that's what Nash had always thought. Until the bastard had gone and proved him wrong.

"Hey there."

Tempe's voice pulled him from the memories.

"Tempe," Phillip said, and looked up at Nash before turning around.

Nash curled a hand around the back of Phillip's head and nodded, trying to escape the flashbacks that were making him feel extra protective. He hated the strength with which they hit and struggled to push them away as he turned to face her, praying she wasn't wearing a red shirt.

"Green," slipped out with his unstoppable smile. *Bright fucking green. Thank God.* But it was the light in her eyes that finally shoved his harsh memories away. He set down his tools and wiped his hands on his jeans, wishing he could take her in his arms and kiss her again. But he had a set of little-boy eyes watching every move he made.

Her lips curved up and she said, "Green," as she approached. "Thank you for the flowers. They were a beautiful surprise." She held his gaze for a few long seconds before turning those dazzling eyes on Phillip. "And thank *you* for the delicious cake."

Phillip glanced at Nash, and Nash nodded again.

Tempest gave him a curious glance.

"You're welcome," Phillip said, and wiped his hands on his pants just as Nash had.

"I have to run into town to pick up the flyers and hang them up at a few shops, and then I was thinking about going to the grocery store so I don't mooch all of your food. I thought I'd see if you needed anything." She looked over their workbenches. "It looks like you two have been busy this morning."

"Typical day. We gathered the eggs, fed the animals, and

came out here to work for a while." He had to put in as much time as he could each day, and it came in fits and spurts, depending on Phillip's attention span. Some days Nash was lucky to get an hour's work in. Other days, he could fit in a solid two or three.

"Looks like you have a very willing apprentice." She surveyed the plastic tools piled up on Phillip's workbench. "What are you making?"

Phillip looked to him again, and Nash gave him the go-ahead.

Phillip took her hand and led her around the workbenches to the far end of the barn, where the rest of the cabinet was waiting for its doors, along with several other pieces in various stages of creation. "Daddy maked it."

"*Made*, buddy." Nash joined them, watching as Tempest ran her fingers over the intricate designs he'd spent weeks working on.

"This is gorgeous." She looked over the other pieces of furniture he was working on, admiring each with Phillip on her heels. Each time she touched a groove or pressed her hand to a design, the corners of her mouth lifted in appreciation.

Nash was proud of what he'd created, but it was nothing compared to what he was capable of, and he stifled the urge to say as much.

She glanced around the barn, her eyes drifting over to the opposite corner, where he'd built a child-size table and chair for Phillip. His drawing papers were scattered over the top, a pile of crayons in the center. He'd used nails to hang several of Phillip's drawings, and several other nails were bare, waiting for his boy to create his next masterpiece. She smiled as her eyes sailed over the cubbies he'd built with a wilderness scene carved into the sides, each cubby home to a variety of toys. Along the same wall was a futon-like bed he'd built. *The Old Man and the Sea* lay facedown on the pillow beside one of Phillip's blankets. Curtains of fabric with pictures of animals on them swayed in the breeze, hanging from the three-sided canopy Nash had built around the bed. The sides of the bed were hidden behind the fabric, but he'd carved scenes with cats and dogs along them. He'd picked up a few old end tables and cleaned them up, painted them to look distressed, and set them up around the barn for Phillip to use. Several of the animals Nash had carved were set up on two of the tables. Beneath each table was a cat bed, one of which was home to two sleeping kitties.

Tempest gazed up at one of his pre-Phillip pieces, an iron and wood chandelier in the shape of a boat, hanging from the center of the barn ceiling. The light fixtures were positioned as railing posts around the perimeter of the boat.

"The lights dim," he said. "Sometimes Phillip likes to nap here instead of in his room."

"Did you make all of this?" She motioned around the barn and picked up one of the animals he'd carved.

"Mostly. Not some of the tables."

"These?" She ran her index finger along the long neck of a wooden giraffe he'd made last winter.

"Yes. Phillip and I read a book about Africa and he was really into the animals." He shrugged. "So I made them. No big deal."

"He maked a lion," Phillip said. "And a leopard, and a snake, and a hyena."

"This is all a very big deal. How do you get any work done if you're creating such an amazing world for your son?"

"We figure it out." He had the overwhelming urge to show

her the parts of himself he'd put away a long time ago.

"I guess so," she said, setting the giraffe on the table. "I saw some of your sculptures online, but there was no mention of furniture."

He took off his hat and ran a hand through his hair. "There wouldn't be. I didn't start selling furniture until after Phillip was born, and I only sell it locally. Gotta make a living, right? The local newspaper had asked to do an article about my sculptures when I first moved here, but I like my privacy. Good thing I turned it down, given the changes we've gone through."

She looked around again. "Do you do any sculpture work anymore?"

"No." He glanced at the door leading to his metalworking and wood-sculpting workshop, debating showing her his unfinished work.

Phillip crouched beside the kittens and petted them.

"And who are these little guys?"

"Moby and Manolin," Phillip answered. "Want to pet them?"

"I would love to." She plunked right down on the concrete floor beside him. "Manolin is an interesting name."

"It's from"—*fwom*—"the old-man book Daddy reads," Phillip explained. "He takes care of the old man."

"*Old Man and the Sea*," Nash reminded him.

Tempest picked up a kitty and cradled it, rubbing her chin over its fur. "That's a very big-boy story. Do you like it?"

Phillip nodded enthusiastically. It was one of his favorite stories. Of course, Nash skipped over the parts he thought might be too upsetting.

He listened as Tempest asked Phillip what other stories he liked and what animals were his favorites. Phillip thought hard about each question, his face pinching in concentration as he petted the kitty, looking to Nash often for approval before finally giving her one-word answers. Tempest was patient with him, and engrossed him in a story about where she'd grown up and the stories her father used to tell her and her siblings around a bonfire on the beach. Phillip moved so close he was practically sitting in her lap. She gave his son her undivided attention, listening to every word he said and asking more questions based on his answers. She transferred the kitten to Phillip's lap and brushed her fingers over his cheek. Her eyes warmed, and a wave of fullness crowded Nash's chest, followed almost instantly by an ache of longing for the close-knit family he'd once had.

"Daddy boated, but he didn't catch big fishes," Phillip said. He pushed the kitten off his lap and stood up to play with his wooden animals.

Tempest picked up the kitty, nuzzled it against her face for a moment, then set it back in the bed beside the other one. She smiled at Nash, still speaking to Phillip as she rose to her feet. "I bet he caught some good-sized fish, though." She looked up at the light again. "Do you still make things like that?"

"No. As I mentioned, metalwork demands heat, and the tools I use to manipulate the metal are dangerous for Phillip to be around." He glanced at his son, who was happily playing with his animals, and this time he didn't try to suppress the urge to show her what he was capable of. He cocked his head toward the door to his other workshop. "C'mon. I'll show you what I mean."

"I stay here?" Phillip moved his toy giraffe along the table.

"Sure. Don't leave the barn."

Phillip nodded.

Nash unlocked the door to the workshop, and Tempest

followed him in. It was a strange feeling, having someone else in his shop. He'd been in there a few times since he'd stopped working with metal, but usually with blinders on and with the sole intent of storing something out of Phillip's reach. Now, as Tempest's nearness lured him in, he wore a different type of blinders. Gone was the urge to share his work, replaced with the need to feel her against him again. He gathered her close and moved behind the open door, out of Phillip's line of vision.

"Hi, beautiful." He brushed his lips over hers, making sure the heat he felt wasn't one-sided. "You smell incredible."

"So do you. I hope it's okay that I came down to the barn while you were working. I didn't mean to interrupt. I really did want to see if you needed anything from the store."

"I need something, but not from the store." It was like she'd uncorked the passionate parts of him.

She breathed harder, a rosy blush spreading rapidly over her cheeks.

"Does that green shirt mean what I think it means?"

She wrapped her arms around his waist. "It means you should kiss me before Phillip gets bored."

He kissed her slowly at first, running his hands up her back, keeping her close. The feel of her soft curves was intoxicating, and when he intensified the kiss, she was right there with him. They stumbled back against the wall, and he fought the voice in his head telling him to slow down. Slowing down was the last thing he wanted to do. Her hands were like fire moving up his body and around his neck, spurring him on to kick up the heat. He crushed her to him, kissing her forcefully and earning a sweet moan like he'd heard in his dreams last night.

"I thought about you all night," he said between kisses.

"Me too," she said breathlessly.

He couldn't get enough of her, ravaging her mouth, her neck—and wanting to take things much further. Seeing her with Phillip had flipped a switch inside him, and in his kisses there was as much lust as there was gratitude. But he knew better than to let this train run its course, and forced himself to put on the brakes.

"Sorry," he said, but he wasn't sorry for kissing her. He was only sorry for being so aggressive. She didn't need that, but she'd unleashed a beast that had been tied up for too long, and now that he had a taste of her, every touch of her lips made him want more. He put some space between them, sliding his hands to her hips.

"Sorry," he said again. "I only meant to kiss you hello, not attack you."

She held tightly to his forearms. "I think I attacked you right back."

He took her hand and peered around the door to check on Phillip, who was still playing with his animals. He hugged her close again, feeling her uneven breaths on his cheek.

"I'm really not this guy," he said.

She laughed softly, and he deemed that sweet, nervous sound as quintessential *Tempest.*

"Should I worry about that?" she asked.

"No. I meant I've gone years without so much as a kiss, and suddenly I can't keep my lips off of you."

"I like your lips," she said shyly.

He kissed her again, savoring every second of their closeness. "Tempe," he said as their mouths parted. "I'm not a guy who *takes* recklessly. I've never been that type of guy, and with Phillip in my life, I can't become that guy. But there's something about you that makes me *trust*, and want, and..." He snapped his mouth closed to keep from sounding like an idiot.

"Thank goodness it's not just me who feels that way."

"You do?"

"Yes," she whispered. "I'm usually so careful, but something about you has turned me into one of those girls who share their bodies like candy. I'm not candy." She dropped her eyes and ran her finger up his arm. "But with you, I kind of want to be M&M's and Skittles and lollipops all wrapped up in one big sugar-coated—"

His mouth swooped down and captured hers. He couldn't help it. The need to possess her, to taste the sweetest dirty thoughts he'd ever heard as they slipped from her tongue, was too strong to fight. She clung to him, making hungry, sensual sounds like she'd made last night and driving him out of his mind. Somewhere in the recesses of his mind thoughts of Phillip broke through, and he once again forced himself to release her. They both came away breathless.

"I need to check on Phillip," he said, moving toward the doorway again. Phillip was sitting at his drawing table, playing with his animals. He turned his attention back to her, knowing this wasn't fair, to tell her he didn't want to be that guy and then to come on so strongly. *Talk about a walking contradiction.*

A thoughtful, nervous expression washed over her face, and she placed her finger over his lips. "Don't say anything. I see it in your eyes, and I know you see it in mine. We need to get this under control before someone gets hurt."

He kissed her hand and laced their fingers together. He had everything at risk—not just his son, but also the first person he'd wanted to let into his life in years. "We should talk about it."

"Let's not," she said, surprising him, and by the look on her face, surprising herself, too. "I always talk things to death. Just this once I'd like to see what happens *without* analyzing it. I'm in Pleasant Hill to start over, so this is as good a time as any to really put that into practice. We were brought together for a reason, and we're connecting. Let's not overthink it. How about if we're *carefully present*, and see where we end up?"

"I'm trying, but being careful around you seems to have the opposite effect."

She pressed her finger over his mouth again. "No analyzing. This is the new, risk-taking Tempest."

Chapter Eight

THE NEW, RISK-TAKING Tempest? When had some other woman taken over her voice box? Shocked by her sudden boldness, Tempest took stock of herself and what she'd suggested, while Nash showed her around his metalworking shop. *Carefully present.* She'd suggested the very thing she was trying not to be—*careful.* But *carefully present* implied her desire to see where things went, and that *was* what she wanted. Her mind was already tripping over the *not analyzing* part of her suggestion. It was a struggle not to overthink the way her heartbeat had gone wild the second she'd set eyes on Nash and how her chest felt full at the sight of him and Phillip working side by side. And then there were the things she was trying not to overanalyze about *Phillip.* Like the way he mimicked his father's every move, looking to him for approval over the tiniest of things. She felt like there was more to his quietness than just shyness, but she couldn't pinpoint what.

She tried to tuck all those thoughts away as she took in the magnificent sculptures surrounding them. Nash had swept her into his arms so fast, she hadn't had time to look around, and now she had no idea how she'd missed the enormous wooden and metal pieces of art.

"Nash," she said with every bit of awe she felt as she admired a half-finished wooden carving. The figure's chest and arms were still in rough form, but even with the blocky cuts, she could see his arms were meant to be outstretched behind him. His hair was rough, but discernable, and appeared to be blowing away from his face. His undefined face angled up toward the ceiling, as if he were preparing to fly into the clouds. The bottom half of the figure had yet to be carved. She moved to another sculpture that must have been at least six feet wide, made of thick pieces of metal and polished slabs of wood curled upward like a baseball glove, with two half-carved children in its palm. One roughly carved child sat with his knee bent, the other tucked beneath him. Beside him, another, more defined boy sat on a stump.

"These are incredible," she said as she moved to another piece, of three tall metal figures, their arms and legs as skinny as twigs, their heads warped, with no facial features. Each was encased in a piece of rusty metal, fashioned like a blanket or a towel around their bodies. Their misshapen faces exuded sadness.

Tempest turned to Nash, struck by his pained expression. His arms were crossed, his biceps twitching, his eyes haunted and dark. She followed his gaze, seeing a multitude of machines and tools on a wooden workbench. Off to the side sat an enormous brick forge, black with wear, and just beyond, a dusty old wooden trunk sat beside a pile of wood and metal.

"Nash?" She touched his arm.

He startled, as if he'd been lost in a memory.

"These are amazing. I don't understand why you don't finish them."

"I told you—it's too dangerous with Phillip around. Believe

me, if it were possible, I'd do it. I got a call yesterday morning from the guy who gave me my big break years ago. He's opening another gallery in Virginia and wants to feature my work."

"That's great. You can get started again. Finish these pieces, and—"

"It's not happening, Tempest. I can't travel with Phillip. He needs structure. His room, his bed. The animals need to be fed and the property here needs to be maintained. I have barely enough time to breathe as it is. Besides, my work—my *real* work—takes more time for each piece than I have in a month. I haven't touched this stuff in years. It's *not* happening."

"Can't you work when Phillip's in preschool?"

He scoffed. "He's not ready for preschool."

She peeked out the door at Phillip again and lowered her voice. "Kids go to preschool when they're three. He's never been?"

Nash took off his hat, ran his hand through his hair, then settled it low on his head again. "Nope. No need."

The pieces of Phillip's quiet world were beginning to fall into place. "Of course there's a need. He's a little boy. He'll learn to socialize and read and write."

His eyes narrowed, and she knew she was overstepping her bounds.

"He's too young. He doesn't need the influence of other kids getting him in trouble."

She followed him out of the workshop, waiting as he locked the door, and trailed him to his workbench. He picked up a chisel and wiped it with a cloth.

"It's *preschool*, Nash," she said quietly. "You're not sending him off to meet delinquents. What kind of trouble can he get in to?"

She wanted to understand his aversion to preschool. When he set down the tool and stalked out of the barn, she went with him. He told Phillip he'd be right outside the doors, but Phillip was too busy with his toys to care.

"Does he have a weekly playgroup or friends he visits?"

"He's got *me*." He paced just outside the barn doors.

"And you're a great father, but you're not his *peer*. How do you get any work done?" She watched his eyes shift to Phillip, then to the two workbenches, and finally, to Tempest.

Boy, he and his son had sure mastered their nonverbal communication skills. She got the message loud and clear. She was overstepping her bounds.

He stopped pacing and crossed his arms again. "I really don't need my life picked apart. He's not ready for school. He's barely done being a baby. When he's six, I'll send him to first grade with all the other kids."

She knew she was pushing him, but this rubbed her the wrong way, and for Phillip's sake, she wanted to understand why he was holding him back. Softening her tone, she stepped closer, tension filling the space between them like a razor's edge. "Nash, he'll be behind the other kids if he doesn't go to preschool. Kids nowadays are using computers when they're four. If you don't like the mainstream preschools, there are all kinds of options, alternative schools, smaller classes, less structure—"

He glared at her, and she held her breath, ready for him to tell her to butt the hell out. But he shifted his gaze to his son, and his shoulders sagged; the tension in his face slowly dissipated, replaced with sorrow? Guilt? She couldn't be sure.

"Did something happen?" she finally asked. "To him? To

you? That makes you so against enrolling him in preschool?"

"No," he said flatly.

"Did *you* go to preschool?"

"Yes," he snapped.

"And public school after that? I mean, until the last two years of high school?"

His eyes narrowed again. "Yes."

"Then you must know how good it can be for a child."

He shifted angry eyes away.

She didn't know why she felt the need to push, but she was doing it for Phillip, and she had to try one more time to get through to him. "He's really quiet, Nash, and I noticed that he looks to you for *everything*. Even before answering simple questions."

"*I'm* quiet," he countered. "He's a good kid. He's careful, like me."

Despite the tension simmering between them, she sensed a fissure in his guard. "He's a great kid, and he *is* careful, but you know how you asked if I was *too* careful?" She paused, giving him a second to respond, and when he didn't, she said, "Maybe you're enabling him to be *too* careful. Maybe not, but it wouldn't hurt for him to socialize with kids his own age."

He set a steely gaze on her, looking like he was going to either walk away or tell her off. As the seconds ticked by, she waited for the time bomb to explode. But he didn't say a word, and he didn't walk away. He stood right there—studying her? Processing what she'd said? She couldn't be sure, and she knew how out of line she was, especially since she had no experience with children of her own to draw from, but something told her he needed to hear this.

"Your mother must believe in sending kids to school," she

said even more softly. "Does she see Phillip?"

He ground his teeth. "She's seen him twice. She lives in Washington State."

Her heart ached for all three of them. He was truly raising his son alone, and what kind of a grandmother doesn't make an effort to see her grandchild? "Do you take him to parks or playgrounds where he can interact with other kids?"

"He's been a few times. We're busy from dawn to dusk, Tempest. You have no idea what it's like to raise a child and try to run a business. Between taking care of him, caring for the animals, taking care of the property, doing laundry, and working to make ends meet, there's not a lot of downtime."

"You're right, I don't have children of my own, so I can't know how difficult that is. But I do know how difficult it is to acclimate to other kids for children who haven't been around kids their own age. I work with them. Several of the kids in my music playgroup are there *for* socialization. I just...It's not easy to be six years old and thrown into school where you don't know anyone and suddenly you're expected to listen to someone who isn't your parent and sit at a desk for hours and eat lunch at a certain time." She watched him grind his teeth together, but the worry in his eyes told her she was getting through to him. "Has he ever stayed with a babysitter?"

"I don't know anyone around here well enough to trust with him."

"Oh, Nash." She ached for him for so many reasons. She tried to wrap her head around what he was saying. "So, you've lived here for all this time and you've never struck up a friendship with another family with a kid his age? Or hired a teenager to babysit?"

"Teenager? No frigging way." He began pacing again. "And

in case you've forgotten, I'm not a social butterfly. He's my responsibility. Why would I hand him off to someone else?"

"It's not *handing him off* if you send him to preschool, or use a babysitter so you can get your work done or run an errand." Tempest might be inherently careful, but she was also a Braden. Bradens didn't give up when things got tough, especially where children were concerned.

"He's fine," he insisted. "He's smart, he's happy, and he's *safe*."

"You're right. I'm sorry for putting my nose where it doesn't belong." The way he emphasized *safe* made her wonder if there was a bigger issue. Was he so untrusting that he couldn't let Phillip out of his sight? If so, then this was a whole different issue than simply not wanting his baby boy to be taken away for a few hours a day for preschool. She needed to tread carefully. But she couldn't stop thinking about him, too. He'd put his whole life on hold. His gorgeous sculptures were just sitting there, waiting to be finished. He would have much more free time if Phillip was in school. He was holding them both back, and he didn't even realize it.

"I have an idea, and you might hate it, so feel free to tell me to shut my piehole. But why don't we take Phillip out together?" she suggested. "There's a wonderful playground with slides and a jungle gym right outside the community center where I hold my music playgroup. We could go there, and he could play with the kids for a while." *And maybe we can figure out what's really going on.*

He rubbed the back of his neck, and a small smile lifted his lips. "You're not going to give up until you see he's fine around other kids, are you?"

"I can't help it," she admitted. "Kids come to me with *real* issues they need to overcome to learn to interact appropriately with others. It's not an easy road, and I'd hate to see Phillip struggling to catch up when all it would take is a play date every now and again. The playground is a perfectly safe place for him to socialize with other children his age."

His eyes hardened again. "If you were anyone else, I'd tell you to stay the hell out of our lives." He stepped closer, bringing them nose to nose, and touched his fingers to hers on the far side of their bodies, out of Phillip's sight.

He was breathing hard, his intense stare kicking up her pulse, but behind the darkness, she saw him struggling to make sense of what she'd said, and that endeared her to him even more.

"Why aren't you?" she asked carefully.

"I thought we weren't analyzing right now." He squeezed her hand, the anger in his eyes softening.

"We're not, or at least I'm trying not to. But it's hard. Just tell me one thing. Should I worry that you have some awful secret, like you're hiding from the police? Or, I don't know, that Phillip is in some sort of danger and you have to keep him out of the public's eye?"

Worry lines crept across his forehead. "No dark secrets that put Phillip in danger. No hidden abuse of him or me or anyone in my family. Just an overprotective father who didn't realize his three-year-old needed to be in school." He shifted his eyes away and said, more to himself than to her, "And worries about his son being influenced by people who can do him harm."

She breathed a sigh of relief. "You realize you live in Pleasant Hill, right? This place is like Mayberry on steroids."

The haunted look returned to his eyes. They both turned at the sound of Phillip's boots approaching. He let go of

Tempest's hand and lifted Phillip into his arms, the haunted look floating away. He kissed his boy's cheek, and Phillip wrapped his arms around his neck, softening all of Nash's sharp edges.

"Hey, buddy. How would you like to go to a playground with me and Tempe?"

Phillip nodded and wiggled out of his arms. He ran back into the barn and grabbed his plastic hammer.

"I was a little worried he wouldn't know what a playground was," she admitted.

"I'm a busy guy, but I'm not an a-hole. At least not on purpose. I may be a loner, but I'm not trying to keep him hidden away from the world. The last thing I want to do is anything that makes his life harder."

"DID YOU KNOW this playground was built by the community?" Tempest asked as they crossed the lawn toward the playground. "A group of residents donated their time and local businesses donated the materials. I think that makes it even more special, don't you?"

"I didn't know that, but yes, I agree." Nash had a feeling he was just getting to see how special Tempest was, too.

Kids laughed as they ran from the slides to the wooden climbing equipment, their parents chatting casually nearby. A young mother pushed her daughter on a swing, and a father, he assumed, paced by the jungle gym with his cell phone pressed to his ear. Spending an afternoon at the playground was normal for most families, but he hadn't thought about how different his and Phillip's *normal* was until now.

He glanced down at his son to get a read on his thoughts. Phillip squinted up at him against the bright sun, clutching his hammer in one hand and his father's fingers tightly in the other. "What do you want to go on first?"

Phillip stared uncomfortably at the equipment.

"How about that cool fort?" Tempest pointed to a wooden climbing fort with slides, a ramp, and a fireman pole down the center.

His son shrugged.

Two young boys ran in front of them, hollering and giggling. Phillip grabbed Nash's leg, huddling closer.

Concern pressed in on Nash as he knelt beside him, taking in his worried expression. "Hey, buddy, this will be fun. I'll be right here with you."

Tempest moved to Phillip's other side and reached for his hand. "How about if we all go in the fort?"

She smiled at Nash, and he was relieved not to see even a hint of judgment in her eyes. There was enough of that going on in his own head.

They climbed into the fort, where a little blond girl with two pigtails was turning a steering wheel like she was driving the fort and a boy who looked to be around Phillip's age was looking out a window talking to another boy who was standing on the ground. Phillip remained glued to Nash's side.

"Want a turn?" the blond girl asked.

Phillip moved behind Nash's leg. As he tried to pry his son from his leg, he realized that if Tempest hadn't said anything to him, he would have written this off as Phillip's typical shy behavior. And maybe it was, but her words nagged at him. *I'd hate to see Phillip struggling to catch up when all it would take is a little interaction every now and again.* He found himself analyzing his son, and he hated that. His son was perfect just the way he was. He glanced at Tempest, who was reaching a hand out to another young girl as she climbed up a ramp and into the fort.

Taking a page from her playbook, he said, "Come on, buddy. I'll do it with you." Nash smiled at the little blond girl as she moved past them toward the slide. He stood behind Phillip and placed his son's hands on the wheel, turning it both ways. "You're the captain of our ship, buddy. Where are we going? Do you want me to hold your hammer?"

Phillip shook his head adamantly, clutching the hammer against the steering wheel. "Fishing!" He moved the wheel and said, "Put your hands in the water."

Nash smiled and pretended to dip his hand over the edge. "It's mighty cold."

As Phillip called out directives and pretended to battle a raging storm, the knots in Nash's chest unraveled. He was fine. His boy was A-OK. He moved away from Phillip and joined Tempest by the window of the fort.

"Do you believe me now?" he asked. "He's fine."

"I never said he wasn't fine," she said quietly. "I just thought it might be good for him to socialize a little."

"Here comes a wave," Phillip hollered.

The girl who had been playing with the steering wheel rushed up the stairs and landed in the fort beside Phillip with a loud, "Hi!"

Phillip made a beeline for Nash, clinging to his leg again.

Maybe he'd spoken too soon. Nash looked at Tempest with his heart in his throat, but her attention was solely focused on his boy as she bent to eye level.

"It was nice of you to give her a turn," she praised him.

"Why don't you introduce yourself, and maybe you can play together."

Phillip looked up at Nash.

Nash nodded his approval, feeling the weight of this interaction like lead on his shoulders. Phillip didn't move. Nash set a hand on his son's back, urging him forward. "It's okay, buddy."

Phillip looked at the little girl again, pushing back against Nash's hand.

Nash took his hand and stepped toward the girl, but Phillip was rooted in place, shaking his head. All Nash's protective urges surged forward. He scooped Phillip into his arms and climbed out of the fort.

"Nash?" Tempest called after him. She caught up to them in the grass and grabbed his arm. "Where are you going?"

"He was scared. Couldn't you see that? He's obviously not ready." He didn't dare look at her. He wasn't just angry that he'd allowed his son to be put in an uncomfortable situation, but he was angry at himself for not realizing this could happen in the first place. Guilt gnawed at his gut. He'd been so damned busy trying to keep their lives going, he'd missed the most elementary of things—and possibly one of the most important.

"Nash," she said, coming to a stop. "Of course he's a little intimidated, but he'll ease into meeting other kids if you give him the chance."

Nash huffed with frustration and turned to face her. Her gaze was soft, and it struck him again that she wasn't judging him. She looked as kind and patient as she had the day he'd met her, and to top it off, knowing she was trying to help his son made her appear even more beautiful. He pressed a kiss to Phillip's forehead, forcing his overprotective urges to settle down, feeling stupid for overreacting.

Tempest ran a soothing hand down Phillip's back. "This isn't a race or a contest," she said sweetly. "This is as new for you as it is for him, and it takes some getting used to. How about if we take a walk?"

He was torn between wanting to protect his boy from feeling any more uncomfortable and wanting to help him get over that feeling. If only fatherhood came with a handbook. *Then PJ might still be alive.*

Tempest's hand slid from Phillip's back to Nash's arm, pulling him from the dark thought. "It's a beautiful day," she urged.

He couldn't argue with that, despite the guilt and confusion twisting within him. "Sure." He pressed another kiss to Phillip's cheek. "Want to take a walk, buddy?"

Phillip buried his face in Nash's shirt and nodded, all those springy curls bouncing around his cherubic face. He ached with love for him, and the thought that he might have made any part of his son's life more difficult made him sick to his stomach. He set Phillip on the ground, and they followed a path around the perimeter of the playground. Every step was a measure in self-control as he watched Phillip like a hawk to make sure he didn't get overwhelmed.

A young mother walked behind two young children far ahead on the path. Phillip gripped his hand tighter as they passed a family sitting on a blanket in the grass. He watched a little boy playing with a puppy, and his grip on Nash's hand loosened. A short while later they passed another family in the grass. A baby slept beside a pregnant woman while a toddler picked at something in a plastic bowl.

"My folks were big on picnics," Nash said out of the blue. "I haven't thought about that in so long, it's almost like it happened to a family I once knew. But when I was younger we had picnics all summer long. It's weird that Phillip and I haven't once had a picnic."

"But you eat outside. That's sort of the same thing. Except there aren't other people around." She looked at him thoughtfully, her message loud and clear. He was doing well, but he could do a little better. "We grew up on the beach, and my parents were always taking us into town for festivals and community get-togethers—which reminds me: I saw a flyer for a fall concert in two weeks. I have to go back to Peaceful Harbor that weekend, but maybe you can take Phillip."

"A concert might be a bit much for him, don't you think?"

"It's a Sunday-afternoon concert at Pleasant Hill Park. I'm sure there will be lots of kids there. I wish I could go. There's no better way to get to know people in your community than those kinds of events. Now *I'm* excited about it." She laughed. "That's the weekend my brother Cole's medical practice hosts a patient picnic, which I've never missed, and I have to see a client in the late afternoon. But *please* tell me you'll take him. It would be so good for him." With a teasing smile, she said, "That is, unless it's too much for his daddy."

He nudged her with his elbow and her laughter sailed into the air, shattering any remaining tension. He hadn't realized he'd been so tightly wound for so long, but just being around her made him feel lighter.

"Okay. I'll take him. But I make no promises about how long we'll stay. If he has a hard time, without you there to push me into staying, we might bolt."

Phillip let go of his hand. It was something that happened many times each day, but now he found himself putting more importance on his son's independence, and he made a mental note to try to encourage that.

Phillip squinted up at him, and Nash realized Tempest was right. Phillip sought his permission for everything. He wasn't sure that was a bad thing, but it was definitely a *thing*. Worrying that he could be accidentally hamstringing Phillip's independence, he made another mental note to pay closer attention to those types of things.

He nodded, and Phillip walked a few feet ahead of them, his head bobbing to the right, then to the left, as he took it all in. Nash tried to remember the last time they'd been to a playground or a park, and he realized it had been *months* ago.

"I have a feeling that you'd do anything for Phillip. So if you do want to *bolt*, just remember how much better he's done in the short time we've been here."

Phillip crouched by a rock and began hitting it with his hammer. He squinted up at Nash, and out of habit, Nash nodded his approval. Phillip sat back on his heels, banging the rock and then inspecting it more closely.

"Sometimes I look at him," he said, "and I can't believe he's the same human being as the infant I held in my arms. People talk about how fast time goes by, but when you're in the thick of it, changing diapers, making sure he doesn't crack his head open when he's learning to stand, worrying when he spikes a fever, it seems like every day takes a hundred hours. But sometimes, how much he's grown and changed—how much *I've* changed—hits me so hard it's difficult to comprehend that we were ever anything other than what we are right now."

"You've done a good job with him, Nash. I know I upset you by suggesting that you put him in preschool, but you really have raised a lovely, happy boy."

"He's so little. The idea of sending him off to school seems wrong. I mean, look at him." He watched Phillip push to his feet and walk down the path again.

"It's hard for lots of parents," Tempest said. "My mom said she worried every time she sent one of us off to a new school—preschool, elementary, middle. *College.* Even though we knew most of the kids we went to school with from community events and playdates, she still worried about how we'd adjust to new surroundings, schedules, the whole deal. And when we went away to college she said that flipped around on her. She knew she had taught us well and given us the tools we needed to succeed and the confidence to adjust to being away from home, but she hadn't prepared *herself* for being without us. Parenting has got to be the hardest thing a person can do."

His parents had never had a chance to deal with one of their sons going off to college, and he had no idea how his mom had dealt with his going to preschool, or any school for that matter. He was a kid. It had never even crossed his mind. But when they'd lost PJ she had been inconsolable for weeks. He'd seen PJ's ghost everywhere before they'd packed up and left town, and even on the boat his brother's ghost followed him like a shadow. He was sure that was one of the reasons they'd packed up and left everything he'd ever known behind. Two years was long enough for each of them to shove their feelings so deep they'd need goddamn shovels to unearth them. Long enough for his parents to be able to function again and not walk around like zombies. *Long enough for Dad's cancer to take hold.*

"You can try out preschool for a day and see how he does. They have observation days. They're like trial days, where you can observe him in class to see how he adjusts."

"Thanks. I'll think about it."

Tempest lowered her voice and said, "Do you mind if I ask

what it was like for you in the early days when you were by yourself with Phillip? It must have turned your life upside down."

He heard her question, but he wanted to tell her about *PJ*, to try to finally get it out of his system with someone he trusted. How could he trust her after just a few days? One look in her honest eyes was all it took for him to find his answer. *How can I not?*

But one glance at his son was all it took for him to hold back that confession. This wasn't the time or place to talk about his loss. Trying to help Phillip learn how to interact with other kids was enough to deal with.

"Actually," he finally answered, "I think he turned it right-side up. I'd been living out of my car and in tents for so long, I hardly remembered what it was like to stay in one place for more than a few weeks. I had no one to answer to, no one to take care of."

"No one to take care of you," Tempest added.

He'd never thought about it that way, but as he fought the urge to reach for her hand, he realized she was right.

"I guess, yeah. But I've never thought like that. I liked being on my own." *The only person I wanted to be around was PJ, and I hated that he wasn't there.* "I hung out with other artists, used a portable forge, hauled my stuff in my truck. And my guitar was the best constant companion."

"You play?" Surprise lit her eyes.

"*Played.* After Phillip's mother left, I was too mad to play, and honestly, there was no time. Have you ever taken care of a baby? If they're not eating or pooping or crying, they're sleeping. And when he was sleeping I was trying to do laundry or clean up. I was afraid to leave the house to go to my workshop, even with a baby monitor. Most of the time, when he finally fell asleep, I crashed, too."

He patted his chest. "He used to sleep right here when he had a stuffed nose or when his stomach hurt. I can't tell you how many nights I sat up on the couch while he slept sprawled across my chest."

"That's so cute. I wish you had pictures."

"Trust me. That was not a time of my life you'd want to see in pictures." He laughed. "I got so little sleep I looked like a zombie. I was afraid to leave him alone, so I only showered while he was asleep, and worried the whole time that I'd miss his cry."

"Somehow I think you looked a lot hotter than you think. But it's the love I wanted to see, not your looks."

Jesus, she stopped him cold. How did he get lucky enough that she was the one who'd called about his ad? *We've been brought together for a reason, and we're connecting. Let's not overthink it.*

"Tell me more," she said. "Suddenly you're a homeowner, *and* a single parent, *and* you gave up creating the art you loved. I can't imagine dealing with so many changes at once. I know you said you weren't in love with Phillip's mother, but you must have missed her, too, which I'd imagine made it even more difficult. I have friends whose parents are divorced, which I know you're not, but it's sort of similar. It seems like so many of them see their ex in their children and have a hard time dealing with that. When you look at Phillip, do you see her?"

Phillip got up and continued walking around the playground. They followed close behind.

"No. When I look at Phillip, I see *Phillip*. Obviously, his skin is darker than mine, and he has the same type of thick ringlets she did, but those are *his* attributes, not hers. When he was born, his skin was much fairer. I thought he looked a lot like"—*PJ*—"me when I was younger. But as I told you before, it wasn't like you think it was between us. We met at an art show in North Carolina. There were a bunch of artists camping at the same place, and after the show we'd hang out, have a beer, talk, and she and I hooked up. Over the course of the show, we got to talking and realized we were heading to several of the same shows over the next few weeks, so we stayed at the same campgrounds. We did our own thing and got together a few times each week. It's not like we lived together. We weren't even a couple. We just...hung out." Damn, he hoped that didn't make him sound like an asshole, but it was what it was.

"Then it makes sense that you don't necessarily see her when you look at Phillip. Maybe that makes it easier than if you did."

They walked for a while in comfortable silence. Nash was watching a guy teach his dog to play fetch, and Tempest grabbed his arm, stopping him from walking forward. She pointed to Phillip, who was watching three kids spinning in circles with their arms stretched out to their sides. They tumbled to the ground in fits of giggles, and Phillip laughed.

Tempest whispered, "Has he ever spun around like that?"

Nash shook his head, wondering if all three-year-olds spun in circles.

"He will now," she said.

Phillip glanced at him, and Nash nodded, giving him approval to do whatever he wanted: watch the other kids, walk around the park, spin in circles...

Phillip watched the kids for another few seconds, then started down the path again.

Tempest wrapped her hands around Nash's arm and whispered, "That's huge. He's noticing what other kids are doing and taking pleasure in their fun. This is what socialization is all about."

He loved the feel of her hands on him, and it stirred all the heat that had been simmering beneath his lengthy confession. But a public playground was not the best place to get aroused, so he tried not to focus on the feel of her delicate, soft hands on his skin, or the alluring look in her beautiful blue eyes, and focused on what she'd said instead.

"I never realized he was missing out on this stuff."

She looked at him like he'd said the most ridiculous thing on earth. "How could you? You're a single dad trying to keep your business going and making sure he's safe and happy as he gets through each day, while *also* doing the million other things it takes to raise a child and run a household." She looked at Phillip and said, "You cannot be all things to him. No parent can be to their child."

"I can try," he said honestly.

She leaned in to him as they walked. "There's a world of difference between a three-year-old and an adult, which is why it's important for him to be exposed to other kids. They're supposed to have silly thoughts, spin around, play chase, catch frogs. It's all part of growing up." She poked him in the arm and added, "And *you're* supposed to have time to finish those sculptures."

He shook his head at her pushiness, but threads of happiness were forming out of the knots that had held him together for so long. She was understanding, easy to talk to, and she made him want to talk more than he ever had. The words *You would have liked my brother* were on the tip of his tongue.

He shifted his gaze to Phillip, who was twisting his hammer in his hands, watching two teenagers toss a football. They needed to play ball more and spin around until they were too dizzy to stand and whatever else three-year-olds were supposed to do. They needed to step outside their comfort zones and live a little more.

Tempest's hands slid off his arm and he reached for her. Her eyes darted to Phillip as he laced their fingers together. Knowing she would put Phillip's well-being ahead of her own desires tugged at his heartstrings, making it even harder to resist the urge to pull her close and kiss her.

We needed this. We needed you.

Chapter Nine

NASH AND TEMPEST had held hands and talked for most of the morning. He'd been sharing pieces of himself, washing away the cloud of mystery, showing Tempest the sweeter sides of the man she didn't want to miss out on. She was dying to kiss him again, but she knew they had to be careful not to confuse Phillip. And now, as he leaned inside the truck to buckle Phillip into his car seat, she didn't even try not to take an eyeful of his ass, all wrapped up in rugged denim. She nibbled on her lower lip, wishing *she* were that denim so she could hug every inch of his glorious lower half.

Nash finished with Phillip and took Tempest's hand, walking toward the rear of the truck. His eyes darted through the rear window, and she realized he was making sure Phillip couldn't see them. His eyes flashed dark as night, and when he slid a hand to the back of her neck, heat pierced her skin.

"Thank you," he said with a husky voice that made her nipples stand at attention. "I never would have realized Phillip should be in school already, or how much he needed mornings like this, if it weren't for you."

"You would have," she said, but her mind was focusing on the proximity of his mouth. If she tipped forward and up just a hair, she could taste him again. They'd kissed only hours earlier, but it felt like a lifetime ago.

"Maybe one day, but it wouldn't have been soon enough." He stepped forward, his thighs pressing against her, and the rest of his incredibly hard body touched her, too. His eyes glowed with a savage fire that made her heart race.

He leaned down, bringing his mouth a whisper away from hers. "I can't wait another second to kiss you."

"Then stop wasting time."

She went up on her toes as he pulled her to him, taking her in a rough and demanding kiss and sending bursts of lust zinging through her. The kiss was frantic and messy. A rushed kiss. A stolen moment. Both of them were acutely aware of the small child waiting for them to return. She didn't have a hope of remaining in control as he pressed her up against the truck, grinding from hips to chest. Her body moved on its own, arching into him without any directions from her brain, which was *done. Finished. Mush.* She was driven by an internal blaze no other man had ever stoked, soaking in everything he had to give and hoping it would never end. When he eased the intensity, the rest of his body was still plowing forward. Every soft press of his lips brought a hard bump and grind of his hips.

More, more, more.

Several tender kisses later, he drew back, still holding her around the base of her neck and breathing so hard their chests collided with every inhalation. He touched his forehead to hers and whispered, "Phillip."

It was all she could do to nod.

He pressed his hands to her cheeks and stared deeply into her eyes. "I'm trying to behave, but I need to be closer to you." He glanced at the rear window again, and she finally found her voice.

"Later." *Holy cow, did I just say that?*

His gaze went predatory.

She swallowed hard. *Yup.* She'd said it all right.

But this wasn't *her*. She didn't sprint right past getting to know a guy before moving on to all the dirty things that were racing through her mind—naughty things she wanted to do with and to Nash. She'd slept with only three men in her life. *Three.* And she'd dated each of them for a few months.

He pressed his lips to hers again, brushed his scruff over her cheek, and whispered, "No pressure. I love kissing you. I just want more of it."

Relief swept through her, and then his hands were in her hair, and he rose to his full height, holding her against him.

"Tempe," he whispered.

She'd heard her name millions of times, but never with so many emotions threaded into it. Nash took her hand and walked her to the passenger door. "FedEx, drop off flyers, and hit the grocery store?" he asked casually, as if this were the way they spent every Saturday morning, sneaking kisses in a parking lot.

"Don't you need to get your work done?"

He shook his head as he opened the door. "Work, or spend the day with you and Phillip?" His lips curved up in a sexy smile. "I'd be crazy to pass up a chance at spending the day with two of the funnest people around."

"You must not know many people," she teased.

"Not many like you, that's for sure."

The honesty in his eyes told her it wasn't just a line. She climbed into the truck. "What do you think, Phillip? Want to go hang up flyers and pick out some goodies at the grocery store?"

Phillip nodded, his eyes wide. "Spaghetti and ice cweam?"

Could you be any cuter? "Sounds perfect to me."

Half an hour later they walked into Emmaline's Café with a flyer in hand and headed for the ad board.

Emmaline nearly bumped into Nash as she whipped out of the kitchen.

"Whoopsie!" Her eyes sailed over Nash, down to Phillip, standing beside him, and then to Tempest. "Hey, Tempe! I see you met Mr. Mysterious."

"Nash," Tempest said with a laugh. "This is Emmaline, the owner of the café and Jillian's bestie. Emmaline, Nash and Phillip Morgan. My new housemates."

Emmaline gave Nash a long, lascivious look and crouched beside Phillip, who slipped behind Nash's legs. "Well, hello there, cuteness. I just baked some cookies. Would you like one?"

Nash lifted Phillip into his arms, his face serious.

Emmaline rose, giving Tempest a curious look. "I should probably have asked Dad first. Sorry. Is it okay to give him a cookie?"

Phillip turned a hopeful gaze to Nash, who nodded curtly. "Sure. Thanks."

"One cookie coming right up." Emmaline hurried over to the counter.

"Nash," Tempest whispered. "That was a little intimidating."

"Hm? What do you mean?" He kissed Phillip.

"Oh boy." She smiled and wiggled Phillip's foot. "I think we need to bring Daddy out for a little more socialization, too."

Phillip buried his face in Nash's neck.

"Was I that unfriendly?"

As Emmaline approached, Tempest said, "A smile goes a long way."

"Here we go." Emmaline handed Phillip a cookie wrapped in a napkin, and then she handed one to Nash. "One for cuteness and one for his very serious daddy." She winked at Tempest and said, "I've got your favorite muffin all ready for you after you hang that up."

Nash flashed a noticeably forced smile. "Thank you, Emmaline. It looks delicious."

Tempest stifled a laugh. "Thanks, Em."

"Thank you," Phillip said with a mouthful of cookie crumbs tumbling out of his mouth.

When they left the café, Nash said, "I smiled."

"That you did, and did you see how Phillip smiled, too?"

He seemed to mull that over as they walked down the block. They left a stack of flyers at Mommy and Me, a local clothing boutique, the ice cream shop, and the post office, and she noticed Nash made a concerted effort to smile at each of the people who said hello as they breezed in and out of the shops.

At the grocery store Phillip helped Tempest push a grocery cart down the ice cream aisle, which left Nash's hands free to touch her every chance he got. When Phillip was busy picking out sprinkles, she reached for the ice cream, and Nash's hand grazed over her lower back. When she stood behind Phillip, helping him push the cart, Nash took full advantage, sneaking kisses to the back of her neck and placing a possessive arm around her waist. Every furtive glance, every secret touch, made her hotter, needier, and by the time they put the groceries in the back of the truck, she not only anticipated his touch, but she *craved* it.

When they finally got home, Tempest put away the groceries while Nash made Phillip lunch. He brushed against her back while reaching for a cup, and when she turned to put the milk in the fridge, he was *right there*. The gallon of milk hit him in the stomach. When had the kitchen become so small?

The edge of his lips tipped up in a devilish grin, and his hand moved over hers as he took the jug of milk. "Can I make you some lunch?"

In her head she heard, *Would you like to eat me for lunch?* She was definitely losing her mind, and he must have noticed her quandary because he chuckled as he put the milk in the fridge.

"Are you hungry?" he asked. "I can make you a sandwich."

Phillip held up a carrot stick and said, "Or *cawits.*"

She blinked up at Nash, who was looking at her with an amused grin. "Um, sure. Thanks." She needed air, and space, and she needed it *now*, before she jumped him right there in the kitchen. She grabbed the last grocery bag with her shampoo and conditioner in it and headed for the stairs. "I'm going to take this up to my room. I'll be right back."

She'd been a hot mess since they'd kissed in the parking lot, and now she was like a nymphomaniac needing her next fuck. She dropped the bag on the bed and went straight out to the deck. She leaned her palms on the railing, closed her eyes, and inhaled a deep, cleansing breath. She could do th—

A pair of big, strong arms circled her waist. Nash's hips pressed against her, his hands crossed her body, bringing her back flush with his chest. *Oh Lord.* He felt so good. Smelled so sexy.

"Are you okay?" Even his tone dripped with sensuality.

She was sure he could feel her heart pounding through her back. She turned in his arms. Her stomach tumbled beneath the heat of his piercing stare.

"Yeah," she said breathlessly.

He kissed her neck. "You sure?"

"Yeah, I just needed some air. It's been a…" She tried to drag her eyes from his, but he had her under some sort of spell. "A busy day. I need to play my guitar or something."

"You're trembling. Are you sure you're okay?" He tightened his grip on her, rubbing his cock slowly against her belly.

"Yes, fine. Just—"

His finger traced the edge of her jaw, making it impossible for her to think, much less speak. Was she even breathing?

"Just what, Tempest?" He lifted her chin with a gentle touch, and she felt her insides melting.

"Just. Just." She inhaled sharply. There was only one way she was going to regain control. She needed to get far away from him. But she didn't want to move an inch. *Then I have to take what I want.* But Tempest had never wanted to *take* before. And she felt a bit lost. She needed guidance. She needed CliffsNotes. She needed to learn fast, or she was going to be a needy mess for as long as she lived under Nash's roof.

"Just kiss me—" The words flew from her mouth, and then there was no way to stop the rest from tumbling out. "My heart is going crazy, and my body's on fire, and if I don't kiss you soon I'm afraid I'll go up in flames."

He cradled her jaw in his hands, lowering his smiling mouth so close she could taste his breath, and *hovering* there. Like a candy bar just out of reach.

"We wouldn't want you to go up in flames." He nipped at her lower lip.

Her breath left her lungs, her pulse quickening in anticipation. But he didn't grace her with those perfect lips. He buried his face against her neck and brushed a kiss there.

"Are you sure, Tempest?" He slicked his tongue along the base of her neck and then he put his mouth beside her ear and whispered, "You know how hard it is for us to stop kissing."

His whispers were like liquid sex, and she felt herself go damp. She heard herself whimper and grabbed his waist, curling her fingers into his skin. "Phillip?"

"He's coloring downstairs." He pushed his hands beneath her hair, angling her mouth beneath his.

God she loved when he did that.

"I need to kiss you," she pleaded. "But I don't know what to do if we can't stop. We *have to* stop."

"We do have to stop," he agreed, moving his hips seductively against her so she felt every inch of his arousal.

Her entire body throbbed in anticipation of his kiss. How could she be this desperate for the taste of a man? She'd never felt so out of control in all her life. She arched forward, wanting his heat, needing his kiss, craving his touch. He ran his tongue over her lower lip. She inhaled a shaky breath, licking her own lips, as if she could taste him that way.

"One kiss." He touched his mouth to hers in a slow, tender kiss, settling all the jumpiness that had claimed her.

This was right. This she could take.

LATER THAT AFTERNOON, while Phillip was napping and Tempest was working on the itinerary for her Girl Power group, Nash made headway on the cabinet he was working on for Country Charm. As he sanded the grooves on the door, he thought about Tempest's reaction to seeing his sculptures. He used to thrive on the look of awe in customers' eyes when they'd fall in love with his work. Seeing that look in her eyes? That had blown him away. He pulled his key from his pocket and went into the workshop. The two barns were the primary reasons he'd chosen this property above the other rural homes he'd looked at. He'd once dreamed of making the smaller barn, the one near the pond, into a gallery. It had seemed so plausible at the time. Now it was where he stored the metals he wasn't able to work with, and a few boxes of holiday decorations his mother had planned to throw away after his father died.

He ran his hand over the sculpture of the young man gazing up at the sky. He'd begun sculpting it when he bought the property, two months before Phillip was born. He'd had a son on the way, and his creative juices had not only been flowing like a river, but they'd opened tributaries to the past. For those two months he'd disappeared into the barn from sunup until long after midnight, pouring his emotions into his work. He'd tried to clear out the ghosts of his past and pave the way for his future as a father. It had helped, but it wasn't enough. He and Alaina had never talked about his family, and pouring his emotions into his art was a lot like pouring them into the songs he'd written those two years on the boat. It was an outlet, but not the one he needed. And then Phillip was born, and his hours in the workshop had dwindled. He'd eventually locked up his past to try to build his future, hoping the skeletons wouldn't find a way out.

"Knock, knock." Tempest peered into the room, clutching a notebook to her chest, looking as gorgeous as ever. The color green had never looked so good. "Are you busy?"

"No. Come in." He offered a hand, and she took it with a shy smile. They'd kissed only once on the deck, but it had been quite possibly the most intense kiss he'd ever experienced. Then again, every time they kissed seemed more powerful than the last. "I thought you were working on your Girl Power stuff."

"I am. The meeting's not until next weekend, so I have plenty of time."

"But you're going back to Peaceful Harbor tomorrow?"

"Yeah. I'm working with one of my clients. She had a stroke and she's suffering from aphasia, which means she knows what she wants to say, but she's unable to speak the words. She's also trying to regain motor function on her right side. She's the sweetest woman, and her husband is so good with her. She's coming along, but it's a tough road."

"Aphasia. I've heard of that. That would be frustrating, not being able to communicate."

"It is, but she's pretty good at nonverbal communication. Not as good as you and Phillip, of course," she teased. "Their fiftieth wedding anniversary is in the spring, and last time I saw her she handed me a note when her husband left the room. She must have written left-handed, because it was barely legible, and it said, 'I want to say my vows.'"

"That's sad *and* beautiful."

"I know. We'll get there. We have to." She exhaled loudly. "On a happier note, would you mind if I helped you and Phillip feed the animals tonight? I've never taken care of chickens or goats, and I'd love to learn. I think it would be fun."

"Seriously?"

"Yes, seriously. I love animals."

"It's stinky and dirty, and the goats may try to eat your clothes." He reached up and tucked that unruly lock of hair behind her ear, and it sprang free like a rebellious child.

"I don't care about dirt and smells."

"Then, absolutely."

"Thanks. But I call dibs on the bathtub after Phillip's done taking his bath tonight."

He laughed to distract himself from thoughts of her naked. "You've got it." He'd have to remember to take a look at her bathtub and see if he could fix it. Great, now he was thinking about her naked in the claw-foot tub, just a few feet from her bed, which brought more dirty thoughts.

"Did you decide to work on these?" She pointed to the sculptures.

"Uh…" He cleared his throat to try to shake those thoughts loose. "No, but you did get me thinking about them again."

She walked around the piece with the two boys in the baseball glove, and his chest tightened. Her fingers trailed over the polished wood of the glove, and her pretty skirt flitted around her ankles. She had no idea how many heartstrings she was pulling.

"I think this is my favorite." She tapped the wood. "You always wear that red baseball hat. I figured you're a fan."

"Used to be," he said honestly. He took off the hat, memories of the day PJ gave it to him rushing in.

"Do you think you'll ever finish them?"

He looked at the piece for a long moment, the urge to tell her about PJ so strong he had trouble fighting it. "What do you see when you look at that piece?"

She walked around it again, her hand at her chin as she assessed his work.

"There's a lot of emotion in this, even though it's unfinished, with the two kids and the way they're resting in the palm of the glove, like it's their cozy nest. Their safe place. I like how this boy is sitting up higher, like he's the older one, and the other one is looking up to him. It's great symbolism. I have two older brothers and three younger siblings, and when I look at this I get the same feeling I do when I look up to Cole, my oldest brother, or Sam. And as the older sister, if I put myself in this boy's place"—she touched the head of the boy sitting on the stump—"I feel that sense of responsibility and pride that comes from being looked up to. You're an only child, so it probably seems weird when you hear me say that. But when my younger sister, Shannon, comes to me for advice, it makes me feel special in a way nothing else can."

She was so open with her feelings, it made him want to be open with his, which was exactly how he'd been brought up before PJ had died. But it went against everything his parents had inadvertently taught him during their two years at sea.

"That piece is actually finished," he managed.

Her brow wrinkled in confusion. "I don't understand."

He tugged his hat low on his head, fighting to draw air into his constricting lungs. "It's called 'An Unfinished Life.'"

"Oh." She seemed to mull that over. "That's so sad. I'm obviously not the best art critic. I got the sense this was a happy piece. You know, two young boys who share the love of baseball."

"It is." He thought he could tell her about PJ. He thought the words would come once he started, but they were trapped beneath the pain and bound by years of repression, stealing his ability to string words together. Memories of the night of the accident slammed into him. *The policeman at the door. The disbelief. "Liar! Fucking liar!" His mother dropping to her knees. His father's face draining of all color as he collapsed beside her. And the anger. The all-consuming, gut-fucking rage that sent Nash flying at the police officer, fists and curses landing with near-deadly impact. He could still feel the strength of the two men it took to pry him off the police officer.*

"But An *Unfinished* Life…?" she asked. "That doesn't sound happy."

Because it's not fucking happy. There was a time it was, but it's not anymore. It fucking sucks. He turned away. "This was a mistake." He stalked from the workshop. "Let's go."

She hurried after him. "What was a mistake?"

Trying to let you in. He ground his teeth together as he locked the door that never should have been reopened.

Chapter Ten

AFTER STORMING OUT of the workshop, Nash had gone back to the piece he was working on and Tempest had outlined more of the itinerary for her Girl Power meeting. She'd called Leesa, and they'd come up with a great idea for a team-building activity: a ropes course that the girls would have to help each other through in order to complete. Luckily, they were able to wrangle her brother Sam into constructing it at Rough Riders, the outdoor adventure company he owned. She'd tried to work on a goal chart to go along with it, but she'd had a heck of a time concentrating and had turned to writing songs instead.

She sat on the back porch, but every tune sounded wrong. She hated leaving tomorrow with things so up in the air. Why couldn't she have the type of job where she could take a mental health day when she needed it?

When Nash had gone inside to get Phillip after his nap, he'd flashed a tight smile before disappearing into the house. Whatever had spurred his anger was clearly still hanging around. Tempest wanted to push. She wanted to pick apart what had happened, the way she analyzed everything else in her life— except what was happening between them. Despite this momentary clash, something was definitely happening between them. She brought her guitar and notebook up to her room and decided to take a walk and try to clear her head.

She pushed open the front door and found Nash and Phillip sitting on the porch, a dozen wooden animals in the space between them. Nash looked incredibly broad and sexy sitting across from Phillip with one knee bent, the other leg acting as a barrier around the tiny animals.

"Hey," he said with an apologetic expression as she stepped outside.

She agonized over the doleful look in his eyes. He needn't apologize for battling whatever demons she'd unearthed. She just wished she knew what they were so she could help him deal with them, or at least keep from triggering them in the future.

"Hi," she said, a little uneasily. "You two have quite a menagerie out here."

Phillip lifted a toy lion and said, "We're"—came out like *weah*—"playing zoo and teaching the animals to talk to each other."

Nash arched a brow, as if to say he was trying. He was using the animals to help Phillip learn about making friends? *Oh dear Lord.* How would she survive the cuteness?

"Heading out?" he asked.

"Just for a walk."

He nodded. "Joining us for dinner?"

Her first instinct was to accept, but she worried that she might trigger whatever she had earlier, and she didn't want to hinder his time with Phillip. "I'm still stuffed from lunch, but thanks anyway."

She took a step forward, and he reached out and touched her leg, gazing up at her with an apology lingering in his earnest eyes. She wanted to tell him it was okay, that they could talk about it later. She wanted to ask him what had happened back there. But in the burgeoning silence, those messages seemed to expand between them.

Phillip moved a tiger across the porch and set it in front of a giraffe, where he hummed a conversation between the two instead of using words.

Nash's lips quirked up and he shrugged. When his hand slipped from her leg, she longed for it to return.

"It's a great start," she said, and headed into the yard to try to regain control of—*what? The situation? My emotions? My sudden inability to relay my feelings coherently?* She didn't have the answer, and two hours later, after a long walk around the pond and a slow meander through the vegetable garden, she was no closer to understanding what had gone wrong in the workshop. She nosed around the locked barn, but the windows had dark curtains over them, leaving her even more curious about it, and *him*, than ever.

She returned to the house just as Nash and Phillip came out the front door with buckets in hand.

"Perfect timing," Nash said with a casualness that hadn't been there earlier. "We're going to feed the animals. Still want to come along?"

"If you don't mind."

He eyed her outfit with a look of uncertainty. "Do you have boots? You probably don't want to ruin your sandals, or that pretty skirt."

"Sure. Give me a sec." She hurried upstairs and put on jeans shorts, cowgirl boots, and her favorite pink hoodie, excited to get involved with the animals, and that Nash's mood seemed to have lifted.

When she walked outside, Nash raked his gaze over every

inch of her, from her head to the tips of her boots. His lips curved up in a smile of pure, male appreciation as he took an equally slow leer north again, leaving a trail of heat in his wake.

Feeling empowered by his nonverbal compliment, she skipped ahead, flashing a smile over her shoulder. "Ready, boys?"

Phillip toddled up to her with his father on his heels. She took Phillip's hand as Nash fell into step beside her, leaning in close and speaking quietly.

"You're killing me with those boots. And those skimpy shorts."

"Thank you." *I might have to wear shorts more often.*

"Listen," he said softly. "I'm sorry about before. I shouldn't have snapped."

"It's okay," she said as they came to the bottom of the hill.

"It's definitely not okay," he said under his breath.

When they reached the chicken pen, Phillip reached his hands up and Nash lifted him into his arms.

"The chickens get a little wild when we go in. Want me to carry you, too?" He waggled his brows.

"I think I'm good, thanks." She followed him through a wood-framed screen door, into the penned-in area outside the chicken coop. The chickens squawked and flapped their wings, scurrying away.

Nash hooked an eyehole latch at the top of the door. "I always lock this in case Phillip decides he's had enough. The chickens will escape faster than you can blink."

"I thought pet chickens roamed the yard."

"Some do, but catching a chicken is no easy feat. When we first moved in I let them have the run of the yard, but we lost quite a few to raccoons and foxes. It's safer for them to be penned. At night we keep them in the coop just in case an animal finds a way in."

The coop stood about eight feet tall and ten or fifteen feet long, with a shingled roof and wood siding. Nash set Phillip down, and the little cutie reached for Tempest's hand and tugged her toward the coop.

"Phillip." Nash set a hand on his son's shoulder, slowing him down. "Why don't you tell Tempe what you'd like to show her?"

Phillip nodded, his dark eyes serious as he turned his attention to Tempest. "I want to show you how to collect the eggs." He pulled her inside the coop and said, "I don't shovel the poop. Dad does."

Tempest laughed. "That sounds like a daddy job to me." She heard Nash chuckle.

She'd expected the coop to stink, but it didn't smell like much other than hay and wood. The floor was covered in fresh hay, and there were vents along the roof and two small, partially open windows. Eight cubbies with plastic nesting boxes lined the back wall. Nash obviously worked hard to keep the coop clean.

Phillip grabbed an egg from a cubby and set it carefully inside the bucket. "Mm-hm." He grabbed another, setting it beside the first. "Mm-hm." He repeated this pattern for the first six eggs.

"May I collect a few?" Tempest asked.

He nodded, and she picked up an egg and pretended to inspect it. "One." She set it in her bucket and picked up another, repeating the close inspection. "Two." She picked up a third egg. "Three."

Phillip watched her every move.

"Want to count yours with me?"

He nodded eagerly and reached into his bucket. He held the egg carefully in both hands, looking it over as she had.

"One," Tempest said.

"One." Phillip set the egg in the bucket and picked up another.

"Two." She smiled as he cradled the egg and counted it off. When he put the egg in the bucket and picked up the third, she said, "Three."

Phillip began plucking eggs from the cubbies and counting them out as he placed them in his bucket. "One. Two. Thwee." He picked up another egg. "Tempe, what now?"

"Four," she answered, pleased with his enthusiasm and wishing she could call Nash into the coop, but she was afraid it would interrupt Phillip's momentum.

"Four," he repeated with a soft "r."

They counted the eggs together, and when they reached the last cubby, Phillip counted them by himself.

"One." He grinned at Tempest as he set it in his bucket. "Two," he said louder. "Thwee!" He launched himself into Tempest's arms.

"Yay!" She was surprised when tears of joy welled in her eyes. Phillip wiggled out of her arms and ran around her. She turned just in time to see him leap into Nash's arms. She covered her mouth in an effort to keep her emotions in check, but there was no stopping a happy tear from falling. She spun around, wiped it away, and reached for the buckets.

"That was awesome, buddy." Nash kissed Phillip's cheek and set him outside the coop. He waited for Tempest. "You taught my boy to count?"

"Sorry?" Had she overstepped her bounds? Did he want to

teach Phillip himself?

A slow grin spread across his handsome face, reaching all the way up to his eyes. "You're showing me how bad a dad I am."

Her heart sank. "Oh no. That's not—"

"I'm kidding." He placed his hands on her waist. "I have a lot to learn, but now that a certain gorgeous blonde has gotten my head out of my butt, I'm pretty sure I'll be a quick study."

Her heart was beating a mile a minute, and she was certain it had just as much to do with Phillip's counting as it did with the tension easing between them. "He was so proud of himself. Did you see?"

"I saw it all, and I was jealous that my little buddy got a hell of a hug."

She moved to hug him, but he clutched her wrists, keeping a few inches between them.

"Tempe, I *am* sorry for getting upset in the barn, and don't tell me it's okay, because it's not. You don't deserve the brunt of my baggage."

"It's..."

He cocked his head to the side, looking at her out of the corner of his eyes.

"I think you have a master's degree in nonverbal communication. That was the best don't-even-try-it look I've ever seen." She laughed, earning another sexy grin. "Fine. You're right. It's not okay, and I accept your apology. But, Nash, I'm a really good listener if you ever want to talk about whatever it was that set you off."

"One!" Phillip's high-pitched laughter interrupted them as a chicken scurried past and Phillip chased her yelling, "Two!"

"I think you've created a monster." He gave her a quick pat on her butt and stepped from the coop, scooping Phillip into the air and holding him over his head as his son tried to wiggle free, squealing with laughter. "What's the rule about chasing chickens?"

"I was counting them! Down, Dad. Put me *down*!" He kicked his feet, and Nash lowered him until they were eye to eye.

"Are you going to chase the chickens?"

Phillip nodded, bursting with giggles. Nash threw him over his shoulder, causing another round of laughter. "Come on, Tempe. Before my boy scares these chickens to death. I'll come out later and get them in the coop."

As she watched Nash carry the wiggling, giggling little boy away from the coop, she no longer needed a mental health day. She wanted to stay right there tomorrow instead of going to Peaceful Harbor to enjoy a *happy-heart* day, and she wanted to spend it with them.

NASH STOOD IN the doorway to his sculpting studio Sunday night clutching the baby monitor, his chest constricting like a vise. He couldn't tell which part of his life was causing the constriction: Tempest's absence, which he felt like a missing limb, the unfinished sculptures standing like ghosts before him, or the locked wooden chest pushed off to the side like a forgotten relic, though its contents were anything but forgotten.

He stepped into the studio and another wave of guilt hit him, for how he had stormed out the other morning. Tempest's voice played in his mind, as it had a million times since then. *I'm a really good listener if you ever want to talk about whatever it was that set you off.* Talk about it? He could barely think about it. And despite his asshole behavior, she remained sweet, caring Tempest. She deserved much more than a guy who might lose his shit over skeletons in his closet. *In my studio.*

He paced, cursing his parents for forcing him to leave everything he had known and then pretending as if his brother had never existed. He couldn't live like this anymore, perpetuating the cycle of repression his parents had unknowingly taught him. Not if he ever expected to have a stable life without continually losing his fucking mind. He needed to deal with this shit once and for all.

His eyes fell to the chest that hadn't been opened since his parents had packed it up when they'd sold their house in Oak Rivers. A bead of sweat formed on his brow as he approached the heavy wooden tomb. He paced, like a lion stalking its prey, his heart hammering against his chest. *Fuck. Fuck, fuck, fuck.* He dropped to his knees and sat back on his heels, willing the oppressive sensation of the walls closing in on him to stop. How had he ended up here? Alone and angry on a cold barn floor surrounded by demons he loved *and* hated.

What the fuck, PJ? You had everything. You were supposed to be the next Ken Griffey, Jr. You were supposed to be here. You were supposed to be the guy I believed you were. How am I supposed to deal with this shit?

Tears rushed into his eyes, and he squeezed them closed, cursing his parents, the fucking baseball team, the police who'd chased his brother's car. Gulping for air, he tore the hat from his head. It was frayed along the seams, stained from years of daily wear, and still, when he looked at the damn thing, he saw his brother's face after his last game. *Wear it proudly, little brother. I'm on to bigger, better things.*

Tears streamed down Nash's cheeks, anger burning in his

gut. His fingers turned white against the red hat.

"Bigger and better? You *asshole*. You fucking asshole." He tossed the hat on the ground and shoved the keys to the chest in the lock, panting like he'd just been in a fight. His eyes shot to the hat, seeing the bright light of excitement in his brother's eyes and bringing fresh tears to his. *Goddamn it.* He tugged the hat back on and pressed his palms to his thighs, dragging air into his lungs. His head dropped between his shoulders. He didn't look at the chest as he lifted the top.

A musty smell assaulted him. Hands fisted against his thighs, he lifted his gaze, meeting the ghosts of his past head-on. Phillip's voice rang out in his head as his eyes drifted over each of his family member's smiling faces in a framed photograph—*One, two, three, four.* He stared for a long time at his father's face. God, he missed him so fucking much. There was a time he could feel his father's hand in his if he tried hard enough, or recall the weight of it on his shoulder. But that had faded like the night swallows the sea, in stages of darkness. Breathing harder, he took in PJ's awards and trophies, his winning jersey from his senior year, the picture of the two of them arm in arm after that last winning game. With a trembling hand he lifted his brother's jersey, revealing PJ's favorite baseball mitt and ball beneath. Memories pummeled him like bullets, knocking him off-balance. He shoved the shirt into the chest and sank down to the floor, too overwhelmed to process a damn thing.

Pushing unsteadily to his feet, he stumbled forward and turned away from the offending items, only to find himself face to face with more ghosts from his past.

He stared at the finished sculpture, *An Unfinished Life,* his fingers curling into fists. He wanted to create magnificent pieces that came directly from his soul more than he wanted to breathe. He could feel the chainsaw vibrating in his hands, the adrenaline pumping through his veins as he carved away layers to find the heart of the wood. He could smell the hypnotizing scent of fresh-cut wood and feel the grit as he sanded it to perfection. He looked at the forge that hadn't been touched in years, and the scent of hot metal filled his senses, the *clank* of the hammer as he bent metal to his will rang out in his ears. He wanted this part of his life back—the excitement of gallery openings, the security of large commissions, creating pieces he could take pride in. He wanted to make *Phillip* proud. And he wanted Tempest. *Damn, do I want Tempest.*

She'd come into their lives like a tree trunk became a work of art, revealing more of her true self with each impassioned moment they spent together, chipping away at the armor that had sheltered his heart for so long. She'd given Phillip more in a handful of days than he'd ever known his son needed.

She gave me this moment of clarity.

His hands shook as he closed and locked the chest. His legs felt like lead as he left the studio and locked it up tight, his chest aching even worse than before. He counted his steps up to the back porch, remembering how adorably flustered Tempest had been the night her sister asked her to be her maid of honor. The first time he'd held her in his arms. *That was the start of it all.*

He'd trusted her with so many parts of himself already. Maybe it was time to trust her with this, too.

Chapter Eleven

NASH HAD NEVER heard *one, two, three* as many times in his life as he had over the last week. Phillip continued counting the chickens, the number of cups of food they fed the goats, the steps down to breakfast each morning and again on the way up to bed at night. It had been nine days since Tempest had taught him to count. Eight days since Nash had opened the chest—eight days since he'd begun gathering the courage to tell her about PJ. She'd already become so entrenched in their lives, reading to Phillip and dragging them out for walks in the park, where Phillip had begun exploring more independently. She'd taken them out for a drive and ended up at the local preschool, where Phillip had loved playing on the playground equipment. She'd gone back to Peaceful Harbor again yesterday to see a client, and he'd forced himself to revisit the items in the chest again. It was less traumatic this time, but nowhere near easy. He didn't feel like he was suffocating, just like he was being punched in the gut repetitively. He'd wanted to tell Tempe about PJ last night when she'd returned home, but she'd taken a bath and gone right to bed.

It was Monday night, and Phillip was counting good-night kisses. Nash brushed his curls from his forehead and gave him a final good-night kiss. "Thanks for all the extra kisses buddy."

"Kiss me more?" That soft "r" tugged at Nash's heart. Phillip's heavy lids fluttered closed, and Nash kissed each pillowy cheek one last time.

When he finally left Phillip's room, he closed the door behind him and heard Tempest singing in the bathroom. She took a bath nearly every night. Afterward she usually sat outside playing her guitar. On the nights the heat between them seared so hot he knew he couldn't control himself, he listened from the confines of his bedroom. Other nights, when he trusted himself not to take more than passionate kisses, he joined her. Inevitably she ended up snuggled against him, and they'd talk about Phillip and the progress he was making, or she'd tell him about the kids she was working with and how much she enjoyed them. She talked a lot about her family. He felt like he knew each one of them. He loved living in her world for a little while each night, and learning about her big, happy family, which not only brought them closer together, but it also helped him to lower his guard and made him want to share the most private parts of himself. But holding her in such an intimate embrace, their fingers laced, her hips nestled between his legs, was both heaven and hell.

He leaned against the wall outside the bathroom and closed his eyes, listening to her sweet, melodic voice. He couldn't believe she'd been living there for less than a month and she already seemed like family. They'd only shared a few hot kisses since the day he'd stormed out of the barn, and it had been hell refraining from taking things further. But first he had to deal with his demons.

He listened to the cadence of her voice as she sang about never growing up, telling himself tonight was the night he would tell her about PJ. She sang soft and slow, about little brothers' favorite songs and a new apartment in a big city. The song was clearly written about parents and children, but his thoughts turned to PJ. Her voice was like feathers drifting over his skin; each word brought rise to happier memories.

Nash sank down to the floor, crossing his arms over his knees, and tipped his head back against the wall, closing his eyes and struggling to hold on to the image of his brother's face. He could see him so clearly right then, he wanted to burn PJ's ever-present smile and square jaw into his mind, to make it easier to recall when his mind became clouded with pain and his brother's face eluded him.

As she sang, he dug deeper, remembering the sound of PJ's laughter as his older brother drove him around town the first week he'd had his license. The feel of his brother's strength as they wrestled in the yard. His hand burned with the sting of catching one of PJ's pitches when they were playing ball in the yard. Tears burned his eyes as she sang of wishing she'd never grown up and wishing life could be that simple again. How many times had Nash wished he could go back in time and somehow bring Phillip with him, just to have more time with his brother? He thought of the pride in PJ's eyes when he'd pitch a winning game. More childhood memories slammed into him, each dragging him deeper into the past. PJ harassing him about his artwork and then showing up at each of his school art fairs. He was Nash's biggest fan, just as Nash was for him.

"Nash?" Tempest touched his arm. "Are you okay?"

He hadn't even heard her come out of the bathroom. His fingers curled into fists as he tried to climb out from under the weight of the past. But it wasn't enough. The tears still burned. His throat was too tight to swallow. Whatever portal he'd opened refused to close. He lifted his face, bringing her worried, beautiful eyes into focus. Emotions swelled inside him, battling for space with PJ's ghost—and he knew it was time to finally face his past.

He pushed to his feet with Tempest watching him so intently it was like she was reaching into his thoughts. He imagined her coaxing them out, as she'd already done in so many ways. Something inside him softened, taking the sting of fear out of his waiting confession, and replaced it with trust.

"Is your offer to talk about what happened in the barn still good?"

Surprise shone in her eyes. "Of course," she said with a sweet smile. "Let me just put my stuff in my bedroom."

His eyes dropped to the toiletry bag in her arms. "I cleaned out a drawer in the bathroom vanity for you last weekend. I must have forgotten to tell you."

"You did? Thank you! Give me one sec."

She disappeared into the bathroom, and he listened to the drawer opening and her setting her things inside. He was eager to share more of himself with her, both emotionally and physically, and he hoped that tonight he'd finally be able to.

Tempest came out of the bathroom with a bounce in her step. "That's so much easier than carrying it back and forth. I just have to remember to bring my shampoo and stuff when I go back home next weekend."

He hated the idea of being without her again next weekend, but he was too distracted by the alluring bounce of her braless breasts and the tantalizing peak of her nipples pressing against her soft white cotton tank top to focus on it. The ends of her hair were damp from her bath, causing transparent wet spots along the swell of her breasts. He dropped his gaze, hoping to slow the heat flooding his veins, but got stuck on a flash of taut skin between her top and her flannel pajama pants. He dragged his eyes back to her face, hoping that would be safer. Her hair was tousled in that devastatingly sexy, just-had-a-good-mattress-romp way she wore it. *Holy shit.* How could he possibly concentrate with all of her accidental sexiness on display?

As she tucked that always-unruly lock of hair behind her ear with another adorable bounce and said, "Should we go outside?" she had no idea what she was doing to him.

I'd rather go to the bedroom. "Sure, but you need to put on a sweatshirt."

"Why? It was pretty warm today. Did it get chilly?"

"Not chilly enough," he said under his breath. If only it were winter, maybe then he could stand outside and cool the hell down. Like metal to magnet, his eyes found her breasts, and he felt himself get hard.

She followed his gaze to her breasts, and her cheeks pinked up.

"Sorry." She hurried into her room and he followed her, knowing she'd throw on her favorite pink hoodie with the white stripe on the sleeve that she wore nearly every night.

He couldn't believe he was already cataloging her favorite clothes, among which were her strappy leather sandals and those minuscule cutoffs she wore just about every night when they fed the animals. She was slowly torturing him, but it would be an awfully enjoyable death.

"I forgot you were going for the whole weekend. How long do you think you'll keep going back to Peaceful Harbor on the weekends? You seem to be picking up quite a few clients." Three more kids had signed up for her music classes this week.

She pulled her hoodie on and zipped it up with her back to

him. "I don't have enough kids yet to afford full-time space for the classes and still earn a living. So until I do, I'll continue with my patients there. And even when I'm here full-time, I'll still go back for the Girl Power meetings. The Girl Power meeting isn't until next Saturday, and Cole's company picnic is the following day, and of course then I'll see my music therapy client. *That* weekend will be crazy."

She spun around with a playful glint in her eyes that nearly made him forget anything but the desire to take her in his arms and devour her.

"Better?"

"Hardly." He strode through her room and opened the door to the deck. As she stepped outside, he said, "Remind me to buy you a big, bulky sweatshirt."

She laughed, and they sat on the bench, their legs brushing. He uttered a curse and moved a few inches away.

"What's wrong? We always sit close."

There was a slight pout to her voice that drew him close again. He draped an arm around her, pulling her against his side and trying to ignore the lust coiling low in his gut. Impossible.

"I know we do, but...Maybe it's seeing how much good you've done for Phillip, or how you've made me feel things I haven't for a very long time. Or how much happiness you've brought to our lives. Or maybe it's because of what I want to talk to you about—or how incredibly hot and sexy you look every minute of the day and night. I don't know why, but it's getting damn hard to keep my emotions in check. Being close to you like this makes me want more, and at the same time, I can't give you more until I get this off my chest."

"Okay," she said softly, and wiggled out from beneath his arm, sitting beside him. "Then let's get to the root of the matter. What do you want to talk about?"

"You're so ready to take on whatever stands in your way. How do you do it?"

She fidgeted with the edge of her hoodie, but her eyes never left his. "This is the new, risky Tempest, remember?"

"I hear you, but I'm not buying it, angel." He took her hand, brushing his thumb over her knuckles and wondering where the endearment came from. The surprise in her eyes told him she was wondering, too. He laughed, earning the same from her. "You are like an angel, the way you came into our lives and opened our eyes to a fuller, happier life, when I didn't think we were missing a damn thing."

She dropped her eyes, a shy smile on her lips.

"You're not risky, Tempe. You're careful, and you're giving, and without even trying, you make me want to open up. There's an innocence about you that is so intriguing, I keep forcing myself to hold back."

"You don't have to hold back." She met his gaze with a sultry look in her eyes. "I'm not *that* innocent." Her tone belied her words.

"I don't mean 'naive' or 'inexperienced.' You have *goodness* about you. You trust and you share like it's as easy as inhaling and exhaling. And you deserve to be with someone who can do the same."

He pressed a kiss to the back of her fingers, and her eyes darkened. He loved that look so much, he leaned forward and kissed her softly. Her lips were moist and warm, and when he deepened the kiss, she leaned in to him, her hands wrapping around his neck. She kissed him hungrily, her tongue moving swiftly over his as he slid his hands beneath her hair, angling her mouth so he could take the kiss even deeper. She was sweet and hot and tasted so damn perfect. He didn't have a chance in hell of backing off, and when she moaned into his mouth, all his blood rushed south, taking his ability to think rationally with it. He palmed her breasts, earning another sweet, needy sound. Lust coursed through him, spurring him on to *take* more, but somewhere in the back of his mind were the words he'd just said, reminding him of what she deserved, of what he *needed* to give her. She was good, and open, and honest, and she deserved the same.

Silently cursing his conscience, he forced himself to pull away. "I'm sorry."

He fixed her hoodie, taking in the flush of her cheeks, her pink, swollen lips, and the crystal-blue pools of desire in her eyes, luring him in again. Like an addict unable to go cold turkey, he had a burning desire, a *dire* need, to kiss her again. He hauled her against him, pressing his mouth to hers again and again and telling himself he was easing off. But her mouth was liquid heat, and he couldn't pull away.

One more kiss.

Their kisses turned fervent and messy, then sweet and sinful.

Just one more.

They were both lost in their wild, frantic kisses, as if they were the last kisses they might ever get.

When he finally gathered the strength to break their connection, they both came away breathless.

"Keep kissing me, Nash," she pleaded. "I lay in bed every night wishing you had kissed me more. I can't wait any longer. We can talk later. Please, I *need* you to kiss me again. *Now.*"

His emotions whirred as their mouths crashed together. She made a low, sensual sound, and it vibrated through him, arousing his primal instincts, and he was gone. *Done.* Too into her to think at all. He pulled her onto his lap, deepening the kiss as she straddled him. Working the zipper of her hoodie down, he palmed her breasts, a desperate sound escaping his lungs.

"I need more." His words came fast and hot, his voice unrecognizable as he tore her shirt up, exposing the most spectacular breasts he'd ever seen. Her nipples pebbled tighter as he took one taut peak in his mouth. He palmed one breast, running his other hand over her waist, her ribs, her hips, her ass. No matter how much he took, he still needed more.

She clung to his head, arching against his mouth. "Feels so good," she panted out, guiding his mouth to her other breast. "I want you so bad, Nash."

He drew back, searching her eyes and knowing he should stop, but the raw desire looking back at him drove him to lower her to the bench. He captured her mouth again, taking her harder, kissing her deeper, and getting so fucking lost in her he didn't know if he'd ever find his way back.

"I need to touch you," he said between kisses.

"Yes," she pleaded.

He took her in another sensual kiss, pushing his hand beneath her shirt, over her stomach. She quivered beneath his touch. It had been so long since he'd touched a woman, he was shaking a little, too. He traced her lower lip with his tongue, teasing her until she was bowing off the bench. She was so fucking sexy his cock throbbed behind his zipper. He tore her shirt up again, taking her breast into his mouth and sucking so hard she cried out. He moved higher, cupping her jaw, and brushed his thumb over her lips. Her tongue slicked over the tip, making him ache to see her mouth wrapped around his cock.

"Tell me you're with me, Tempe, or tell me to stop. I need to hear it from you."

FROM THE LOOK of lust in Nash's eyes to the heady need in his voice, his raw sensuality electrified her. She pressed a kiss to his thumb, wishing she were brazen enough to suck it and send the green-light signals other girls doled out like smiles. But she wasn't bold enough to do something so visibly naughty. Instead, she gathered what courage she could, took his hand, and guided it beneath the waist of her pajama pants.

"I'm right here with you," she assured him.

Her breathing shallowed as his thick fingers moved beneath her belly button, and along the edge of her panties. The heat of his hand was intoxicating. Her hips rose, urging him lower, to finally touch the part of her that had been aching for him. His hand moved south, and his eyes smoldered as his mouth covered hers, kissing her slow and sweet. His fingers slid up and down along the crease between her sex and her thigh, brushing the side of her sex, making her wetter, more needy, with each stroke. She focused on the feel of his lips against hers, his tongue thrusting deeper as his hand moved beneath her panties. His fingers moved up and down, up and down, in a dizzying pattern as he opened his mouth wider, claiming more of hers. He thrust his fingers inside her, and a low moan traveled up from her lungs, escaping into his mouth. He delved deeper with both his tongue and fingers, quickening his pace and hitting all her magical spots.

"There. God, *there*," she begged, feeling him smile against her lips.

Each time his fingers pushed in, an electric current pulsed through her, and at the same time, he kissed her harder, possessing all of her at once and creating an erotic rhythm. Her thoughts spiraled out of control, unstoppable pleas spewing from her lips—*"More. So good. Yes."*

When he brushed his whiskers over her cheek and said, "I want to feel you come," the guttural sound of his voice and the naughtiness of his words shattered her last shred of control. She grabbed his head, crashing her mouth to his, her body a trembling, pulsing mess as he took her up to the edge of sanity. His cock rubbed and ground against her thigh as his fingers moved in and out between her legs, sparking involuntary tremors in her thighs that traveled to her sex, growing stronger, pulsing tighter as she neared the peak. Her senses reeled, overwhelmed by his touch, his scent, his taste. She gave herself over to the inferno that had been mounting for days. Fire spread through her limbs, consumed her chest. Cries of ecstasy poured from her lungs, but he didn't relent. He continued his pursuit of her pleasure, eating at her mouth as he fucked her with his fingers, holding her at her peak so long she thought she might explode. Heat rippled beneath her skin with each pulse of her climax. Her body shook and shivered as she rode the crescendo of their passion. He kissed her softer, pressing his lips to the corners of her mouth, along her lower lip, stroking her slowly between her legs as she came back down from the clouds. Warmth spread over her, enveloping her in a blissful feeling. When he withdrew his fingers, she heard herself whimper.

He brought his slick fingers to his mouth and dragged his tongue along the length of them, a wicked smile forming as he sucked them clean. She'd never seen anyone do that before, and her body electrified anew, with much more than sexual desire.

She wanted whatever that was. *Dark pleasures? Erotic pleasures?* She didn't know. She only knew it was naughty and sexy and so exciting she could hardly wait to see him do it again.

"Ohmygosh," slipped out before she could stop it.

He chuckled. "Too dirty?"

"No. I like it. I've just never...I've never seen anyone do that before." She whispered, "I like it."

He kissed her again, long and slow and oh so delicious.

"My sweet, sweet angel, you unleashed years of pent-up sexuality. I have a feeling you might need to tame me."

Reveling in his endearment, she said, "No. No taming, please." Feeling bold, she reached between his legs, taking in the full girth of his arousal. "That's big enough to share. But I'm really not into sharing."

He chuckled and moved her hand to his hip, kissing her again. She tasted herself on his tongue, and when he deepened the kiss, his whiskers prickling her cheeks, sparks flamed inside her again. She ground her hips against his arousal, and he laced their hands together.

"Soon," he promised, and held her tight. "I wanted to talk to you before we even went this far, to let you into my world. But your kisses consume me."

"How could I be any more in your world? I live here," she pointed out.

After another languid kiss, during which she may have sighed dreamily, he said, "You are. But what happened that afternoon in the barn? That wasn't okay."

A look of grief came over him, and she remembered how troubled he'd looked when she'd found him in the hall.

"You already apologized for that," she reminded him.

"I know." He brushed her hair from her shoulder and

pressed a kiss there. "But I didn't explain why I was upset. I think we should sit up for this." He pushed up to a sitting position.

She sat sideways on the bench, giving him her full attention. He lifted eyes so troubled, she reached out and stroked his arm to comfort him.

"Whatever it is," she said, "I hope I can help."

"You already have." His lips twitched, as if he might smile, but they never made it. He reached for her hand, absently caressing her fingers between his.

"There's no easy way to say this, so I'm just going to lay it out there." He looked out over the yard, his jaw clenching tight. After a long moment, he let out a breath and met her gaze. "The reason my parents took me out of school and we traveled for two years was because…" His voice cracked, and his eyes darted away again. He blinked several times. "I had a brother, and he was killed when he was a senior in high school."

"Oh, Nash." She moved closer, remembering what he'd said about his childhood. *It was just me and my parents…We were close.* "I'm so sorry."

He stared out over the deck, blinking against tears. "He was my idol, you know? My best friend, and at times," he said with the hint of a smile, "my worst enemy." He half laughed, half scoffed, still blinking against damp eyes. "He was um…It was after the last baseball game of the year. He pitched. They won."

She moved so close she was practically in his lap, fighting her own tears.

"PJ was everything I wasn't. He was popular, into sports, and so sure of himself. He wanted to play for the Nationals."

"Your hat," she said softly.

He nodded. "*His* hat. He was being scouted for the major

league free-agent amateur draft. We all knew he'd make it. He gave me the hat he'd worn every day for eight years after that game, and the asshole got himself killed later that night." A tear slipped down his cheek. He swiped at it, and she touched his hand, gently moving it away from his face, and kissed the wetness away.

"It's okay to cry." She wiped her own tears, wishing she could take his pain away.

He took her hands in his and held on tight. "Oh, I cried. Tears of fucking anger. He wasn't who I thought he was. He'd gone out celebrating their win with a buddy from the team and his cousins, who were in from out of town, and they robbed a goddamn convenience store two towns away. He had everything to lose and nothing to gain. Our family wasn't rich, but we had enough money. He had a *future*. He was nothing like the person I thought he was. It was all a fucking lie." He released her hand, curling his into fists.

"You never knew he was hanging out with a bad crowd?" she asked.

The deadpan look he gave her nearly stopped her heart.

"Hanging out with?" he scoffed. "He was *driving* the *getaway* car. The police chased them for seven miles before he took a turn too tight and rolled the fucking thing. He died instantly. The other three guys were all messed up. I lived with the guy for fifteen years. How the hell did I miss that he was a thief?"

"Nash." She didn't even know what she wanted to say, but she felt the need to say something. He looked so mad, so sad. So *broken*.

He shook his head. "Don't. Please don't try to tell me that I shouldn't judge him. You can't imagine what it's like."

"No. I can't, you're right."

"Neither could we," he said harshly. "Everything changed that night. The police showed up at the door, and I went ballistic. I didn't believe them, and when I look back now, I realize how crazed I was. But that night?" He turned away again. "That night I wanted to kill the motherfucker. It didn't matter that he was just the bearer of the most horrible news we'd ever heard. All that mattered was what he said. I hated the police officer almost as much as I hated my brother."

"No, Nash." Tears tumbled down her cheeks for his pain, his loss, and the anger he still carried. "You can't take all your years together, all the good things that made you look up to him, and throw it away like it wasn't real. You have to hold on to the person you knew him to be. He wasn't a thief *to you*; you just said as much."

He pushed to his feet and paced. "He wasn't who I thought he was, Tempe. Not by a long shot. And it wasn't just me. We went from being a family of four to a family of three and a ghost. PJ was *everywhere*. Memories bombarded me every single day, and I analyzed every goddamn one of them, looking for clues that he was a thief. I know it was even harder for my parents. I swear, in the days after his death, my parents put up walls so thick even their best friends couldn't get through. They didn't take phone calls, didn't answer the door. They had him cremated, buried his ashes with only the three of us there, packed up our shit, sold the house, and went out on the boat."

"Your family ran," she said. "I can't imagine leaving all those memories behind."

"You mean all those *lies*. You have no idea what it was like. Your brothers call and check on you; they go to work and have significant others they love. They're living their *truths*. PJ's life was a *lie*, Tempest. And my parents made damn sure that we left all his lies behind. And you know what the suckiest part was? They pretended he never existed, and at first I didn't get it, because...*Fuck*." He turned away, hands fisted. "I wanted to talk about him. I *needed* to talk about him. But they couldn't. *Wouldn't*. When I tried, my father told me I was upsetting my mother, and she'd cry for days. My family died right along with him, and I had to learn to move on with his ghost by my side. To this day my mother clams up if I mention his name."

He faced her again, his lips pressed into an unforgiving line. "I'm pretty sure that's why she doesn't see Phillip. I think seeing him stirs too many painful memories for her. PJ's name was Phillip John." Fresh tears welled in his eyes. "I had to honor him, despite it all." He breathed heavily. "I loved him so damn much."

"Oh, Nash." Unable to give him the space he was trying desperately to keep between them, she embraced him. He was so tightly wound, his arms hung stiffly by his sides, but she held on tight, pressing her cheek to his chest. "I'm so sorry."

"I'm sorry I lied to you," he said sharply. "I know that makes me no better than him."

She drew back, saddened by the anger in his eyes. "Nash, I understand why you didn't tell me the truth. You didn't even know me."

"No." He pushed from her arms, shaking his head. "It's not okay. None of this is okay. I can't even bring myself to tell my own son about my brother. How fucked up is that?" He sank down to the bench.

She sat beside him, grasping for the right thing to say. "You've carried this around for all these years? Didn't your parents try to help at all? Or get you a therapist to talk to when you got back from your trip?"

He sat back, his head resting on the railing, and stared up at the sky for a long, silent moment. Exhaling a long breath, he sat up and squared his shoulders in a practiced move.

"Once we left Oak Rivers, we never went back. After the trip, we rented a house in Charlottesville. We were three people who were once a family and had become strangers living in a painfully silent house. I couldn't take it. I packed up my stuff, grabbed my guitar, and hit the road. I didn't even know where I was going. I met this artist in Pennsylvania who needed an assistant to do his grunt work, and within a few weeks he taught me to do chainsaw sculptures. Within six months we were selling more of my work than his." He looked at his hands. "It was like my hands were made to do that work. After a few months I took off on my own. I called home every few weeks, and we'd talk for a few minutes. My father taught at the university, but his health deteriorated fast."

"I can't imagine what it must have been like when you were at sea, and then losing your father so quickly." She tried to wrap her head around how much he'd lost.

"We went days, *weeks*, without communicating. My father buried himself in books, and my mother painted."

"And you?" She reached for his hand, and when he didn't take it, she laced their fingers together and curled her fingers around his.

"I wrote songs, played my guitar, studied. But mostly, I tried to escape it all—the pain, the memories." He met her gaze, fresh tears wetting his eyes. "Basically, we buried my brother, and then I had to learn to bury everything else deep enough that I could move on."

"So you never got any real closure?"

He shrugged, as if that didn't matter.

"Nash, how can you move on if you haven't had a chance to mourn your brother? You never talked about him? You've never gone back to visit his grave or make peace with your loss? Regardless of what secrets he had, the years you shared are important. They shaped your life. They shaped who you are, and you're an amazing man."

He shook his head, as if he didn't believe her. "I spent two years mourning him," he said halfheartedly.

"It doesn't sound like it. It sounds like you spent two years repressing your feelings about him." She wrapped her arms around him again, pressing her cheek to his chest and feeling the panicked beat of his heart. She held him until the tension in his body eased, until his breathing slowed. "How can you mourn a person you can't talk about?"

His arms came around her and he said, "I'm talking about him now."

Chapter Twelve

TEMPEST COULD PRACTICALLY hear the clicking of gears in Nash's head as he pondered her offer to take Phillip with her to her children's class at the community center. They were in the barn talking while Phillip played with his toys in the grass just outside the doors. It was Thursday afternoon, three days since he'd begun telling her about PJ. He'd been sharing more details about his family, and his feelings, every day, and it had brought them even closer together. She thought having a window of opportunity without Phillip to worry about might do him a world of good.

"He's never gone anywhere without me," Nash finally said.

She knew this, of course. The two were attached at the hip. "But you've seen him with me. He trusts me, Nash." Earlier that morning, while Nash showered, she and Phillip had made silver-dollar pancakes—counting each one—and had surprised Nash with breakfast. Phillip was coming out of his shell more and more each day. "Being around the other kids will be good for him, especially if you're really thinking about signing Phillip up for an observation day at preschool. It would be like practice, and it would give *you* a few hours to get some work done without a three-year-old underfoot."

He rubbed the back of his neck. "I called the preschool and set up an observation day for next week."

"Wow. That's wonderful." She hadn't realized he'd come so far in his decision. But she knew letting Phillip go with her was hard for him to consider, and she wound her arms around his neck and kissed him.

They hadn't gone any further than they had the night on the deck, but she wanted to. Every magical kiss made her want more. But they were sharing so many other intimate parts of themselves, the speed with which they were moving felt *right*. Each night they kissed and talked for hours as Nash unburdened himself of the secrets he'd been holding on to for so long. The more he shared about what his life was like before—and after—they lost PJ, the more he wanted to hear about Tempest's family, too. They shared private moments and memories, pieces of their lives that had formed their personalities and values and stories about the people they loved most. Each night Tempest went to bed breathless and wanting the man who was just as careful as she was, but they were building a solid foundation, and there was no rushing where that was concerned.

"I don't mind having Phillip here while I work," he said.

"I know. You're a wonderful daddy, but you're also a single, working father, and you need independence as much as he does. Maybe you can get a little work done on those sculptures that are waiting in your locked shop." She smiled, and the tension around his mouth eased. "Letting him go to a class with me doesn't mean you're being selfish or letting him down. You're giving him a chance to succeed on his own, and you know I'll watch him every second. I would never let anything happen to him."

"I trust you, angel. You know that." He circled her waist with his arms, and his eyes drifted over her shoulder at Phillip. "I just…What if he has a hard time?"

"That's what cell phones are for. I will be there to help him if he needs anything at all. You've seen me with him. You trust me, right?"

He nodded, conflicting emotions evident in his trusting eyes and tense expression.

"Let me do this," she urged. "For both of you. Think about it, Nash. This will give you a taste of what it might be like when he goes to preschool. Pick up the chainsaw; see if it still speaks to you the way it once did."

He glanced over her shoulder again. "How can it be this hard? I trust you. I really do."

"Because that's what love is." She stepped back in case Phillip walked in. "You love him so much you don't want him to stumble, but kids have to know they can figure things out and stand on their own two feet. He can't do that without being given the chance. And he's like your security blanket, too. It's a big step for both of you."

Nash's lips tipped up and he pulled her close again, giving her a chaste kiss. "You must have been a mom in a previous life."

"I have lots of younger siblings, and my parents were big on teaching us to be independent."

"Let's ask Phillip, okay?" He took her hand and together they went out front. Phillip looked up from where he was playing, and Nash crouched, still holding Tempest's hand, as he brought her down beside him.

"Hey, buddy, would you like to go with Tempe to play music with other kids?"

Phillip's brows knitted. His eyes moved between the two of them, settling on Nash. A silent message she couldn't read passed between them.

"Just you and Tempe," Nash explained. "I'll stay here and work, and I'll see you the minute you get back." He squeezed Tempest's hand so tight she knew he was channeling all his worries in an effort to sound positive, and it made her fall even harder for him.

Phillip's eyes found their joined hands and then skipped up to Tempest's face, and he smiled. She felt like she'd been holding her breath waiting for an answer, and when he reached for her other hand, her heart nearly exploded.

Nash walked them to the car and transferred Phillip's car seat to her backseat. After strapping him in and kissing him a dozen times, he took Tempest's hands with a loving look tinged with worry. "Thank you," he said. "I think you're right. This will be good for us. All three of us."

A swarm of butterflies let loose in her belly. "I hope so. I'll make sure he's fine. If he's doing really well, I'll text you. If *you're* also doing well," she said lightly, "I'll take him out for a while longer so you have more time. Try to remember who Nash Morgan the man, the artist, the creative genius is, and let Nash Morgan the daddy take a break."

His chin dropped for a beat, a small smile lifting his lips. He looked at her from beneath the bill of his ball cap, giving her another trusting gaze. "I'm becoming more of the man I used to be every day, only better. Thanks to you."

THE FIRST FEW minutes in Nash's sculpting studio were the

hardest. He was flooded with excitement one minute and drowned in guilt the next. Was it wrong to be pumped about getting back to sculpting if it was at the expense of being separated from his son? What if Phillip wasn't having a good time? What if he was clingy and making it difficult for Tempest to teach the class? That thought stopped him in his tracks, and his eyes hit the door. He'd been so worried about his son, he hadn't weighed the reality of what Tempest's offer had meant for her. He felt for his phone in his pocket, but she'd promised to text if there were any issues. *You trust me, right?* Yes, he definitely did.

It had been so long since he'd cared about anyone other than family and even longer since he had *wanted* someone to care about him. Since she'd moved in, he'd greedily soaked up their closeness like a sponge. He wanted to watch the sun come up with her in his arms every morning, but he couldn't risk Phillip finding them together like that. It had been especially hard to leave her the first night he'd told her about PJ, but when they'd finally gone to their separate bedrooms, with the burden of his secret lifted, he'd slept better than he had in years. She was good for both of them in so many ways.

He pushed open the back doors to the barn, his gaze landing on his heavy leather tool belt hanging by the tool bench. There was a time when he'd worn it so often the leather had been soft and pliable, but now it was stiff. He didn't wear it when he worked on furniture. But he wore it when he was sculpting larger pieces, after the bulk was removed and the piece was molded into form and he was refining his work. His eyes shifted to the unfinished sculpture of the boy looking up at the sky.

Hope fluttered in his chest. Would there actually come a

time when he might finish this sculpture? *When I might make more?* Guilt perched on his shoulders again. Tempest and Phillip had been gone for twenty minutes and were probably at the community center by now. Was he okay? Was Tempest regretting her decision? He pulled out his phone to check his messages and was mildly relieved to see there were none.

Am I going to worry about you two every minute?

Returning his attention to the reason Tempest had offered to take Phillip in the first place, he maneuvered the sculpture of the boy looking up toward the sky onto the dolly and rolled it outside. His pulse kicked up at the simple transition. A little while later, after donning gloves, headphones, and safety goggles, his body vibrating from the force of the chainsaw, Nash was completely absorbed in the project. Muscles he hadn't used in forever twitched and burned as he maneuvered the edge of the blade to carve away the blocky wood. When his muscle memory kicked in, the light touch he'd spent years honing returned. He expertly maneuvered the blade, getting just the right depth on each cut as he carved the child's elbows and knees, hips, and feet. Wood shavings flew around him like confetti, covering his clothing and puddling at his feet. The smell of gasoline and fresh-cut wood hung in the air. *Heaven.*

A rush of adrenaline hit as the form took shape, and he swiftly moved from the chainsaw to the wood shaper and then to smaller tools, defining wrinkles in the denim around the boy's knees and ankles and the creases around his fly. He took off his hat and brushed the wood shavings from it as he stepped back to admire his work. Grinning like a fool, he marveled at the piece he'd created. There was still a lot to do, but hell if it wasn't exactly what he'd envisioned when he'd first begun making it all those years ago. *Sonofabitch. I've still got it.*

"DADDY!" PHILLIP RAN through the barn and bolted out the back doors toward Nash with a handful of colorful pipe cleaners.

Shocked that they were back so soon, Nash scooped him up before he could get too close to his tools. "That was fast. Did you have fun?" He reached for Tempe and she took his hand. Feeling exhilarated, he tugged her closer, putting his arm around her waist.

"We were gone three hours," she said, taking his hand. "I texted to let you know we were going to get ice cream, and then we walked through some of the shops. Didn't you get the message?"

Three hours? He hadn't spent three hours apart from Philip since his son was a baby. He must have been so into his work, thoughts of Phillip had slipped away completely. He didn't know what that said about him. He didn't have a chance to respond to Tempest because Phillip was talking as fast as he possibly could.

"We played music with xylathings and tamberns and shaky sticks, and we had ice cweam. I made fwends. Know what else? Dad? Dad!"

Nash's jaw hung open as he listened to his boy say more in sixty seconds than he'd said in the last two days. "I'm listening, buddy. Tell me more."

"Look what Miss Hattie gave me!" Phillip shoved the pipe cleaners in Nash's face. "Tempe's going to help me make animals with 'em." He wiggled out of his arms and pointed at the sculpture. "Who's that?"

"Don't go near those tools, buddy."

Phillip stopped walking, and Nash put a hand on his shoulder. "That's just a boy I made. Do you like him?" He kissed Tempest's cheek and lowered his voice. "Who's Miss Hattie?"

"She owns the art boutique where I'm playing Friday afternoon. We stopped by so I could see the setup. She has the most incredible kids' area. Phillip loved it." Tempest stepped closer to the sculpture with an awestruck expression. "You cannot keep making furniture when you have *this* inside you."

"What do you have inside you?" Phillip asked.

Nash laughed, kissed Tempest's cheek, and then bent down and kissed Phillip's. "Just a lot of love, buddy, and probably a whole lot of sawdust."

After Nash cleaned up, they fed the animals and made pipe cleaner pets. Or rather, Tempest made them, because Nash wasn't nearly as adept with pipe cleaners as he was with a chainsaw. Phillip told him all about his afternoon with Tempest again while they ate dinner. In one afternoon she'd managed to show both of them what they were capable of with a little trust.

Later that night they sat around a bonfire singing "Five Little Monkeys." He'd never seen his son giggle as much as he had when they sang about a monkey falling off the bed. It might have helped that Nash pretended to fall off the log he'd been sitting on each time he sang the line. Nash had done it as much to earn one of Tempest's sweet laughs as he had for Phillip's entertainment.

Phillip leaned against Nash's shoulder as Tempest sang one of the songs she'd written for a client. "*They crossed their hearts, swore on stars. Promised to keep you safe, to love you through.*" She hummed a few more bars and then she stopped playing and motioned for Phillip to come to her. "Let's let Daddy play now."

She held her guitar out toward Nash, and Phillip climbed up on her lap. "Daddy doesn't play guitar."

She wrapped her arms around him and whispered, "Daddy is so talented. There's nothing he can't do."

Their eyes met and he felt all the emotions he'd been holding back come tumbling forward. He'd wanted to take things slow because he was worried about Phillip, and if he were honest with himself, he was also a little scared. And now, as he watched her loving up his son, other emotions warred within him. He'd loved being back in the throes of carving today, but he was still struggling to figure out how Phillip could have escaped his mind during those three amazing hours.

"Play, Dad," Phillip said, bringing him back to the moment.

"I haven't played in years."

"You also hadn't sculpted in years, and look what you did. It's like riding a bike. You never really forget." She kissed Phillip's cheek. "Right, Phillip? You want to hear Daddy play music, don't you?"

Phillip nodded and yawned. He snuggled against Tempest as Nash's fingers fell into place, and one of his favorite songs, the one that had kept him company for all those years on the road, came out. *Guess it is like riding a bike.* The words to "Something" by George Harrison came as if he'd been singing it every day of his life. As he sang about something in her eyes, and something in her smile, his brother's words came back to him. *When you meet a girl who rocks your world, this is the song you'll play.*

Damn, bro, you were right.

He played the whole song, and then he played another and another, feeling lighter than he had in years. But as his eyes fell on Tempest, his little boy fast asleep in her arms, there were no words for what he felt. He set the guitar down and reached for Phillip, but Tempest shook her head.

"Do you mind if I carry him?"

Never in a million years would he have thought he could feel what he did at that moment. "Sure."

With his hand on her back, they headed upstairs.

"I love listening to you sing," she said as he changed Phillip into his pajamas.

"Then I'll sing for you more often." He tucked Phillip into bed and brushed a kiss over his forehead.

"May I?" She motioned toward Phillip. Just when he didn't think his heart could get any fuller, she whispered, "Good night, sweetheart. I was so proud of you today," and kissed his little boy, proving him wrong.

Chapter Thirteen

NASH CLOSED THE door to Phillip's bedroom and started down the hallway with Tempest, so overcome with emotion, it was a struggle not to take her in his arms and finally show her just how much he cared for her. But his loving thoughts were clouded by something he'd been grappling with all evening.

"Tempe, about this afternoon."

"Thank you for letting me take him." She stopped walking and smiled up at him. "He had such a good time, and he did really well with the other kids."

"I'm glad, but I have to tell you something. I haven't had time away from Phillip since he was an infant, and then today I got so caught up in what I was doing, I didn't think about him." He shifted his eyes away, a stab of guilt piercing his chest. "At first I did, but once I got busy, I don't know what happened. I just...didn't. What does that say about me as a father?"

She stopped walking and touched his hand. "It says you trusted me, and you trusted Phillip. You knew I'd call if there was an issue, and if there had been, and you didn't answer the call, I would have brought him home. But that didn't happen. We both had an amazing time. Actually, I think all three of us did. You needed that time, Nash. You're a different man than you were before you had that time alone. I see it in your eyes, and I feel it in your touch, and even in the way you look at Phillip. He's your baby, but he's not a baby. He's a smart, friendly, curious little boy who is loved beyond this world. You are an incredible dad, Nash. Let yourself be an incredible man, too."

She grabbed his shirt, tugging him closer and setting his body ablaze. "There is *nothing* bad about what happened today. Please don't twist it into something it's not."

When she flattened her hands against his chest and kissed the center of it, he angled her face up, needing to see her, to feel their connection even deeper. A stream of silent messages passed between them—*I want you. I'm right here. I'm nervous. I've got you.* She touched his cheek, caressing his jaw with a desperate look in her eyes. He was right there with her, and he was done trying to fight the pressure building inside him.

"Tempest," he whispered, and lowered his mouth to hers, intending to kiss her tenderly, to take things slow. But she tasted sweet and hot, and all of the emotions of the past two weeks surged forward, unshackling his inner savage.

His mouth opened wider, and his tongue thrust deeper. He groped her ass, tightening his hold on her hair like a beast, tugging her head back and exposing her luscious neck for him to claim. He ground against her hips, spurred on by her heady pleas and the feel of her knee sliding up his thigh. He grabbed hold of it, rocking against her as he captured her mouth again, and when that wasn't enough, he lifted her into his arms. Her legs circled his waist and he stumbled forward with the force of their kiss. Her back hit the wall with a *thud*, and they broke apart, both of them panting, eyes wide with alarm, listening for Phillip.

After an interminable number of seconds, their mouths crashed together again. Their teeth clanked, tongues thrust in urgent, wet kisses so frigging good he got swept away, and her back thudded against the wall again. He reluctantly tore his mouth away. Her eyes widened, but a soft laugh escaped her swollen lips, and it did him in. He carried her into her bedroom, and she clung to him as he lowered her to the bed, her arms and legs wound tightly around his neck and waist, her gorgeous eyes appeared electric in the dimly lit room. His mouth swooped down and captured hers again as he came down over her. They both moaned as their bodies sank deeper into the mattress. Her hands played over the back of his neck, sending shivers down his spine. He deepened the kiss, opening his eyes with the need to see her as she writhed beneath him. Her hair fanned out over the pillow, her eyes fluttered open, and he drew back, gazing deeply into them.

"Tempe," he whispered, wanting to say much more. But lost in a world of lust and need, he was incapable of forming another word.

She pushed her fingers into his hair and pulled his mouth to hers, lifting her hips off the mattress, she moved against him in a slow, sensual rhythm. A raspy groan left his lungs as he met her efforts with a thrust of his hips. Emotions warred in his mind. He wanted to stay right there, drowning in her taste, reveling in her hungry mouth, but he also wanted to fast-forward, tear off every shred of her clothing, and bury himself so deep and hard they'd both lose their minds. A long, low moan vibrated up her chest and into their kiss, driving him out of his fucking mind. And then another thought crashed into him—
Phillip.

Fuck.

He needed to close the door. Why hadn't he thought of that before? Tearing himself away was torture, and his mouth refused to obey, going back for more again and again before he finally found the strength to pull away.

"Phillip," he said hastily, and backed off the bed. His erection strained against his jeans as he closed her bedroom door.

He tugged off his shirt and ran a hand nervously down his chest as he came down over her. Her cheeks glowed with the flush of arousal. Her lips were slick from their kisses. She looked delicate and feminine, and exquisitely tempting. He perched on his forearms, his heart beating so fast he was sure she could feel it pulsing in the air between them.

"Hey, beautiful."

She ran trembling fingers up his arms. "Hi," she whispered. "I missed you."

He brushed his lips over hers. "I'm right here, and I'm not going anywhere."

He kissed her then, with all the tenderness he'd meant to before, bracing himself with one arm so he could touch her face, stroke her cheek, and brush his fingers through her hair. She was so soft, and her skin was so warm. He wanted to feel all of her, to revel in every breath she took.

"I couldn't love kissing you more," he whispered, and pressed his lips to the tender spot beside her ear.

Her fingers curled around his arms, and he brought his mouth to hers again, more demanding and possessive, wanting to brand her as *his*. Their bodies moved in perfect sync, rocking and grinding as he moved lower, running his tongue over the frantic pulse at the base of her neck. Her breasts pressed against him with each anticipatory breath. He kissed a path down the center of her chest, feeling her breathing hitch as he tugged down the neckline of her dress and dragged his tongue across the swell of one beautiful breast.

He lifted his eyes, but hers were closed, her lower lip trapped beneath her teeth. Her fingernails dug harder into his skin. "Angel, do you want me to stop?"

"No," she whispered. "God, no."

Grinning like an idiot, he thanked his lucky stars and slanted his mouth over hers again. Jesus, he could kiss her until the sun came up and never feel like he'd missed out on a thing. She was strength and delicacy, trust and happiness, all in one devastatingly sweet woman. His hand moved down her side, squeezing her waist, her hip, her thigh, wanting to claim every piece of her. When he reached the edge of her dress he felt her tense up and stilled his hand, giving her the reins.

She kissed him slowly, carefully, and then her hips lifted off the mattress, shifting slightly. She covered his hand with hers, pressing his fingers into her thigh. It was the green light he needed, and he felt grateful and proud and so fucking happy he grinned into the kiss again.

She was smiling, too, and they both laughed. He wrapped her in his arms and rolled them onto their sides, cupping her ass with two hands and aligning their bodies once again.

"Three years is a long fucking time," he admitted. "I'm out of practice."

She wiggled against his erection. "You don't *feel* out of practice."

God, she was so fucking sexy. "I'm afraid of going too fast, or misreading a signal. And I really don't want to screw this up."

"I promise," she whispered, "if you misread anything, I'll tell you. But I'm right here with you, and I'm not going anywhere."

His heart turned over in his chest. He touched his lips to hers again, and their mouths fused together in a scorching kiss that burned away all the remaining anxiety, leaving no room for anything but white-hot desire. He didn't ask permission, didn't slow down, as his hands coasted over her ass and legs, up her back, until the thin material of her dress was tangled in his fists, and they both rose. He drew her dress over her head and tossed it to the other side of the bed. In the space of a breath he drank in her sweet curves, restrained by pretty pink lace, and the wicked look of lust in her eyes. Adrenaline surged within him as he took her in another demanding kiss. His hands moved over her skin like water claiming new territory, touching her everywhere at once, and when he went for the clasp on her bra, his thick fingers fumbled. She reached behind her back and removed it for him. They both went a little wild, kissing and groping as they fell to the mattress in a tangle of limbs and loud, greedy noises.

"More. I need more of you," he said urgently, tasting her flesh as he moved down her body.

"Yes—"

He lowered his mouth to her breast, swiping his tongue over and around one rosy peak. Her back bowed off the bed, but he kept up the tantalizing tease. He'd waited so fucking long for her, he was determined to enjoy every minute of it. Three years felt like nothing compared to these last couple of weeks.

"*Please*—" she begged.

He greedily sucked her breast, lust thrumming through him with each of her needy whimpers. He lavished the other breast with the same taunts until she bucked beneath him, demanding more. Sealing his mouth over that luscious breast, he sucked so hard she cried out. He tried to release her, but she clutched his head, holding him in place. *Fuck yeah.*

TEMPEST WAS LOST in a world of scintillating pleasure and emotions she was too swept up in to define. *Out of practice?* Who was he kidding? Every swipe of his tongue set her nerve endings on fire.

"Good Lord," she panted out. "I want to live in your mouth."

He touched her with gentle power despite his massive size. His teeth clamped around her nipple, and she sucked in a sharp breath, feeling the effect like a bolt of lightning between her legs. He sucked her breast into his mouth again, deep and hard, for so long she felt herself climbing toward the edge of release. She heard herself whimper, and he released her breast, claiming her mouth again, and just as quickly, moved back to her body, pressing hot, openmouthed kisses down the center. He clutched her ribs with both hands as he killed her brain cells one kiss at a time. She arched up, needing more, wanting to submerge herself in each and every sinful moment at the same time. Her consciousness rolled out like the tide. He slicked his tongue over her skin again, and she surged toward the edge of oblivion. He pushed his hands to her hips, pressing his fingers into her flesh, and brought his mouth to her inner thigh. *Holy cow.* She fisted her hands in the sheets as he sucked her sensitive skin to the point of titillating pain. She arched off the mattress and he pushed her down, eyeing her hungrily. The man knew how to take control, something she never thought she'd like, but she was so turned on her whole body was shaking.

She shifted her hips, giving him the signal she knew he was seeking. His lips quirked up, and a devilish look came over him, causing her pulse to spike as he hooked his fingers into the sides of her panties and tore them off. *Tore. Them. Off.* Two shreds of silk and lace drifted down on opposite sides of the bed. He didn't waste any time—*thank God*—and slicked his tongue along the center of her sex. Her eyes slammed shut, and she heard a stream of noises sailing from her lungs. He was *all in*, eating at her sex, one hand holding her down, the other playing over her clit with perfect pressure. She felt the pulse of an orgasm building inside her, and when he shifted, thrusting his fingers inside her, and brought his mouth to that oversensitive bundle of nerves, fireworks exploded behind her closed lids.

"Nash—"

Her toes curled under and her heels dug into the mattress, but he was relentless, taking her up, up, *up*, and *higher still*. She couldn't breathe, couldn't think, could only give herself over to the burning sensations that seemed captive within her. Words sailed from her lips—"*Ohgod, ohgod, ohgod. Right there.*"

He stopped.

Her head shot off the mattress and she looked between her legs, frustration rising inside her.

Nash looked at her with a playful smile, his lips glistening with the evidence of her arousal. He pressed a finger over his lips and pointed at the door. She slapped her hand over her mouth and fell back to the mattress, mortified. And then his mouth was on her again, causing one heart-stopping orgasm after another, until she lay in a cloud of ecstasy, trying to catch her breath. The mattress sank as Nash moved beside her. His jeans brushed against her legs. She'd forgotten he was still dressed. Embarrassment seeped in again. She'd just come too many times to count and he was *still clothed!*

She opened her eyes and found him gazing down at her with so much emotion swimming in his eyes, there was no room for embarrassment. He pressed a series of shivery kisses to her lips, his hands roving over her skin. His chest was hot and hard, and he felt delicious. When she'd first seen him shirtless, she'd been mesmerized. He wasn't perfectly sculpted like those models she'd seen in fitness magazines. He was *real*, with a dusting of chest hair that led south like a treasure trail, disappearing beneath his jeans. His physique was hard and defined from physical labor, not from lifting weights, and it must do something different to a body, because she could pass up models any day, but she was pretty sure those seams on her panties had melted open when she'd set her eyes on him.

He hauled her to him, taking the kiss deeper. She felt his frantic heart beating against her own.

"You still have your pants on." Reaching for the button on his jeans, she said, "Off, please."

His face clouded with uneasiness. "*Fuck.* I don't have a condom. I didn't think we were going to…"

"I'm on the pill. Are you clean? *Please* tell me you're clean."

His expression didn't ease. He wrapped his hand around her wrist, moving her hand from the button of his jeans to his hip. "I'm clean, Tempe, but…"

His eyes drifted to the door, and her lust-addled brain finally realized the reasons for his hesitancy. The pleading look in his eyes made her wish she'd realized it sooner. "But you don't want to take any chances," she answered for him. "Was Phillip's mom on the pill? It's ninety-nine percent effective."

He shook his head. "Broken condom. Christ, Tempe. I don't want to bring her into the bedroom with us. What we have is already a hundred times more than she and I ever did. But I'm just starting to figure out mine and Phillip's life, and"—a hopeful smile split his lips, and he ran his knuckles down her cheek—"I'm so into you, I don't want to chance something going wrong when we're just starting out."

Her heart was so full of him it felt near bursting. She touched her lips to his, and he slid his hand to the back of her neck, drawing her closer, kissing her deeper, and igniting all that warmth into flames. How did he do it with just a kiss? She pushed him onto his back, his eyes widening as she tugged the button of his jeans open.

"Tempe, I'm serious. I don't want to chance it. Not when you're just getting started with your business and Phillip is about to go through more changes with preschool."

She came down over him, as he'd done to her, kissing him until he was all over her again, pawing, and groaning and rocking his formidable cock against her.

Any shyness she once felt was gone. She wanted him, and she wasn't about to let tonight end until he knew it. "Take your pants off," she said, tugging at his zipper.

He grabbed her hand again. "Angel, I can't."

She palmed his erection. "Oh, you *can*. But we're not going to. I respect your concerns, Nash. I'd never try to push you into changing a decision about something so important. But if you think you're walking out of this bedroom without feeling as good as you made me feel, you're wrong."

His brows knitted with confusion, and she ducked her head, slicking her tongue along his stomach and dipping beneath the waist of his jeans. "Unless I can get pregnant this way, I think we're safe."

His jeans were off in three seconds flat, and her mind reeled at the first sight of his long, thick, perfectly sculpted baby maker. He gathered her in his arms, and she forced her eyes up to his.

"Lie back." She pushed him onto his back, earning the sexiest smile she'd ever seen, but she caught only a glimpse of it, because she was already moving south, her eyes locked on the junction of his powerful thighs.

Tempest wrapped her fingers around his heavy, hard length and dragged her tongue across the broad tip. He sucked in air between gritted teeth, and she did it again, craving that heady noise. He groaned—*just as sexy*. She licked him from base to tip, gliding over the glistening bead at the crest, his essence bursting in her mouth. She lowered her mouth over his shaft, and his hips bucked up. His hand came down over her hair, stroking it as she followed every deep suck with a tight stroke of her hand. He picked up her rhythm, rocking with her. He fucked her mouth hard and fast, hitting the back of her throat with each thrust.

"Angel, I need you." He grabbed her ankle, shifting her body so they were side by side, his impressive erection stretched past his belly button, and he buried his face between her legs.

"*Ohmygod.*"

She was struck dumb for a moment, too lost in the feel of his mouth to remember that she was supposed to be pleasuring *him*. She bent her leg, opening wider for him, and he held it against his shoulder, thrusting his tongue deep inside her.

Holy mother of God. This man...

His hips bucked and she fisted his cock again, taking him to the back of her throat, stroking and sucking to the same beat as his tongue fucking her. Her insides coiled into a tight knot, and she felt him grow impossibly thicker in her hand.

"Come with me," she panted out.

She tried to focus on bringing him pleasure, teasing his sac with one hand as she worked him with her mouth, but he was too good at what he was doing, and she kept stopping just to bathe in the exquisite pleasures he was doling out. She felt the prickling heat of her orgasm racing up her limbs, burning deep in her belly, and she worked him faster, took his cock deeper. Just when she thought she was going to lose her mind, her orgasm crashed over her, and the first pulse of his release shot down her throat. She swallowed it down, her inner muscles pulsing as he worked his magic—and came, and came, and came.

They both collapsed to the mattress, breathless and sated. Nash wrapped his hand around her ankle, placing tender kisses along her calf. She rested her cheek against his leg, trying to remember how to breathe. It should have been an awkward position, but it felt intimate and sensual.

When they finally found their way to the same end of the bed, he tucked her naked body against his, spooning her from behind. His arm came over her, cupping her breast as if it were made just for him.

"I'm so glad you're here, angel," he whispered.

Angel. For the first time ever, she knew she was exactly where she was supposed to be.

Chapter Fourteen

IT FELT STRANGE to be in town without a secondary agenda of dropping off a piece of furniture or picking up supplies. But as Tempest had so kindly pointed out, Nash and Phillip could both use a little socialization, and there was no better time to socialize than when Tempest was playing guitar at the Downtown Art Boutique. The boutique was a colorful mix of art mediums, ranging from wood and glass to metal and fabric. Every piece was for sale, from the stylish chairs—now filled with customers—to the lights and batik curtains flanking the front windows. Peace flags and wind chimes hung from the ceiling, along with at least a dozen different chandeliers, some boasting candles rather than lights. There were even paintings suspended above their heads. Nash had spent so little time in town he hadn't even known the eclectic boutique existed until Phillip and Tempest had mentioned it. As he meandered through the shop Friday night, picking out a pretty pair of dangling angel earrings for Tempest and a hand-dyed tambourine for Phillip, he wondered what else he'd missed in the quaint town.

The children's boutique took up the rear half of the store, separated only by the change from hardwood in the adult boutique to plush carpeting with pastel animal prints. Nash stood at the juncture of the two, admiring Tempest as she played for a group of children in the center of the carpet and wondering how he'd make it through the weekend without her. She was going to Peaceful Harbor tomorrow for her Girl Power meeting, and she had Cole's picnic on Sunday as well as a client to see later that afternoon. She had such a busy schedule, he was glad she found time for him and Phillip. He smiled as he watched her. Her hair was secured at the nape of her neck with a pretty blue clip that matched her eyes. Blond tendrils framed her face, a few stray strands resting over the shoulder of her sweater. He'd seen so many of her emotions—happy, sad, concerned, *sated*—but sitting on that purple velvet chair, with at least a dozen young faces smiling up at her as the children sang silly songs with her, she looked like she'd found her calling. She mesmerized those children, and Phillip was right in the thick of them, trying to keep up with the lyrics and laughing with the redheaded boy beside him. Nash wondered where his quiet boy had gone. She lifted her eyes as he glanced over again, and he found his answer.

He blew her a kiss, and the adorable blush that often chased her emotions rose on her cheeks, as it had last night. He'd never forget the way she'd looked at him when she'd pushed him onto his back and loved him with her mouth. Or the sweet sighs she'd made as she'd drifted off to sleep in his arms. He'd stayed with her until just before dawn. And they'd snuck kisses every chance they'd gotten this morning before she'd left to come to the boutique. He and Phillip had shown up shortly after Tempest, giving her time to get settled in and giving Nash and Phillip time to swing by the store and pick up a few things, most importantly, a box of condoms. Thank God Phillip couldn't read yet.

A pretty blonde who looked to be around Nash's age sidled up to him, watching Tempest. "She's something, isn't she?"

"She sure is," he said.

"The kids love her. I'm thinking about asking her to play twice a month. You know, bring in some family fun." She paused, then held out her hand. "I'm Hattie Rivers. I don't think we've met."

He glanced over, taking in her bright green eyes, the multitude of colorful necklaces and bracelets like the ones he'd seen for sale in the display cabinets, and her wide, friendly smile, and shook her hand.

"No, we haven't. I'm Nash Morgan, Tempest's boyfriend." He loved the way that rolled off his tongue. "Thank you for being so kind to my son, Phillip, the other day."

"Oh, Phillip is yours? He's the cutest boy. He's got this quiet zest about him that really comes to life once he's comfortable. You are going to have your hands full when he's a teenager." Her eyes narrowed. "Wait. Nash *Morgan*? Are you...? Nash Morgan the *artist*?"

"I don't do much art anymore. Mostly furniture, but yes, unless there are more Nash Morgans around here."

She grabbed his arm and dragged him toward a door with a sign above it that read WHERE THE COOL STUFF HAPPENS. She threw the door open, and Nash's breath left his lungs. In the back of an office, which was as interesting and colorful as the boutique, stood one of his sculptures.

"That's mine," he said absently.

"No way." Hattie laughed. "That beauty is all mine. I bought it five years ago at a gallery in Roanoke." She nudged him forward. "You can go in. You look like you miss it. I get that way with my art, too."

Yeah, he missed it, all right. He'd never been a big believer in signs, but between the song that had come out when he'd played the guitar the other night and the sculpture before him, he was pretty sure the universe was speaking to him.

"I made this piece while I was staying at a campsite. My neighbors weren't too happy with me." They'd complained at first, but once they'd realized what he was doing, they'd put up with the noisy equipment, coming by to bring him coffee and admire his work each day.

The pixie was carved of wood, with wide angel wings. It had taken him weeks to get her wings just right, with layers of scalloped etchings and minuscule carvings of butterflies. He ran his hand over the intricately carved flowers that made up her hair. She sat with one leg folded beneath her, the other leaning against the body of a guitar, which was made of both wood and metal. Her eyes were closed in a tranquil expression. Her chin rested on the back of her hands, which were perched on the headstock of the guitar. He'd carved the bottom of the tree trunk into a sturdy stool, with vines wrapped around each leg. He hadn't wanted to let the piece go, but he couldn't travel with it, and it had brought in more than twenty-five hundred dollars.

"*Love Spirit*," he said. "That's what I called her."

"I know. I love her. She's my good-luck piece." Hattie reached up on a shelf and handed him the card he'd included with the piece.

Love Spirit. She is the embodiment of goodness in humanity. Enjoy her.

—Nash Morgan

He smiled and handed the card back to her. "I'm glad she found a good home."

"It's a sign, you know," she said as they walked out of her office. "Tempest bringing you to me like this."

Chills ran up his spine.

"Maybe so." He glanced over at the children's boutique, where Tempest stood in the center of a mass of children, holding Phillip's hand. She glanced up, meeting his gaze and, along with the sparks he'd come to expect sizzling between them, there was an undercurrent of something much more powerful.

"You said you don't do art much anymore," Hattie said. "Why? I'd love to carry your work."

He shook his head to bring his mind back to the conversation. "It's dangerous with Phillip around." He drew in a deep breath, remembering all the things Tempest had been telling him lately, and added, "But he might be starting preschool soon. Maybe we can work something out then." Selling even one sculpture would pay for the year's tuition.

The longer they talked, the more excited Nash became about the possibility of working toward selling sculptures again.

Jillian and Nick stopped by to listen to Tempest play, and stayed to chat with Nash. Tempest was warm and funny with the children and friendly with the parents. By the end of the afternoon, Phillip was exhausted, Tempest had picked up seven new kids for her music classes, and Nash was head over heels for the woman who was changing their lives one day at a time.

Later that evening, after Phillip played with his new tambourine—*tambern*—and went to bed, and Tempest *ooh*ed and *aah*ed over her new earrings, Nash took a shower and went to work setting up a surprise for her while she soaked in a long, hot bath. He placed the candles he'd also bought from Hattie around the room. He lit them on the windowsills, beside the bed, and on the desk and dresser, filling the room with the scent of lilacs. He set the box of condoms in her bedside drawer, knowing Phillip was less likely to go into her things than his, and he hoped he wasn't jumping the gun. But he'd spent fifteen years bottling up his emotions, and whether he was jumping the gun or not, he didn't want to hold anything back.

His stomach felt like wasps were nesting in it, but he took that as a good sign. He was *feeling* again. He *cared*. His hand shook a little as he lit the last candle, and a gentle hand touched his shoulder.

"Nash…?"

He set the lighter on the table and turned. His body flamed at the sight of Tempest wearing only a towel and a seductive gaze. Crimson spread up her chest and neck, blooming over her cheeks. Her skin was still damp from her bath. Behind her, the bedroom door was closed.

"Angel," he said, taking her face between his hands. "Do you believe in signs?"

TEMPEST GAZED INTO Nash's eyes, trying to think past the blood pounding in her ears. Her body vibrated with desire. She'd felt his eyes on her all day at the boutique, while pretty women gawked at him and men sized him up. She'd wanted to claim him in front of them all—*claim him*! Tempest had never wanted to *claim* a person in her life. Nash hadn't seemed to notice the women vying for his attention. He'd been too busy undressing her with his eyes. She wondered if he had been wishing, as she had been, that they could find a private area and finish what they'd started last night.

"Universal signs?" she asked hopefully. His mouth was so close she smelled his minty toothpaste. When she'd first seen the candles, she'd felt like she'd walked into a scene from a romantic movie, but his question and the look in his eyes brought it all home. This was *their* romance, and it was as real as the hardwood floor they were standing on.

"Yeah."

"Yes, always have."

"I never did," he said, "but in the past two days, I've seen them everywhere. I call you *angel* because it came to me, and it felt right. Then today, when we were at the boutique, Hattie had my *Love Spirit* sculpture, the embodiment of everything good, which is how I see you."

She'd seen the angel after she'd finished playing. It was stunning.

"A sign," she whispered. A lump formed in her throat from his confession, and the look in his eyes, and the candles, and...*him.*

He kissed her, still holding her face like he *needed* her to hear every word he said. And she wanted to hear every last one.

"When I sang to you the other night, I hadn't played that song in years." His hands left her cheeks, and he stared at his fingers. "But when my fingers hit the strings, it came without thought."

His eyes found hers again, and she felt herself getting lost in them.

"PJ taught me that song, and he told me...He told me one day I'd sing it to someone special." His lips curved up, and tenderness rose all the way to his eyes.

The lump in her throat thickened, not because of the things he was saying, but because he was thinking of his brother in a positive light, and she wanted that for him so badly she could taste it.

"Another sign," she said, breathy and soft. "The night I saw you and Phillip getting ice cream was my first sign. I had just thought about how I needed a sign to know if I should move in, and then there you two were. And the candles are another sign, because that's what I always used at night in my apartment. They help me relax."

But tonight they had the opposite effect. His potent male scent overwhelmed her despite the pretty, floral-scented candles, making her mind travel to dark, dirty places. She knew how incredible his naked body felt, the pleasures he would bring with every touch, every kiss. And as he drew her into the circle of his arms, all his tenderness ignited, sparking electric currents like flames beneath her skin.

Holding his gaze, she dropped her towel to the ground. "Your turn."

He took a step back, raking his eyes down her body, and she swore he growled. *Growled!* He made quick work of stripping out of his clothes, and then there were no words needed as he hauled her to him. His fingers dug into her flesh as he devoured her mouth, his cock pressing eagerly against her belly. She felt passion rising like the hottest fire, and she grabbed at his ass, his back, his shoulders, anywhere she could reach as they stumbled to the bed and tumbled down together.

His broad body cocooned her from above. Her hips cradled his. His cock rubbed along her sex as he took their kisses deeper. He groped her breasts, her ass, moving as fast and hungrily as she felt. She dug her fingers into his back, wrapping one leg over his hip, wanting all of him.

"Baby, if you keep doing that, we'll skip all the foreplay."

He captured her mouth in a blazing kiss, and she grasped at the thoughts whirling around her head. She wanted foreplay. She loved foreplay. He was a *master* at foreplay. But she *needed* him buried deep inside her.

She tore away from the kiss. "Condom. Did you get condoms?"

His grin told her he did. He leaned over and grabbed the box from the bedside drawer, withdrew a few, and tossed them on the bed.

"Hurry," she urged, rising beneath him and shoving a little square package into his hand.

He tore it open with his teeth and leaned back on his knees, pinning her in place with a piercing stare as he rolled it on. His eyes were pitch-dark, his abs rippled with each heavy breath. She itched to touch them, to feel them grinding against her. He looked like sin and goodness personified, and she could hardly believe this magnificent man with a heart of gold was *hers*.

He took her in another toe-curling kiss before lowering her gently to the bed and kissing her again, slow and deep. Every slide of his tongue brought a rush of anticipation. She shifted her hips, bringing the broad head of his cock tight against her throbbing sex. When he drew back from the kiss, brushing his hand along her cheek, and smiled down at her, she felt herself unraveling.

"Kiss me, Nash." *Before I lose my mind.*

His mouth came coaxingly down over hers, and he angled his hips and pushed in slowly. She felt every inch of him entering her, until he was buried to the hilt.

"Tempe," he said in a low, long breath.

The look on his face was raw lust and pure, unadulterated pleasure. The heat of his body coursed down the entire length of hers as they began to move.

"Tempe. *Jesus*, Tempe."

Hearing him say her name in such a sex-laden voice sent a turbulent wave soaring through her. She bowed off the bed as they found their groove, but he was too big, thrusting too hard, and she sank down to the mattress. He kissed her possessively and pushed his hands beneath her ass, angling her up as he ground his hips in slow, erotic circles. Sparks of pleasure radiated from her core. How could it have been years since he'd done this? He was beyond talented. He was a sex machine, a master of copulation. He was—*holy shit*. Her thoughts fragmented as he thrust faster, deeper, giving her pleasures she'd only dreamed of. When he sealed his teeth over her neck, the rush of an orgasm raced up her limbs.

"Harder," she panted out.

He covered her mouth with his, kissing and thrusting, kissing and thrusting, in a dizzying pattern, hurtling her beyond the point of return.

"Nash—" she cried out at the same time as he groaned out her name, pushing in so deep he hit some magical spot she didn't know existed, catapulting her to new heights. Suspended at the peak, panting and breathless, her whole body trembled. And then he kissed her again, alighting a tremor between her thighs and sending the orgasm crashing over her in one explosive wave after another.

They lay together long after their breathing calmed, drained and sated. He rolled away and sat up at the edge of the bed, ridding himself of the condom. He tied it off, wrapped it in tissues, and tossed it in the trash can. Then he gathered her in his arms as he'd done the other night and kissed her shoulder.

"I'll take care of that later," he whispered in a thick, gravelly voice. "I need to hold you."

She snuggled against him, his warm breath drifting over her skin. She closed her eyes, feeling his heart beating against her back.

"I want to hold you all night." He kissed her shoulder, and she melted a little more.

She splayed her hands over his arms, wishing he could hold her all night. "I don't want to go back to Peaceful Harbor tomorrow."

"Those girls need you." He nuzzled against her neck, and she closed her eyes, sinking back against him like his body was made for holding her. He kissed her shoulder, her neck, her cheek, and she allowed herself a brief moment of wondering what it would be like to fall asleep like that every night. "But I'll be counting the minutes until you come home."

When she'd left Peaceful Harbor, she hadn't ever imagined thinking of another place as home or associating anyone other than family with that word. But as she lay in Nash's safe, loving arms, thinking about *home* and drifting off to sleep, it was his and Phillip's faces she took with her.

Chapter Fifteen

SATURDAY MORNING WAS bittersweet. Nash and Tempest had made love two more times, and he'd stayed with her until nearly four o'clock in the morning. But this morning, exhausted and still smiling, she'd left for the weekend. Nash sat at the kitchen table designing a cabinet for a custom order, feeling her absence weighing in the silence. He got up and turned on the radio, wondering how he'd stood the quiet before he'd met her.

All this time he'd thought he was doing the right thing by being there for his son twenty-four seven. But now, as Phillip sat on the chair beside him, his little face scrunched up in concentration, Nash worried he was stymieing him with their quiet and happy existence. He needed to make more of an effort to speak and take him places. He'd had a full childhood, but he'd pushed those memories so far away, he'd forgotten how important those experiences were.

He draped an arm over the back of Phillip's chair. "What are you drawing, buddy?"

"Us." Phillip remained hunkered down over his drawing.

Nash took in the two *almost* circles with several straight lines coming out from them. "Look at me, buddy."

Phillip lifted his eyes, and Nash's chest warmed.

"When someone speaks to you, buddy, you should look at them, okay?"

Phillip nodded.

"And when you answer, can you please try to use your words?"

"You don't always use your words."

You are a smart little man. "You're right, but I'm working on fixing that."

Phillip nodded, and Nash cocked a brow.

"Okay," Phillip said, and went back to drawing.

Nash watched him for a few more minutes as he added another almost circle to the drawing and a few scribbles near the bottom of the page.

"What are those?"

Phillip pointed to the scribbles. "Big and Little and the chickens." Then he pointed to the almost circle. "Tempe."

Even his son was thinking about her. Maybe a change in scenery would do them both some good.

He pushed from his seat and held a hand out to Phillip. "C'mon, bud. Let's go someplace."

Phillip took his hand and slid off his chair. "To the cookie lady?"

It took Nash a second to realize he was talking about Emmaline. He was still a little embarrassed by his curt response to her. "How about the park?"

Phillip grabbed his wooden giraffe from the counter as Nash turned off the radio.

"How about the park *and* the cookie lady?" Phillip asked as they headed out the front door.

"Okay. Sounds like a plan. But we have to swing by the

hardware store on the way home to pick up a few things."

A short while later Nash lifted Phillip from his car seat and set his feet on the sidewalk. They fell into step behind a family, and Nash found himself comparing the interactions between the parents and children to his interactions with Phillip.

"I liked the monkey in the movie. Did you, Mom?" one little girl asked.

The woman put a hand on the girl's shoulder and continued chatting with the man. When the other little girl chimed in about her favorite part of the movie, neither parent acknowledged her, either. Nash looked down at Phillip, taking pride in the fact that their nonverbal communication was better than no response at all.

He pulled open the door to Emmaline's just as Jillian walked out with Emmaline on her heels. He'd hoped to avoid Emmaline, and he certainly hadn't expected to see Jillian. Emmaline's eyes bloomed wide with surprise.

A smile goes a long way. He flashed his best smile and hoped he looked less nervous than he felt. "Hi."

"Hi," Phillip mimicked, making Nash's smile one hundred percent real.

"Cuteness!" Emmaline exclaimed. "And cuteness's dad. How are you boys?"

Nash laughed at the endearment. "We're great, thanks. How are you?"

"You guys know each other?" Jillian asked. She was dressed to the nines, in sky-high heels and a tight, silver, glittery dress.

Nash wondered where she could possibly be going dressed like that. "We met last weekend," he answered. "Is there a gala I'm not aware of?" He nodded toward her dress.

"Dad." Phillip tugged on his hand.

"Yeah, buddy?"

"Use your words," Phillip whispered.

Jillian and Emmaline exchanged an approving smile.

"Shown up by a three-year-old. Nice." He tousled Phillip's hair. "You're right, buddy." To the girls he said, "We're trying to learn to communicate better. Jillian, that's a lovely dress. Are you going someplace special?"

Jillian bent to Phillip's height and said, "Your daddy did well."

"Jilly dresses like this a lot," Emmaline said. "It comes with the job."

"I wear my designs so they sell better," Jillian explained. "Speaking of which, I need to get back to the shop. Nice to see you guys. Can you *please* tell Tempe to call me? I miss her."

I miss her, too, and she's only been gone a few hours. "Sure," he answered, thinking it was the perfect excuse to send her a text. "She's in Peaceful Harbor this weekend."

Jillian was turning to leave, and stopped. "Are things going okay with her staying at your place?"

"Yes, great." *Better than great.*

"She teached me to count," Phillip chimed in.

"Tempe is a fantastic counter," Jillian said, flashing a smile to Nash.

He took it as a sign of approval. "She had a Girl Power meeting today," he explained.

"Oh, right. Well, we'll catch up when she gets back." Jillian waved as she headed down the sidewalk.

"I just made some delicious apple pie," Emmaline said. "Can *cuteness* have a piece?"

Phillip gazed up at him with a hopeful look, and just as Nash was going to answer, Phillip said, "Can I please have pie?"

Was it silly to feel prideful for something so small? If so, he didn't give a damn, because his little boy was a very fast learner. And in the last ten minutes, both of them had climbed out of their comfort zones pretty impressively. "Absolutely."

They ate their pie in the crowded café, and he texted Tempest. *Is it crazy that I miss you already? P and I are at Emmaline's eating pie. This is all your doing. It's kind of nice to be enjoying life again instead of just making it through each day. Think you can make the weekend go faster? Can't wait to see you.* He looked at Phillip before sending the text, and changed the last sentence to *We can't wait to see you* before sending it off and giving Phillip, who was counting each bite he took, his full attention.

TEMPEST STOOD AT her parents' kitchen counter chopping vegetables for salad, listening to Sam rave about the ropes course he'd set up for the Girl Power team-building event, and thinking about Nash. He had texted earlier in the day to say he missed her. She'd returned the text after she'd finished up with the Girl Power group, and they'd been exchanging cute and sexy texts ever since.

"I'm telling you, if there were an Olympic ropes course, I could set it up." Sam stole a slice of red pepper from the cutting board and Tempest swatted at his hand.

"It was pretty impressive," Faith, Sam's fiancée, admitted.

Sam brushed her dark hair from her shoulder and kissed her neck. "Thanks, babe."

Cole's wife, Leesa, turned from where she stood in Cole's embrace, and said, "The girls did really well. They didn't leave anyone behind, and the way they cheered each other on nearly brought tears to my eyes."

Cole leaned in and kissed her cheek. "That's because you and Tempe have done such a great job of showing them how to help others."

Their mother pulled the roast out of the oven and set it on the top of the stove.

"Smells good, Mom," Nate said as he and his wife, Jewel, came into the kitchen. "Hey, Tempe." He stole a handful of veggies. "How's life in Pleasant Hill? I hear you're living on a farm."

"Farmette, I guess." Tempe set the knife down and hugged Jewel. "I missed you guys." Even though she'd been gone only a few weeks, it felt like it had been much longer. But as much as she missed hanging out with her family, tonight she was torn, because she also wished she was back in Pleasant Hill with Nash and Phillip.

"I talked to Nick," Cole said to Nate. "He checked out the guy she's living with, said he's a good guy."

"I did, too," Sam said.

"You did what?" Tempe pointed the knife at him. "Don't tell me you checked him out, too."

"Okay." Sam plucked another pepper from the cutting board. "I won't tell you."

She shook her head and finished cutting the vegetables.

Their mother, Maisy, sidled up to Tempest, her thick blond waves framing her smiling face. She snuck a piece of cucumber. "The boys make mine and your dad's lives much easier."

"By doing your spying for you?" Tempest teased. She knew they were only trying to protect her, and she loved them for it, but at her age it felt a little ridiculous.

Their mother laughed. "Of course. Otherwise you know your father would be climbing the walls. He'd show up on the man's doorstep the minute he got wind of you even thinking about living there."

"Dad's not that bad," Tempest said.

"Want to bet on that?" Cole asked.

"Where is Dad?" Tempest asked. "I thought he was going to be here."

She heard the front door open and then the sound of her father's uneven gait coming down the hall. *Speak of the devil.* He never let them down. Thomas "Ace" Braden had been in the military only a few years before a jump landing had gone wrong and had cost him his left leg from the knee down.

He came into the kitchen carrying a big chocolate cake. He still looked like he was in the military, with his short-cropped hair and authoritative stance. "Sorry I'm late." He set the cake on the counter and worked his way around the room, hugging all the girls and patting his sons on the back. When he reached Tempest, he held her by the shoulders, openly assessing her before pulling her into a tight embrace. "How's my girl?"

"I'm doing well, Dad." There was something about her father's embrace that always settled her restless thoughts. But tonight, despite how safe and good it felt to be in his arms, she still felt unsettled, like part of her was missing or she'd left something unfinished.

"You look a little tired. Are you getting enough sleep?" He picked up a slice of carrot and held it up with a smile, seeking her approval.

She nodded, wondering if Nash and Phillip had gone to the same school of communication as her father. "I'm sleeping fine, although I have weeks of *not* sleeping to catch up on." *From late-night make outs with Nash.* "Jillian is a total night owl."

"Always has been," he said. "I brought chocolate cake in case you were having a hard time being away from family." He pressed a kiss to the top of her head, then wrapped his arms around their mother from behind and kissed her cheek. "And how's my beautiful wife tonight?"

"Better now that you're home. Want to slice the roast?"

Dinner was delicious, and it was nice to be surrounded by so much familiarity. Her brothers teased each other relentlessly and showered their significant others with attention. Her thoughts turned to Nash and his family. She couldn't imagine what it would be like to lose one of her siblings, much less lose a sibling, a parent, and then being virtually abandoned by her only living parent all within a few short years.

"Honey, what's happening with your business?" her mother asked as they cleared the plates from the table.

"It's coming along. I put up flyers around town for my classes, and I've been getting phone calls. But the community center only has the two time slots available, and I can't afford to rent retail space until I'm sure I can fill a year's worth of classes."

"And the hospital work you're doing?" her mother asked.

"It's good. My patient's chemotherapy is working, and the little boy I work with hasn't come out of his coma, but the doctors are hopeful he will." She set the plates she was carrying on the counter. "I'm really leaning toward doing the kids classes full-time. Is that awful? That I'd rather do more with the kids outside of the hospital than working with patients in the hospital?"

"Awful? Of course not, sweetheart. Why?" She began washing the dishes, and Tempest touched her hand, gently nudging her out of the way.

"I'll do the dishes. I need something to keep my hands busy."

Cole carried in the salad bowl and set it beside the sink. "Is there something I can help with?"

"Cole, honey, why don't you take Dad and the boys outside for a while?" her mother suggested.

Cole's eyes narrowed skeptically. "What's going on? Tempe? Are you sure everything's okay where you're living?"

She sighed. "Yes, that's the *best* part of my life right now."

"Are you having a hard time at the hospital? I can speak to the docs I know there," Cole offered.

"No. The people there are lovely." She turned off the water and dried her hands on a towel. "I just feel like I'm ready for a change. I thought the change I wanted was just a new area and moving my business. But I think I want to shift my focus away from some of the more heartrending parts of music therapy, and I know that's weak, and a little pathetic, because those patients need my help, but—"

"That's not weak, honey," her mother said.

"It's called picking a specialty," Cole added. "There's a reason I didn't go into oncology. Some fields take a deeper emotional toll than others. There's no shame in knowing where you can do the most good, even if doing the most good means helping people who aren't riding a fine line between life and death."

"That makes sense," Tempest said. She hadn't even realized any of this was weighing on her until the words came out. And now that she was thinking about it more clearly, she was glad she'd brought it up.

"Am I missing out on the powwow?" Jewel asked. Leesa and

Faith followed her into the kitchen, with her father on their heels.

Her father set the glasses he was carrying with the other dirty dishes. "Powwow? Do I want in on it?"

"Just work talk, Dad. No big deal," Tempest assured him. "I'm going to do the dishes. You guys can go relax. I've got this."

"I'll help," Leesa offered.

"Me too," Jewel and Faith said in unison.

"Why don't the guys go hang out and we girls will take care of the rest?" her mother suggested again.

"Mom, you cooked. Go relax." Tempest turned back to the dishes.

"Not a chance," her mother said conspiratorially, and shooed the men out of the kitchen.

After the men left, Tempest filled the girls in on her work situation.

"I think Cole is right," Leesa said. "You should decide what makes you the happiest and focus on doing that. Like we do with the Girl Power group."

"I do love helping the girls," she agreed.

"Where is all this coming from?" Her mother took the plate Tempest was washing and rewashing and set it in the dishwasher.

Tempest shrugged. "I don't know. I've always felt like I should do everything I can to help *everyone* I can. Like there was an endless well of support inside me, but then I met Nash, and I see him with his son, pouring all his love and energy into this amazing little boy." The curious looks passing between her mother and the girls did not escape her. "And it makes me wonder how much of myself I'll have left over if I continue working to build my business in all directions. You know what it was like here. I worked weekends, evenings, and rarely had a day off."

Faith wrapped the extra roast in aluminum foil and set it in the fridge. "Left over for…?"

"Oh, come on, Faith," Jewel said. "For herself. For a relationship. I get it, Tempe. I spent so many years taking care of my brother and sisters, I look back now and wonder how I found time to breathe. Thank God for Nate. He made me take a good long look at my life."

"He made you take a good long look at love, honey," her mother said. "Tempe, tell me more about Nash and Phillip."

The girls moved closer, like they didn't want to miss a word, and Tempe's pulse quickened at the thought of sharing her feelings with them. She'd never been one to kiss and tell. Especially around her mother. But she wanted to share Nash and Phillip with them. She'd just have to be careful how much she shared.

"They're…complicated," she said honestly. "Phillip is Nash's whole world. Like his *whole* entire universe."

"What about Phillip's mother? Is she in the picture?" Leesa asked.

"No. She left when he was only three months old and has never come back to see him, which is really sad for Phillip *and* for her. And for Nash, only he seems more angry at her for leaving Phillip than anything else."

"Oh, the poor boy," her mother said.

"Nash has stepped up to the plate in every way. He's an incredible artist, and he put sculpting, the part he loves the most, on hold because he said it's too dangerous to do around Phillip. Now he builds furniture, which is what he says sells around Pleasant Hill. His furniture is gorgeous, but his sculptures?" She warmed with the memories of the sculptures and immediately became saddened by the thought of his loss. "They're more powerful than anything I've ever seen."

Her mother grabbed the chocolate cake and began cutting it into slices.

"Mom? We just ate dinner."

"You need this, honey. A mother knows these things." She handed Tempest a piece and then cut a slice for each of the girls. Faith handed out forks, and they sat around the kitchen table. "Now. Tell us more about Nash."

"What do you want to know? He's kind and creative, and he can be funny when he's not being super serious. He's protective, and a bit of a loner, but I think that's because he's literally busy every minute keeping up with Phillip and his business. But he *is* a single father. A very *busy* single father. So some things get missed."

"What does that mean?" Jewel asked.

"Well, Phillip is three, but he's not in preschool. Nash had no idea three-year-olds even went to preschool. And you know how sometimes Dad doesn't talk, but he gives you looks and you *know* what they mean?"

"Do I ever," her mother said.

"That's Nash and Phillip *all* the time. Or at least it was before I moved in. From what I can gather, they hardly ever spoke to each other, but they communicate so effectively, it's like they're of one mind most of the time. We took Phillip to the park, and of course he had a hard time interacting with other kids because he's never around anyone but Nash. I started teaching him to count, and he's a fast learner. But should I worry about coming into their lives and suggesting preschool and learning to count and socializing…? Does that make me one of those pushy women we can't stand?"

Leesa laughed. "We can't stand pushy women?"

"Shannon is pushy," her mother said.

Tempe agreed. "But she's not the kind of pushy I'm referring to. I mean one of those women who tries to come in and take over and change who people are."

"Oh, Tempe, that's not you," her mother said. "But you're not a wallflower, either. Do you feel like you're *trying* to change who they are?"

"No, I don't think so. I really like who they are. A lot. Like a *whole* lot. But I see this smart little boy who was being held back. And then there's Nash, whose love for his son is so real and so big…" She sighed, grasping for words.

"And you're falling for them," her mother said carefully.

"What? No, I'm not falling for them." She shoved a forkful of cake into her mouth.

The girls watched her with amusement.

"Good thing it's not peach season," Leesa said. "We might have to buy an orchard."

Tempest laughed, nearly choking on the cake, which caused everyone else to laugh.

Her mother handed her a glass of water and patted her on the back. "See what happens when you lie to your mother? Drink up, baby girl."

That made them laugh even harder.

"I remember when I said I wasn't falling for Nate. That lasted about a day," Jewel teased. She tucked her blond hair behind her ear and leaned closer to Tempest. "All it took was one kiss for me to know Nate was my one and only. Have you kissed Nash yet?"

Tempest felt her cheeks heat up. "That's not the type of thing you ask in front of someone's mother."

"Do you think I live under a rock?" Her mother sat down and crossed her arms, giving Tempest a deadpan stare. "I raised four very *active* boys and two girls. Granted, you are much more careful than the others, but if you think I don't know about your kiss behind the oak tree at the Fall Festival with Billy What's-His-Name when you were fifteen, or the make-out session with Tommy Argway after the tenth-grade dance, then you're sorely mistaken."

Tempest shoved more cake into her mouth and looked away, utterly embarrassed. Her mother leaned closer, and with a gentle hand, she turned Tempest's face toward hers again. "Kissing and loving is all part of life, Tempest. And you've been waiting a long time to find someone you *wanted* to have in yours."

Her heart tumbled over her mother's innate ability to see her true feelings.

"What are you worried about, sweetheart? That you're taking over someplace you shouldn't be, or that you can't control how you feel?"

"Maybe a little of both," she admitted.

"Because you're not Phillip's mother?" Jewel asked.

"Maybe." Tempest couldn't believe she was being so forthright. "But it's not really that, because I know I would give the same advice to anyone who had a little boy that wasn't getting the socialization he needed. So maybe I need to change my answer. I think it's the second thing you said."

Her mother had an assessing eye glued to her. "What I'm hearing is that you *have* had that first kiss and you want more, and all that other stuff is there, and it's real and maybe even a little troublesome, but not like the feelings. That's new and exciting and so very scary for you, my careful girl." A grin lifted her mother's lips and reached all the way to her eyes.

"Ohmygosh. Okay, *fine*, we kissed." Tempest pushed from the table and paced, catching a glimpse out the window of her father and brothers down at the beach. "It was like we couldn't *not* kiss. Trust me, we tried to fight it. Or at least I think I did. I can't know for sure, because the part of my brain that usually is smart enough to make those decisions turns to mush when his mouth is near me. And when we kiss…" She gazed out the window, seeing Nash's face, feeling his breath ghosting over her skin, tasting his kisses. "It's like nothing else exists."

Faith jumped up and hugged her. "That's the best feeling ever!"

It sure is.

"So, what's the problem?" Leesa asked. "Oh wait, you *live* there. That's tricky. You guys, what if she does more and then this doesn't work out?"

"Then she moves out," her mother said way too easily.

"Are you telling me to give myself over to Nash, Mom? Because that sounds weird coming from a mother to a daughter." *And it's exactly what I need to hear regardless of how weird it is.*

Her mother's thoughtful gaze roved over Tempest's face. She wasn't analyzing or judging. All Tempest saw staring back at her was immense love and understanding.

"Sweetheart, I have always trusted you to know what's right for *you*. And I know you believe in universal signs and lovers who are fated to be together. But I'm not sure you trust that for yourself. I know you're looking for answers, but only you can know if this man is right for you. He may be the right one, or maybe he'll be the right one for *now*. You can't know until you let yourself explore whatever it is you are feeling."

She'd been ready to explore since day one, but he'd held back. She was glad he had, given what he'd revealed. It made her respect him even more than she already did.

"All that stuff about your business makes more sense now," Leesa added. "You're getting close to Nash, so you're thinking about your future. Remember when Cole and I got together? He made some big decisions about not working extra hours or expanding the business. You've said you wanted a family the whole time I've known you, so better to make that choice about work now rather than after you've established the business."

Her phone vibrated. She slipped it out of the pocket of her dress and peeked at the screen. *Nash*. She felt a smile tugging at her lips.

"It's from him," Jewel said, and the girls all crowded around her again.

"Geez, you guys." Tempest's heart raced as she opened the text and the girls said, "Aw," in unison at the selfie of Nash and Phillip with a caption below, *Wish you were here*. Nash had one arm around Phillip, who was holding up two fingers, as if he were counting how many people were in the picture. There was a fire in the pit beside them and a bag of marshmallows on the bench behind them.

Her mother and the girls studied the picture.

"He is super-hot," Faith said, then quickly added, "Don't tell Sam I said that."

"Yeah, don't tell Cole I agreed," Leesa said.

"Ditto with Nate," Jewel said.

"You can tell your father. He knows he's my number-one man, but wow, honey. He's a good-looking man, with kind eyes and a beautiful little boy. Seeing that cherubic little face makes me wish I could have another baby."

"Um…" Leesa's cheeks burned pink. She spread her hand over her belly. "We were going to tell everyone later, but how can I keep it to myself now?"

Her mother gasped, tears welling in her eyes. "You're pregnant?"

Leesa nodded. "I'm ten weeks along."

"My first grandbaby!" Her mother embraced Leesa, laughing and crying at once.

There was a round of squeals and congratulations, and many hugs. They must have been really loud, because the guys came rushing inside.

Cole took one look at his wife and laughed. "I knew it."

"My baby boy is having a baby of his own." Their mother hugged him.

"A baby? Come on over here, honey." Their father hugged Leesa.

"Dude, you're going to be a father and you didn't tell me?" Sam tugged Cole into a manly embrace. "Wait until I get my hands on my nephew. He'll be the coolest little guy around."

"It might be a girl," Faith reminded him, pushing between them and hugging Cole.

Tempest returned Nash's text as everyone congratulated Leesa and Cole. The girls began talking about a baby shower. The men devoured the rest of the cake, and an hour later, after giving Shannon, Steve, and Ty, who was out of the country on a photography assignment, the happy news, they sat out back on their parents' deck discussing what it would be like to have a baby around. Tempest tried to follow along, but her mind was back in Pleasant Hill. She didn't know what it would be like to have a baby around, but she knew how much she enjoyed being around Phillip.

She wished he and Nash were there now. Sometimes at night Nash sang to them, and it was easy to imagine him sitting on the deck with his guitar, Phillip curled up in her lap. She looked around at her family. Nate and Jewel were snuggled together beneath a blanket, and Sam and Faith were sitting on the porch swing. Beside them, her parents sat on a lounge chair built for two. Tempest sat on the steps beside Cole and Leesa. With all the love around her, Tempest realized Nash had been right. She wasn't *risky* Tempest. She was simply *Tempest*, and she liked who she was. She was *real* and *cautious*, and she always followed her heart. And right now her heart had her contemplating driving back to Pleasant Hill instead of sleeping at her apartment. It would be late by the time she arrived, but she would have a few hours with Nash and Phillip before driving back for Cole's picnic.

"I'm happy for you guys," Tempest said to Cole, to distract herself from the ache of missing Nash. "Will you announce it at the picnic tomorrow?"

He hugged Leesa a little tighter against his side, making Tempest miss Nash even more. "We hadn't planned on it, but if tonight's any indication, I doubt I'll be able to keep my wife from spilling the news."

"I couldn't help it. With all that talk about Phillip and then your mom said she wanted a baby..." Leesa's eyes danced with elation.

"It's okay, baby. I'm glad the news is out," Cole said. "Speaking of Phillip, Leesa said you have a picture of him and Nash. Mind if I take a look?"

She pulled her phone from her pocket, opened the text with

the picture of Nash and Phillip, and handed it to Cole.

He looked over the picture, the glimmer of joy still hovering in his eyes from sharing their news. "He looks like a nice guy, and that's a hell of a cute little guy he's got there."

"Mm-hm." In her mind she heard Nash say, *Flip.*

Her phone vibrated again, and another text bubble appeared, with a message from Nash. *Be careful driving home tomorrow evening. Text me when you leave so I know when to start worrying if you don't show up.*

Cole laughed. "I like him already."

She reached for the phone, but he was looking at the messages again.

"I didn't mean to snoop, but is this true? Is this how you feel?" he asked, showing her the text below the picture. The one she'd sent to Nash in response to his text saying he wished she was there.

Me too.

Of all her brothers, she was probably closest to Cole because he was the most cautious, and he thought before he acted, much like she did. She knew she could be honest with him. "Yeah, I do."

"You must really like him."

She nodded, feeling herself smiling again. "He's taking Phillip to his first community concert tomorrow, and I wanted to be there, but I didn't want to miss your work picnic."

Cole handed her the phone and wrapped his fingers around hers. "Tempe," he said quietly. "I remember what it was like when Leesa and I first started seeing each other. She was all I thought about. If you want to see him, *go.*"

"But I never miss your picnic." *Although I want to this time.*

"*Exactly.* You've *never* missed it. It's time to put yourself first. Go, Tempe. Be happy."

She felt like she was going to cry, and as she rose to her feet she was a little dizzy with anticipation and from her brother's support. The others must have overheard what she'd said, because suddenly the girls were hugging her and nudging her toward the door with enthusiastic, *Go, go, go*s!

Chapter Sixteen

NASH SCREWED THE last brace into the ceiling and secured the curtain rod into place. He stripped off his shirt and tossed it on the floor as he climbed down from the stepladder. Singing along to the radio, he unwrapped the decorative fabric shower curtain and shook it out. He and Phillip had spent almost an hour picking it out. Phillip had liked one with flowers, and Nash had liked one with musical notes, and just as they were about to flip a coin, a salesgirl had appeared with a box of new stock. They'd both taken one look at this one and agreed it was perfect.

He climbed up on the stool again, threaded the curtain rings through the holes at the top, and took a closer look at the silhouette of a woman with pink angel wings. *Another sign.* It wasn't just the angelic woman that had caught his eye. It was the magical look and feel of the curtain. The soft white fabric and silhouette of the woman's lips as she blew into her palm, creating a swirl of butterflies, flowers, and musical notes that flew up and around the top of the curtain, creating a halo of white around the ethereal-looking pixie, reminded him of Tempest. He felt himself falling deeper in love with her every day, and when they were close, it was like his soul opened and she filled all the parts of him that had been empty for far too long.

He spread the curtain across the length of the rod, hoping she liked it.

The sound of the front door opening snapped him from his reverie, his muscles flexing to life as he stepped from the stool. The familiar padding of Tempest's feet ascending the stairs caused a sudden lightness in his chest. She appeared in the doorway wearing the sexy, midthigh-length hippie-style dress she'd had on this morning, with short suede boots that made her legs look a mile long. The way his body heated up, it was like he was seeing her for the first time. She was sinful nights and heavenly days personified. Her mouth curved up in that beautiful smile that had stopped him cold the first time he'd seen her. Her gaze drifted down his bare chest, and her lips parted. She swallowed hard, her eyes lingering around his abs, igniting the fire she'd already stoked. She dropped her bags, and a puff of air left her lungs. He felt himself grow hard as steel. She stood before him, hardly breathing, staring hungrily at his body and fidgeting with the edge of the dress he wished would melt off. *Damn*, she'd cornered the market on accidental sexiness.

"You came home." *Aw, hell.* He sounded as blown away as he felt. He couldn't believe she was there, after he'd spent the last few hours trying to keep his mind *off* of how much he missed her.

Her eyes moved to the shower curtain, then quickly back to his chest, shifting between the two several times as she closed the distance between them like she didn't know which to focus on. "You...You did this for me?" She touched her mouth with one hand, reaching for the curtain with the other. "It's beautiful, but I thought the tub didn't work."

He stepped to the side and motioned toward the new faucet he'd installed. She didn't need to know about the piping he'd had to replace to keep it from leaking, or that he and Phillip had gone back to the store twice to get the right fittings. It was worth it to see the happiness shining in her cheeks.

"You fixed it," she said breathlessly.

He took her hand, the bathtub forgotten, and pulled her closer. "I thought you were staying in Peaceful Harbor. You have Cole's picnic tomorrow, and your appointment with your client."

"I was." She placed her hand on his chest, making his pulse beat even harder. "But I missed you guys. I'll drive back for Cole's picnic."

You missed us. His thoughts stumbled. She hadn't just missed *him*; she'd also missed Phillip. He'd spent years protecting his son from everything and everyone. Not once had he slowed down enough to think about how it would feel to have someone else care for his son. He hauled her against him, probably too roughly, but the emotions taking hold were too powerful to control.

"We missed you, too." He buried his face against her neck, gathering her hair in one hand and breathing in the scents of the salty sea and the feeling of freedom it induced. "Way too much," he whispered in her ear. "But I don't want to come between you and your family."

"Cole doesn't mind if I miss the picnic tomorrow, but I'd much rather you and Phillip came with me," she said. "I was afraid to ask, because it's been only a couple of weeks and I didn't want to freak you out, but I want you to meet my family. I know it's a long drive for Phillip, and we have plans for his first concert—"

"Yes," he said without hesitation.

"Yes?" She went up on her toes. "You'll go? You don't mind the drive, or—"

"Angel, where you go, we want to go."

"Oh, Nash. Thank you!" She wound her arms around his neck. "We should figure out logistics. I have to see my client at five and the session takes about an hour."

Nothing would stop him from going with her. "I'll take Phillip to the beach and let him run around. We'll be fine. I can't wait to meet the people who raised such a sweet—" He kissed her mouth. "Smart." He kissed her forehead. "Sinful," he whispered in her ear. Gazing deeply into her eyes, he said, "Beautiful, insightful woman."

"I'm glad you're home," he whispered. He nuzzled against her neck, feeling her soft curves melt against him as he gathered the hem of her dress in his hands. "How about we try out the bathtub and I show you just how glad I am?"

"Yes," she said as he lifted her dress over her head and it floated to the floor.

"And the bed." He unhooked the front clasp of her bra and lowered his mouth to her breast.

"Yes—"

He drew her panties down and backed her up—gently this time—against the wall. She stared boldly into his eyes and said, "And the desk? I've never had sex on a desk, and I've—"

He covered her mouth with his, kissing her with the promise of making all her fantasies come true. And then he did just that.

Chapter Seventeen

WHEN NASH THOUGHT of a company picnic for a medical practice, stodgy doctors with big egos, fancy catering, and a plethora of in-your-face marketing campaigns came to mind, but Cole's company picnic was held at a park near his home and was packed with families. It seemed more like a community festival than a picnic. A local band played country music on the bandstand, which was decorated with fall-colored streamers, pumpkins, and haystacks. Colorful awnings covered tables where children of all ages were doing arts and crafts, and the local 4-H Club had created a hay maze and stacked hay bales for children to climb on. Across the lawn there were potato sack races, dunking for apples, and other fun events going on.

"You look so deep in thought." Tempest's hair blew across her cheek. She turned into the breeze, sending her hair over her shoulder. Her cheeks were pink from the chilly afternoon air, but her eyes glimmered with happiness. She wore a pair of skinny jeans with the boots she'd worn last night and a simple peach sweater, and she'd never looked more beautiful.

"It doesn't feel like an office picnic. I thought they'd be hawking their practice every chance they got. It reminds me a little of my traveling days," he admitted. "The only thing missing is a beer garden and artists." They'd arrived just a few minutes ago, and Tempest had made a beeline for the snack table, which he chalked up to her adorableness. She was a responsible adult with an exuberant love of the simplest things he found irresistible. He loved so much about her, and he couldn't wait to meet her family.

"Cole doesn't host these events for marketing purposes. He does it as a way to honor his patients who have gone through traumatic experiences and come out on top. It's all about community and family and letting them know he's there for them not for the money, but because he's a real person, too." She tilted her head with another sweet smile and asked, "Do you ever wish you could go back to traveling?"

He put a hand on Phillip's head, holding her gaze so she would see he meant every word of what he had to say. "There have been times that I've missed it. Or thought I did. But, no. I wouldn't trade my life for anything in the world."

Her eyes moved between him and Phillip as she dug into a bowl of candy corn, grabbing her third handful. "That's good, Nash. That's *so* good."

Phillip didn't look to Nash for approval before stuffing his chubby little hand into the bowl. *Progress.* Just that morning his son had expressed his independence when, instead of following him around the goat pen as they fed Big and Little, he'd taken Tempe's hand and dragged her back to the chickens and asked her to sing one of her silly counting songs.

"I love Cole's picnics because the whole community comes together. I'm so glad we didn't skip it." Tempest waved her hand toward the event going on all around them. "The leaves are turning colors, and there's a *shock* of fall in the air. Don't you love this time of year?" She popped a few pieces of candy corn into her mouth and spoke before he could respond. "What most people don't get is that there's a right and a wrong way to attend these events. Most people get distracted by the pumpkins, dunking for apples, and everything cinnamon. Those are the amateurs. I go right for the candy corn every time. It's a mystery why people don't eat candy corn at any other time of year, but as long as the leaves are falling and the air is crisp, I'm going to rot my teeth every chance I get with the world's finest candy."

He couldn't resist tugging her closer. "You're killing me with your cuteness. You know that, right?"

She fluttered her lashes flirtatiously.

Phillip held a piece of candy up for Nash. His cheeks were as full as a squirrel hoarding nuts for winter.

Nash bent down and let him pop it into his mouth. "Thanks, buddy, but I think after this we've had enough candy. I don't want you to get a tummy ache."

"I won't," he said around a mouthful of candy.

"Oops." Tempest winced. "Sorry. Candy corn is my downfall." She shoved the rest of the handful in her mouth and held her palms up. "Done. No more. Promise."

He tugged her closer. "There are worse things than too much candy, but thank you."

Phillip shoved the rest of his candy into his mouth and held up his palms. "Done." A piece of candy fell to the ground, and when he reached for it, Nash swooped in to retrieve it and handed him a fresh piece from the bowl. "Last one, bud, okay?"

"Time to move away from the candy and meet my family." Tempest held her hand out, and before Nash could take it, Phillip did. Her eyes flicked up to Nash's in surprise, her face warm with affection.

After they'd made love last night, she'd stolen even more of his heart when he'd had to leave her so Phillip didn't catch them in bed together and she'd gazed up with sleepy, loving eyes and said, *I've already had more hours with you than I could have hoped for. You're Daddy first, boyfriend second, and that's one of the reasons I like you so much.* But there was no comparison to what the sight of his son's continuing trust in her did to him.

As they neared the bandstand, he draped an arm over her shoulder and said, "How about a dance first?"

Phillip nodded, and Nash scooped him into his arms and gathered Tempest close with his other arm. Tempest put her arms around both of them, grinning like he'd just given her the world.

"This beats the heck out of our kitchen dances, doesn't it, buddy?"

"Yes," Phillip answered.

"This beats the heck out of any dance I've ever had." Tempest ran her fingers along Nash's neck, with a secret smile meant just for him. They danced and joked about having too many left feet. Nash couldn't remember a time when he'd felt so complete.

When the song ended, Tempest let out one of the happy sighs he loved to hear. He set Phillip on the ground and held his hand.

"Tempe!" a tall, dark-haired man hollered across the lawn as he approached, holding the hand of a petite brunette.

Tempest waved. "That's my brother Sam and his fiancée, Faith."

Nash stood up a little taller with the prideful feeling of wanting to measure up, and held Phillip's hand a little tighter.

Sam and Faith hugged Tempe, and Sam held a hand out to

Nash. "Hi, I'm Sam, and this is my fiancée, Faith."

"Great to meet you both."

Sam crouched beside Phillip and offered a hand to him, too, which instantly endeared him to Nash. "You must be Phillip. It's nice to meet you."

Phillip looked up at Nash. They'd explained to Phillip on the way over that he was going to meet a few members of Tempest's family, and she had told him a little about each one and how nice they were. She always knew just what to say to put him at ease, but this was a big step for his little man.

"It's okay, buddy," Nash said. "This is Tempe's brother, Sam, and his girlfriend, Faith. Say hi." He didn't think Phillip knew what a fiancée was, and there was no need to confuse the situation.

"Hi," he said shyly, and put his hand in Sam's and shook it as Nash had.

"He is too cute." Faith bent down and said in a conspiratorial whisper, "Were you and Tempe hiding out by the candy corn? She loves that stuff."

Phillip nodded with a wide grin, and they all laughed.

"We're glad you could make it," Sam said. "Have you seen Mom and Dad yet?"

"No. I didn't want to make them meet everyone at once," Tempe said.

"There are a lot of Bradens," Faith teased. "But don't worry, Nash. From what I hear, you handled Nick, Jax, and Jilly just fine."

Nash arched a brow, wondering who had told her that.

"Braden grapevine," Tempest explained. "I told you it was over the top. How about we hit the arts and crafts and not embarrass them?"

Nash's phone vibrated. He took the phone from his pocket and saw Larry's name on the screen. He had ditched his calls for long enough. "I don't mean to be rude, but I'd better take this. It'll be quick." He answered the call as they walked toward the arts and crafts booth. As hard as it was to turn Larry down once and for all, Nash cut straight to the chase, leaving no room for discussion. Larry understood, and Nash told him maybe in a few years, when Phillip was older, they could work something out.

After the call Tempest said, "I didn't mean to eavesdrop, but I would have watched Phillip so you could get the pieces done," she said. "I hate to see you turn your back on such a good opportunity."

He put his phone in his pocket, struggling with the finality of what he'd just done. "I appreciate the offer, but you're not a babysitter, and I can't travel for a weekend gallery opening and expect him"—he motioned toward Phillip—"to do well on the road, in hotels, or at the opening. He's what matters right now. Maybe someday I'll reconnect with Larry, but not yet."

"Have you given any more thought to doing a piece for Hattie?" she asked. "Then you wouldn't have to travel."

"Maybe. We'll see how his observation day goes at preschool this week. Thanks for your encouragement. It means a lot to me."

"I saw a few of your pieces online," Sam said. "When you get back in the swing of things, we'd really like one."

He didn't know if Sam was just being nice, or really wanted to own a piece of his artwork, but either way, it felt great to hear it. "You're Tempe's family. You don't have to *buy* anything. Just let me know what you want, and if preschool works out for Phillip, I'll try to get it done."

"Oh, we want one," Faith assured him. "But not at the expense of putting off work you can do for a gallery. That's huge."

With the support of Tempe and her family, doing work for a gallery was beginning to feel more and more like a real possibility.

Phillip pointed at a table in the arts and crafts booth where children were coloring pictures of pumpkins.

"Ooh! Pumpkins!" Tempest said. "Want to color one with me?"

Phillip nodded, and when Nash pulled out a chair for him to sit on, he climbed onto Tempest's lap instead. The grin that brought to Tempest's lips was priceless. Nash sat beside them and couldn't resist taking a picture with his phone.

Phillip reached for a fat orange crayon and began coloring.

"Let me take one of the three of you," Faith offered.

He leaned in close and draped his arm around Tempest as Faith took the picture.

"I want a copy," Tempest said.

"Me too," Faith chimed in.

Nash texted the picture to Tempest with the message, *The first woman to steal my son's heart.* Faith gave him her number and he texted her the picture, too. He was glad she wanted it. It made him feel like he was part of their tight-knit group.

"Hey," Sam said. "Do you have plans for later, when Tempe goes to see her client?"

"Not really," he answered. "I figured we'd knock around on the beach or something."

"Mom and Dad don't know it yet, but we're all hanging out at their house tonight. It's on the beach, so you don't really have to change your plans to come with us. Tempe can join us after she's done."

Tempest smiled up at him with a hopeful gaze. He wanted to be included more than he'd realized, but he knew Phillip would be exhausted, and he didn't want to deal with a meltdown the first time he got together with her family.

"Thanks, but it will have been a long day for my little guy, and he may get overtired. I don't want to hinder your plans with a cranky boy."

"Please don't let that keep you from joining us." Faith took Sam's hand, gazing at Phillip like he was the cutest kid on the planet. "We all love kids, and Jewel, Nate's wife, practically raised her younger siblings. If he gets cranky, we can help. That's what family's for."

A wave of longing for his family swept through him. He cleared his throat, trying to push away the sudden desire to see his mother. Were all of Tempest's family members this openhearted? Would the rest of them welcome him and Phillip so warmly? Could he handle it if they did?

Tempest put her hand on the back of his leg. He loved that she was so openly affectionate. He was all in with her, so whatever her family brought to the table, whether it was warmth or judgment, he would deal with.

"If you're sure," he managed.

Sam patted him on the back. "One hundred percent. It'll be great."

They talked for a few more minutes, and then Sam and Faith left to get something to eat.

"Are you okay?" Tempest asked. "You looked a little pale there for a minute."

"Yeah. Just missing my family a little today."

She reached for his hand. "I'm here if you want to talk."

"I want gween." Phillip interrupted, watching the little girl beside them coloring with a green crayon.

Glad for the distraction, Nash searched the pile of crayons in front of him, and hell if they had every color under the sun except green. He held up a blue crayon. "How about blue?"

Phillip shook his head. "Gween for the leaves."

The little girl held up the green crayon. "I have green. Do you want a turn with it?"

Phillip buried his face in Tempest's neck. Tempest brushed his curls from in front of his eyes so tenderly, it tugged at more of Nash's already aching heartstrings.

"Would you like a turn with the green crayon?" Tempest asked.

Phillip nodded into her neck.

"Can you say, 'yes, please,' to the nice little girl?" she urged.

Still hidden against her neck, Phillip said, "Yes, please," and the little girl handed him the crayon.

Nash let out a breath he hadn't realized he'd been holding. "Say 'thank you,' buddy."

"Thank you," he said, looking at the little girl this time.

"Can I use your red?" the little girl asked.

Phillip nodded and pushed the red crayon across the table.

"Thank you," she said, and began coloring.

"Can I use the wed?" Phillip asked.

Nash chuckled, knowing exactly how the next ten minutes would go now that Phillip seemed more comfortable. Luckily, the little girl didn't seem to mind sharing, even when Phillip asked for each of the next three colors she used.

When they left the coloring booth, Nash said, "Maybe he's ready for preschool after all." He tugged Tempest closer and whispered, "I'm really glad you came into our lives."

She slipped her arm around his waist and flashed a flirty smile. "Maybe tonight you can show me *how* glad."

LATER THAT EVENING, Tempest sat on the stone wall in her parents' backyard with Jewel, watching her parents walking with Phillip along the water's edge. Her father carried Phillip, pointing up at the golden orb of the moon and then down at the water. She wondered if he was telling Phillip the mermaid tale he'd told her as a little girl. She hoped so. She loved her father's stories and thought Phillip would enjoy them just as much. Farther down the beach, the low flames of the bonfire danced in the breeze. Nash, Nate, Cole, and Sam stood beside it, arms crossed over their broad chests. Nash had been stealing glances at both her and Phillip ever since her brothers had pulled him into a conversation about marketing his sculptures. They'd spent all afternoon at the picnic, catching up with her family, sneaking kisses when Phillip was busy playing, and wishing they could do more. She knew Nash could hold his own, but she also knew he was having a hard time missing his family. As much as she loved her family, she couldn't wait to have a few minutes alone with Nash to make sure he was okay.

Faith and Leesa came down from the house with a bag of marshmallows and sticks to roast them with and sat on the wall beside them.

"Are you stressing out about how much everyone loves Nash?" Leesa asked.

Tempest laughed. "No. How could they not love him? He's such a good dad, and he's smart and sweet."

"And hungry," Jewel said.

"What? Why? We ate dinner." Tempest took a long look at Nash, and her heart soared. With the glow of the moon behind him, his face was shadowed, but she felt the heat of his gaze boring into her.

"He looks at you like you're a steak and he's starved," Jewel teased.

"You can see that?" she whispered. "Please tell me my brothers can't."

"It's a girl thing," Faith assured her. "The guys are too caught up in helping figure out his work to notice. Did you hear them earlier? Nate said he could hook Nash up with that gallery down by the marina, and Sam offered to include something in the Rough Riders newsletter about his work."

"I hope they don't push him too hard. He and Phillip are making so many changes at once." She noticed her parents heading back up the beach. Her father handed Phillip to her mother, who brushed his curls from his forehead and pressed a kiss there. "I think Mom's in love with Phillip. You don't think the guys will scare him off, do you?"

"Oh, *please*. Your brothers are like A.1. Sauce to your steak," Jewel said. "They *care*, Tempe. They are not a deterrent."

"She's right," Leesa said. "I fell as hard for you guys as I did for Cole."

"I am falling hard for him," she admitted. "For both of them."

The men headed in their direction.

"Look at these pretty ladies all lined up," Nate said as they approached.

Each of the men reached for their significant other's hand. Nash strode right up to Tempest and stood between her legs, settling his hands on her hips.

"How's my favorite girl?" His gravelly tone gave her goose bumps.

"Better now. Are you okay?" Seeing him with her family had done something to her. She wanted to protect him from their pushiness, but at the same time she wanted him to adore them like the girls did.

"We'll see you guys at the bonfire," Jewel said, motioning for the others to join them.

"Yeah. Your family reminds me of what mine used to be like. Before…" He wrapped his arms around her waist. "It's hard, but it's good."

Emotions whirled inside her. "I'm sorry it's difficult, but I'm glad you like them."

"Tempe," he whispered, and glanced down the beach at Phillip, snuggling in her mother's arms. "It's hard to put into words how much I feel for you. You've given us so much of yourself, and now you're sharing your family. It's all a little overwhelming, in a good way."

"I feel the same way about you," she admitted. "And how you trust me enough to share Phillip."

"It used to be so easy to shut the world out. After we lost PJ, nothing mattered enough to want it to last. Then Phillip came along, and I've never loved anyone or anything like I love him." His gaze softened and then became a little haunted. "And then came you, and I'm falling so hard for you, angel. I'm afraid to also fall hard for your family. I lost PJ. I lost my dad. My mother is off pretending like she never had the family I knew. Phillip's mother abandoned him. I know this isn't the place to bring this up, but I'd be lying if I didn't admit that where we are—you, me, and Phillip—scares the hell out of me."

Tears brimmed in her eyes. "You're afraid I'll disappear?"

He shook his head. "No, not cognitively. The man in me knows our relationship is strong, even if young, and only time will tell what will happen. But the worried father in me, and the needy boy in me? Yeah, those two vulnerable parts are."

A tear slipped down her cheek, and he brushed it away. "I don't want to make you sad. I just want to be honest with you."

"I'm not sad." She laughed a little, swiping at more tears. "I'm ridiculously happy. Geez, that sounds bad. I'm not happy that you're worried. I'm happy that I mean as much to you as you mean to me."

A smile lifted his lips. "So what do we do?"

"Um...*kiss?*"

He cradled her face in his hands. "Your family is watching us."

She shrugged, smiling like the lovesick fool she was. "I don't care. I've waited my whole life to find you and I have no idea how we handle the unknowns, but I know how we handle what we feel. Kiss me, Nash. Kiss me like you mean it."

He covered her mouth with his and her family cheered so loudly they both laughed into the kiss.

He lifted her off the wall. "We should join them." Taking her hand as they crossed the cool sand, he said, "Your brothers asked me what my intentions were with you."

"Oh God. *Really?*"

He put his arm around her, hugging her closer. "I told them I intended not to screw things up."

"You've got all the answers," she teased.

"No. But when Phillip was born I didn't have all the answers either. I didn't have *any* answers. But I had *love* and I had *hope.* And somehow we've made it this far. You've helped us find answers to questions I didn't know to ask. I figure maybe it'll be enough for us, too."

He really *did* have all the answers. Tempest smiled up at him and said, "In a world where apps connect strangers to hook up without even knowing their names, and *likes* and *shares* are sold like commodities, I think *hope* and *love* are more than enough. They're everything."

Chapter Eighteen

BEFORE NASH AND Phillip left for their observation day at the preschool, Tempest's parents had called to wish Phillip luck on his *big day*. They'd bonded so deeply during their visit that Phillip had talked about them nonstop ever since. He'd never spoken on the phone before, and it was fun to watch him pacing, the way Nash did sometimes. Nash had needed to remind him that Ace and Maisy couldn't see him nodding through the phone, but every day Phillip was getting better at communicating.

Her parents should have wished *Nash* luck, too. It was exactly eight minutes since Miss Juliana, the thirtysomething, all-too-chipper preschool teacher convinced Phillip to join the group for story time, and Phillip was still teary-eyed. They should call observation day *parental torture day* instead, because nothing was harder than seeing the fear in Phillip's eyes as a woman he'd only just met led him away. *It'll be hard at first, and he might even cry,* she'd told Nash. *But I've been through this hundreds of times, and I assure you, he'll adjust better if you're behind the two-way mirror.* It had taken all of Nash's willpower to walk out of that room and hide behind the fucking two-way mirror. He felt like he was abandoning his son, breaking his trust. How could this possibly be better than Nash sitting on the frigging carpet with him, holding him so he knew he was safe?

He watched from behind the wall of shame as tears slid down his son's cheeks. Two more minutes—that's all he was giving them. Then they were out of there.

The little girl next to Phillip moved closer, and he inched away, which brought him side by side with another little boy. The little girl moved closer again and reached for his hand. Phillip stared at her. Nash did the same as the dark-haired girl said something to his son. Phillip nodded. Nash held his breath. The little girl smiled. Damn, she was freaking adorable. Phillip smiled.

You smiled.

Holy shit, you smiled!

Nash pressed his palms to the glass. "You can do this, buddy. I know you can do this," he whispered. He watched as the little girl continued talking, and Phillip leaned closer to her. Holy cow. That's how friendships were born. It was that easy—and that hard, for both of them.

He was floored at how much they were teaching the kids. They sang the alphabet song, finger painted, and talked about an upcoming visit from a fireman. By the time class ended, Nash had made a mental list a mile long of things he should be doing with Phillip.

When Phillip saw him, he barreled into his arms. "I made fwends."

"You did? That's great, buddy." He wasn't sure he should tell him he'd seen him with his new friends.

"Mommy!" the little brunette girl who had befriended Phillip exclaimed.

All around them mothers were picking up their children. How long would it be until Phillip asked about his mother? Jesus, he'd thought he had this dad thing pretty well under control. Would he ever?

Phillip pulled him by the hand toward the wall where the teacher was hanging up the finger paintings and pointed to one. "This is mine. It's still wet."

"I love it."

"Know what it is?" Phillip asked.

Nash looked at the brownish-blue-purple blob and tried to come up with a clever answer. Luckily, Phillip was too excited to wait.

"It's a mermaid. She lives in the ocean, and she hooks fishes."

Thank you, Ace.

"I think it's one of our most clever paintings," Juliana said. "You have such a vivid imagination." She touched Phillip's head and smiled at Nash. "He told us all about Papa Ace promising to take him out on his boat to look for mermaids."

Nash's heart expanded. *Papa Ace?* When did that come about?

"We have an opening in the Monday, Wednesday, Friday class," she offered.

"Thank you. I think we'd like to take that spot."

As the parents gathered their children's things from their cubbies, Juliana said, "Remember, Moms and Dads, we're starting our 'family unit' in November. We'll be sharing pictures of our families and pets, so please mark it on your calendar and send in family photographs for the children to share. Feel free to send in extended family, too. The more the merrier."

Grandparents, aunts, uncles. A familiar viselike grip clutched at his chest at the thought of Phillip being the only kid with no pictures of extended family. Not that he had much of an extended family anyway, but goddamn it, Phillip had a grandmother. So what if she had a busy life? So what if seeing Phillip made her sad? Wasn't it worth a little discomfort as an adult to be part of her grandchild's life? Maybe it was time to bridge that gap once and for all and stop hiding behind their ghosts.

They stopped at Emmaline's on the way home to celebrate Phillip's first morning at preschool, and Emmaline made a special peanut butter and jelly sandwich in the shape of a heart for Phillip. He nodded off on the way home.

Nash found Tempest sitting on the front stoop. Her eyes were puffy and red, her nose was pink, and she clutched a wad of tissues in her hand. He carried Phillip up the steps and sat beside her.

"Angel, what's wrong?"

She sniffled and wiped her eyes. "The little boy in the coma hasn't woken up, and the little girl's chemo is working, but she had some sort of reaction to something, and she's having a hard time."

"Oh, baby. I'm so sorry." He shifted Phillip and put his arm around her. "These things take time."

"I know they do. It's so sad, and it makes me so angry. Life is *too* precarious, and they're so young. I hate that they have to deal with this. Sometimes it knocks the wind out of me." She drew in a deep breath, exhaling slowly. Wiping her eyes again, she said, "The hospital offered me a full-time job." Fresh tears tumbled down her cheeks. "Darn it." She swiped at them again.

"That's good, right?"

She shook her head. "I have all these new clients for the music classes, and I thought about what you said about *hope* and *love*. I have *hope* that I can make a go of it, and I *love* what I do, so when they offered me the job, I turned it down."

"Tempe, you're confusing me. You didn't take a job you didn't want. You have more students for your classes. I know I'm thickheaded sometimes, but shouldn't that make you happy?"

"Yes," she said sharply. "But I went to see two office spaces today and the rent in town is crazy high. The community center can't give me any more days, and—" She wiped her eyes and her hand flew to her mouth. "Ohmygosh. I'm sorry. I'm blubbering like a selfish fool, and you had your observation day today. How was it?"

"You're not a blubbering, selfish fool." He kissed her, tasting her salty tears on her lips. "I'm sorry you had a hard day, but I'm sure we can figure something out for your classes."

She drew in another deep breath and squared her shoulders, nodding as she regained control of her emotions. "I'm sorry. I feel better now. What a mess. Sorry. I know something will come through. It was just an emotional day. The spaces I looked at were real eye-openers. I had dreams of holding kids' classes full-time, and it's going to take a miracle to make those dreams come true. But you're right. I'm not giving up. I'll figure something out. Tell me about Phillip. The class wore him out, huh?"

"It wore both of us out." He told her about the class and what it was like watching Phillip try to acclimate. "There are so many things I need to start doing with him. Singing the ABCs, teaching him about firemen and policemen, and, basically, start explaining everything in the *world* to him."

"I'm so proud of you for taking him. I know that must have been hard, and I wish I could have been there with you."

He leaned in and kissed her. Phillip sighed in his sleep, and they kissed again.

"Let me put him down for his nap. I'll be right back."

He came downstairs and found Tempest sitting on the couch.

She patted the seat beside her. "I thought you'd want to be able to hear him if he woke up."

"Thanks. He's zonked. We have an hour or so." He ran his hand up her thigh and kissed her neck. "We could fool around."

She lay back, allowing him to move over her. "First tell me what else happened at preschool. It sounds like it was a pretty good morning."

"It was a great morning." He lifted her sweater and kissed her belly. "I think I'm going to sign him up for three days a week starting in two weeks." He lifted her sweater higher, teasing her nipple through her sexy black lace bra.

"That feels good. I mean, *sounds* good."

She slid lower on the couch, and he pulled the lace material down.

"Finish telling me, because in a few minutes I won't be able to think."

He chuckled. "They're starting a family unit in November, which means it's time for me to start talking to him about his mother."

She lifted her head with a serious expression. "Oh, Nash. That's a biggie. Have you said anything to him about her yet?"

"No. He's never asked. But he will. There were a dozen moms picking up their kids today. It's only a matter of time. I won't make a big deal of it, but I have to say something." He brushed his mouth over hers. "Do you want to talk about your work? We can talk about Phillip later."

"No. This is important. If you want to hash it out, I'm happy to try to help, or get some advice from my mom maybe?"

"I might take you up on that. I want to go back to Oak Rivers. You were right. I need closure." He pushed his hand beneath her skirt and up her inner thigh. They'd made love every night this week, but he could have her ten times a day and it would never be enough.

She pushed up on her elbows. "I'll go with you."

"You would do that for me?"

"There's nothing I wouldn't do for you."

"I WAS HOPING you'd say that." Nash lifted her skirt and tore off her panties.

Tempest giggled, secretly loving how much he desired her. "I'm going to need all new lingerie."

"I'm not sure why you wear them at all. *Shit.* Condom." He pushed to his feet and lifted her into his arms, heading for the stairs.

"I can walk!"

"This is faster." He took the steps two at a time and carried her into her bedroom, closing the door behind them. "Wait a sec."

He disappeared and came back a minute later with the baby monitor. She loved that even in the heat of passion he watched out for Phillip. They stripped down fast, and he lowered her to the bed.

"Baby, you are gorgeous. I like naptime." He wrapped his

fingers around his shaft, giving it one slow stroke.

She couldn't hide the widening of her eyes.

"You like seeing that?"

"Maybe," she said shyly, though she didn't feel shy. He made her feel sexy and wanted. She'd never been particularly confident in the bedroom, but with Nash she'd never been anything *but* confident. *Another sign.*

"Do you like seeing this?" She moved her hand between her legs.

"Holy shit. I hope Phillip has a long nap, because, baby, I want to do so many dirty things to you." He kneeled between her legs, stroking his hard length. When she stopped, he grabbed her wrist and sucked her fingers clean, his eyes locked on her.

"*Ohmygod*," she said breathlessly. "You're so naughty."

"You haven't seen naughty yet." He lowered her fingers to her sex again, and then his mouth followed.

Her hand stilled at the sheer pleasure he was bringing her.

"Don't stop, baby. I want to watch you come."

She closed her eyes, forcing her fingers to move over her clit as he devoured her. He pushed his fingers inside her, and she moaned. She slapped a hand over her mouth, arching off the bed as he adeptly found the magical spot that sent her spiraling over the edge. Her inner muscles convulsed, and he stayed with her, loving her through the very last shudder.

He grabbed a condom and sheathed himself, then laced their fingers together, aligning their bodies.

"Don't cry out, sweet girl," he said.

She'd never been a noisy lover, but like everything else with Nash, who she'd been and who she was were two different things. She didn't have a chance in hell of not crying out every time they made love. He entered her in one hard thrust. Each time he withdrew, her body rose, wanting him back.

He kissed her as he drove in hard, swallowing her cries and moving in a vigorous rhythm. Holding her hands firmly beside her head, he brought their lovemaking to a new, even more thrilling level. She wrapped her legs around his waist, allowing him to go deeper. With the next thrust, electricity arced through her, and he grunted out her name as they found their mutual release.

Nash collapsed on top of her, kissing her tenderly.

"Shower with me," he said as he sat up on the edge of the bed. "I'd suggest a bath, but I think it'd take too much time."

"What about Phillip?"

"We'll bring our clothes and the baby monitor, and we'll shower quick." He grabbed the monitor and said, "That is, if you can behave yourself."

She gathered her clothes and followed him down the hall, watching his naked butt the whole way.

She didn't behave herself. Who could with a six-four, kindhearted, sexy-as-hell beefcake like Nash naked and wet standing before her? Not to mention that the minute their bodies glided against each other he got hard again. She happily sank to the edge of the tub and loved him with her mouth. But that wasn't enough for her hungry man. He lifted her to her feet, lowered her onto his cock, and ravaged her mouth. Good Lord, he felt even better without a condom. *Oh shit.*

"Condom," she said between urgent kisses.

He stopped, a low groan rumbling up from his chest.

"Nash, the pill is ninety-nine percent effective. I think we're okay." *Please don't stop. Please don't stop.*

Fear and hunger coalesced in his eyes, and in the next

breath, love pushed that fear to the side. He kissed her again. Her back met the cold tiles, and she arched away from them.

"Oh, baby, do that again."

She arched forward as he slid her up and down along his shaft. "Damn, that makes you tight."

"You're embarrassing me. Now you have to make it up to me by making me come."

And he did. *Twice.*

Chapter Nineteen

OVER THE NEXT week they fell even more into sync. The three of them fed the animals, took walks, and picked wildflowers, which Tempest and Phillip had started putting in vases around the house. It was amazing how little touches could make a house feel even more like a home. Although Nash wasn't fooling himself. He knew that had little to do with the pretty flowers and everything to do with Tempest and his son making their house a home *together*. Phillip was as captivated by her as Nash was. After they put Phillip to bed each night, they fell into each other's arms. Most nights they made love, remaining together until four o'clock in the morning, when Nash reluctantly returned to his own room. To ensure his early-bird son didn't stumble upon his empty bed, they'd begun setting an alarm, as they'd both slept so hard one morning, they'd barely woken up in time for him to race down the hall before Phillip got out of his bed. Luckily, his needs-her-sleep girl had gotten adept at sleeping through the four o'clock alarm. And on the nights they didn't fool around, Nash loved singing to her as she caught up on her sleep within the safety of his arms. It was getting increasingly difficult to force himself out of her bed.

Parting this morning had been the hardest yet, because

today was Friday, and they were on their way to Oak Rivers. Tempest's parents were watching Phillip so he and Tempest could make the trip in one day. It was a huge leap of faith for Nash to leave Phillip with them, but it was time he added *trust* to his repertoire of *hope* and *love*.

Tempest reached for his hand. "Are you okay?"

"Yeah. Just nervous. I can't believe it's been fifteen years since we left." He put his hand back on the wheel, his anxiety increasing with each mile they covered. "Thanks for coming with me."

"Of course. Thank you for letting me take Phillip to music class this week."

Phillip continued to come out of his shell, counting everything in sight and stumbling through singing the ABCs. Nash had been surprised when Phillip had asked if he could go with Tempest to music class, though maybe he shouldn't have been. He was constantly holding her hand and sitting on her lap. He couldn't deny that he was elated with the time it allowed for his sculpture work. This week he'd even begun working with metal again, and he'd made a point of checking his cell phone often, ensuring that they were never far from his mind.

"He loves you." He reached for her hand, needing the contact more than the security of the steering wheel.

"I love him, too, Nash."

He knew that. He also knew she loved *him*. They'd skirted around the words, and he wanted to say them, but he needed to be free from his ghosts before he could begin saying all the things he wanted to.

"Think we should call your parents and ask how he is?" he asked.

Her lips tipped up in a clever smile. "I already texted my

mom. She said he and my dad are fishing off the dock at the marina. I have a feeling your boy's going to be just fine."

"Thanks to you." He lifted her hand to his lips and kissed it. He'd asked her parents for advice on how to talk to Phillip about his mother, and they seemed to think Nash had the right idea. *Keep it simple and let him know he's loved.* He'd enrolled Phillip in preschool, and he promised himself he'd talk to Phillip before they covered their family unit. *One thing at a time.*

"I got another lead on office space from Jilly." She'd picked up two more families for her classes from the flyers they'd hung up at Emmaline's Café, and this week she'd checked out more retail spaces. Unfortunately, they were either too expensive or too small. She'd been disappointed, but she'd said the universe would give her a sign and guide her to the right space when it was time.

"That's great. Do you still feel like you made the right decision?" The little boy who was in a coma had woken up last week, and Tempest had been elated. She was going to continue to work with him, as he'd suffered a few deficits, and she'd continue working with her other clients, as well, until their programs ran their course.

"Yes," she said with a sigh of relief. "I'm ready for this change. Now all I need is for the stars to align."

"They will, angel." She deserved to make her dreams come true more than anyone he'd ever known.

As the highway gave way to rural farms and two-lane roads, Nash had a sinking feeling in the pit of his stomach. His hands began to sweat, and he tried to pull away, but Tempest held on tight.

"It's okay, Nash. If it's too much, we'll turn around and go home. You don't have to do this today."

Yes, he did. He saw Phillip's starting preschool as the next chapter of their lives, and he didn't want to start it with his past hanging around his neck like a noose.

They drove past a host of unfamiliar shops. "We used to go to a restaurant on that corner on the weekends. A lot has changed." When he turned a corner, the library came into view. It was the most elaborate building in Oak Rivers, elegant and stately with wide steps and tall marble columns, on its perch at the top of a hill.

"My dad used to take us there on Saturdays when we were kids so my mom could paint in peace. He was always studying something, and we'd play around on the Internet, or PJ would drag me outside to toss a ball around. He always carried a baseball."

"You must miss them both so much. It's too bad those last years with your father were so tumultuous."

"Yeah." He clenched his jaw. Another skeleton about to be revealed. "I've wondered if he knew he was sick when we went away. We lost him so quickly afterward. I just can't believe it would have hit so suddenly. I asked him when he first told me he was sick, but he always skirted the answer." His father's even, calm voice whispered through his mind. *If life offers one guarantee, it's that death is inevitable. All you can do is move forward.*

"He was probably protecting you. As you know better than anyone, that's what parents do." She pointed to a sign for the high school. "Is that where you went to school?"

"Yeah." He turned down the road and drove to the school. The redbrick building looked smaller than he remembered. He parked out front. "I guess this is a good place to start. I haven't been inside the school since the day of his accident."

She watched him intently as he stepped from the car.

"I'm okay, baby. Really." He pulled her closer. "If it's too much, we'll leave. But the worst part was just getting through those first few minutes. I think I'm okay."

"But will you be okay when you see the people who know what your brother did?"

He'd been asking himself that for the last week. "Facing my demons means doing exactly that." He took her hand and headed for the school.

"This is new." He pushed the button on the front door and a buzzer sounded, letting them into the building. "How is that secure? I could be carrying a gun."

Tempest pointed to a sign on the door directing visitors to the front office. The office felt smaller, more oppressive. There was a time when the office had felt threatening because of what it had meant to be sent there. Now it felt oppressive for an entirely different reason. Even though it had been fifteen years, he found himself scanning the faces of the women behind the desk. Luckily, he didn't recognize them. A minor victory.

A dark-haired woman looked up from behind a computer. "Hi. Can I help you?"

"Yes. Hi." Shit, what was he supposed to say? *Hi. My brother was killed and I wanted to see if I could walk through the halls without freaking out.* "I went to this school, and I was wondering if I could walk around and—"

"Nash?"

Nash glanced at the balding man approaching from a hallway on the other side of the room. It took a minute for him to realize it was his brother's best friend, Roy Wagner. Roy had been with PJ the night of the accident. He'd broken his jaw, both arms, his right knee, and his left shoulder. When Nash and his parents had moved away, Roy was still in the hospital with his jaw wired shut, or at least that's what Nash's parents had told him.

He looked him squarely in the eye, anger raging inside him. "Roy" came out icily.

"I'm the principal here now. How crazy is that?" Roy offered a hand.

Nash fought the urge to smack it away. "We just wanted to have a look around." He put a protective arm around Tempest.

"How about we talk in my office first?" Roy motioned toward an office at the far side of the room, and Nash reluctantly followed him in, closing the door behind them.

Roy motioned to the chairs in front of his desk.

"I'd rather stand," he said sharply. "Roy was with PJ the night of the accident," he explained to Tempest. "He was in on the robbery."

Tempest stepped closer to him. He appreciated it more than she'd ever know, because she was about the only thing stopping him from knocking Roy's front teeth out.

"Wait a minute." Roy's eyes narrowed. "Nash, that's not true."

"My ass," he seethed. "The cops told us—"

Roy held up a hand. "No, man. I know what the cops said, but that wasn't true." He leaned against the edge of his desk and crossed his arms. "Didn't you read the papers that summer? The clerk had it all wrong. Yes, we were all in the convenience store, so to him we looked like we were all in on the holdup, but PJ and I didn't rob the place. That was my jackass cousins."

Nash's vision closed in on him, and he stumbled backward. "Is that the story you came up with to save your ass? So you could have this life? This career? Stay in the town and hold your fucking head up high?"

"Nash," Tempest said, reaching for him.

Nash brushed her off. "I heard the police. We were in town for two weeks after the accident. The clerk dropped the charges, but only because of the accident. He made a statement that the families had suffered enough. So don't give me this bullshit."

"Where was I, Nash?" Roy's voice escalated as he pushed from the desk. Nash had a solid four inches on him, but that didn't stop Roy from getting in his face. "I was in the fucking hospital with my mouth wired shut and messed up from a head injury. I couldn't clear up a damn thing. Once my head worked right, I told my parents the truth, but they were my *cousins*. My parents wanted to protect them."

TENSION RADIATED OFF Nash like a furnace. The veins in his neck bulged and his eyes narrowed. He pushed Roy back against the desk.

"Nash," Tempest snapped, but he didn't even look like he heard her. He was breathing too hard, shaking all over.

"So you let everyone believe my brother was a thief?" Nash grabbed him by the collar.

Tempest grabbed his arm, and he shrugged her off.

"No! No, I didn't!" Roy held his hands up in surrender.

"Nash, listen to him," she pleaded, grabbing his arm again. His skin was hot as fire. Rage blazed in his eyes. "*Please*, Nash."

"I told the papers," Roy said as fast as he could. "Really, man. You can look it up. I told them. They ran an article. It was months after the accident. I had to deal with my parents, and in the end I went against their wishes. Please, man. You know I loved PJ." Tears brimmed in Roy's eyes. "He was like my fucking brother, man."

Nash huffed out one harsh breath after another, tears filling his eyes.

Tempest knew he was too hurt to hear what Roy had said, too angry, too lost in emotion to react. She touched his face, forcing his chin in her direction.

"Look at me, Nash. *Please*, let's look it up. He was just a kid when it happened. Listen to what he's saying."

With jerky movements he threw Roy back and wiped his forearm over his eyes. He sank down to the chair, elbows on knees, and buried his face in his hands.

Roy sat beside him, shaking and red faced. "I was messed up, man. Not just physically, but I'd lost my best friend, too. Remember?"

Nash stared blankly at him, breathing so hard Tempest could hear him even from two feet away.

"PJ and I were in the back of the store," Roy explained. "We went up to pay and saw my cousins holding the guy up. They didn't even have a gun. They had their phones pressed against their jacket pockets and the guy was so scared he thought they were guns. Hell, *we* thought they were guns. PJ and I bolted. We ran to the car, and my cousins jumped in the car screaming for him to drive. PJ took off like a bat out of hell. He was hollering at them, 'What the hell was that? Why'd you do that?' and then the cops were chasing us, and he took that turn and— the world went black."

Nash's chin dropped to his chest, tears streaking his cheeks. "He didn't do it," he said in a raspy whisper.

Tempest went to him and he pulled her down on his lap

and buried his face in her neck, unabashedly sobbing as he repeated, "He didn't do it. He didn't do it. Jesus, baby. He didn't do it."

Beside them, Roy's shoulders sagged as he gave in to his own tears, looking guilty and helpless. Tempest wanted to hold him, too. She wanted to take away all the years of pain and guilt and anger both men had endured.

What seemed like a long while later—and not nearly long enough—Nash sat back and wiped his face without apology, without shame, and he reached for Roy. Roy embraced him. Tempest pushed to her feet, but Nash dragged her into the hug. And there in the office of his brother's best friend, she watched the two broken men put themselves back together.

Chapter Twenty

NASH PACED THE deck at a little after one o'clock the next morning with the phone pressed to his ear, relaying to his mother what he'd learned from his visit to Oak Rivers. They'd visited PJ's grave, and he'd broken down again, but it had done him good to finally say goodbye to his brother without a black cloud hanging over them. He'd wanted to call his mother last night, but he'd realized his father had died without knowing the truth, and it had knocked his feet right out from under him. He'd been in no shape to speak to anyone other than Tempest. Even after tucking Phillip into bed, which usually was enough sweetness to make his shittiest days better, he'd been a mess. He and Tempest had talked for more than an hour, but she'd been emotionally and physically exhausted, and she'd fallen asleep in his arms. But he was too restless to close his eyes, and he knew he wouldn't sleep until he spoke to his mother.

"Didn't the neighbors get in touch with you?" he asked.

There was a long silence. He pictured his mother's warm dark eyes clouding over. Afraid she'd clam up again, he said, "Mom—"

"We cut all ties. You knew that." Her voice cracked, and he knew she was crying. "Remember what it was like on the boat?

Daddy couldn't talk about what happened. I couldn't—"

Sobs burst through the airwaves, bringing tears to Nash's eyes. He should have gone to see her, not delivered the news over the phone. But he couldn't wait another day. Not when he knew the news would bring her as much relief as it had brought him—after she got through the initial shock and pain of reliving that awful time.

"We were ashamed. We were broken. Our baby had just died in the most horrific way, and the person we knew him to be was shattered."

"I know," Nash choked out. "But now we know the truth. Mom, I *need* you in my life. Phillip needs you in his life. I can't live with this gaping hole inside me anymore, and if that makes me selfish, I'm sorry. I know you have your reasons for not seeing him, but we need you in our lives."

"I'm sorry, honey. It hurt so badly to see him and to know you were creating this beautiful life with a son you'd given your brother's name, and…" Sobs broke through the line.

Nash pressed his finger and thumb to his eyes, trying to stop the flow of tears, but it was no use.

"I'm sorry," his mother pleaded. "It's not fair to you or to Phillip. I just couldn't stand that PJ was gone, that he'd never have those things."

Nodding, Nash realized his mother couldn't see him. "I know," he managed. "I miss you. I miss you so damn bad, Mom."

"Baby, baby, baby," she said through her tears. "I miss you, too, but I've never stopped thinking about you. I have painted Phillip four pictures. I've knitted him nine pairs of mittens since the time I saw him. I couldn't bring myself to send them."

Nash sank down to the bench, laughing and crying at once.

"And I think I've driven Bradley crazy, I've made mac and cheese so many times." Bradley was her new husband.

"Oh, fuck," he sobbed.

"Language," she said with a laugh, a cry, and so much love it made him ache. "You know, Bradley and I have this little RV. We could close up the gallery the week of Thanksgiving. I could make you some of your favorite mac and cheese."

"I'd like that. And, Mom, I need to tell you something else. I've met someone…"

Nash told her about Tempest and about Tempest's family. And then they talked about PJ again. When they made their way to the topic of his father, his mother told him that his father had never believed what the police had said. Maybe the universe had spoken to him in some magical way. He felt better knowing that and wished his father had conveyed that to him over those tumultuous years. It might have opened lines of communication, at least a little. But he'd come to accept that some ghosts would never be fully put to rest.

He sat outside for a long time after they ended the call doing nothing more than taking deep, cleansing breaths. He looked out over the yard, thinking about the walks he and Phillip and Tempest had been taking together. She made songs up about everything from the number of steps it took to walk around the pond to the *pretty pink flowers* and their *blue-petaled friends* she and Phillip picked.

Feeling more clearheaded than he had in years, at two fifteen a.m.—a time that would forever mark the blending of his new and old lives—he headed down the steps and crossed the dew-drenched grass toward the locked barn by the pond.

"ANGEL, BABY, WAKE up."

Tempest groaned and rolled onto her stomach. "Is it four o'clock already?"

"No, but I want to show you something."

She opened one eye and Nash smiled down at her.

"Morning, beautiful."

"Why do you look like you've downed seven barrels of coffee? Aren't you tired?"

"Nope." He lifted her up to a sitting position and slid one of his T-shirts over her head.

"What are you doing?" She fell sideways onto the mattress and closed her eyes.

"Just getting started," he said, struggling to get a sock on her foot.

"Nash...?" He got one sock on, and she grabbed his head, her foggy brain finally clearing. "Are you delirious? It's—" She grabbed her phone and checked the time—3:45 a.m. She groaned and fell back to the mattress again.

He managed to get her other sock on and was busy shoving a pair of his sweatpants up over her knees.

She groaned again. "Why are you dressing me like a street urchin at three o'clock in the morning?"

He pushed her feet into her cowgirl boots and pulled her upright. "I need to show you something before the sun comes up." He guided her out the back door, and she snuggled against him, warding off the cold.

"*Brr.*"

"Sorry, baby." He held her close as they traipsed across the grass to the barn by the pond. "Stay here."

"As opposed to going to a ball in my new clothes?" she grumbled. As he pulled open the barn doors and disappeared inside, she called out, "Do you remember me telling you I need my slee—"

Tiny white holiday lights sparked to life inside the barn.

She shuffled forward. Lights shimmered around each window. The dark curtains were gone, the glass sparkling clean. A bright red Christmas tree skirt sat in the middle of the concrete floor beneath a partially finished metal table and chair. A pile of metal was stacked along the far wall.

"What is this? Are you going to have a holiday party in here?"

He took her hand, flashing a smile even more radiant than the one she'd seen in the article the first day they'd spoken on the phone. "This is your classroom. Or it will be if you want it. We can put down carpet and paint the walls. I only put the Christmas tree skirt down to give you an idea of how a carpet would brighten it up."

Her hand flew over her mouth, and tears filled her eyes.

"You said the universe would give you a sign." He wrapped his arms around her waist and smiled down at her. "The universe got confused, and it spoke to me instead. It doesn't look like much yet, but we'll make it beautiful and comfortable for the kids. It's yours, angel."

"Nash." She laughed and cried and kissed him so hard their front teeth knocked. They both pulled back, holding their mouths. "Are you sure? I mean, how much rent—*Ohmygod.* I never signed the lease. Or paid my rent. Nash! How could you let me get away with that?"

His deep, loud, hearty laugh filled the air. "Do you know how much I love you? How could I charge you rent after making out with you?"

Fresh tears flooded her cheeks as he cradled her face in his big, warm hands and said, "I love you, Tempest. I love you more than life itself, and I want to help make your dreams come true, just as you've helped us." He sealed his vow with a kiss. His alarm went off and he kissed her again, tender and sweet.

"Come on. I know you need your sleep. Let's go to our room." He turned out the lights, and they headed toward the house.

"You mean *rooms*."

"No, I mean *room*," he said casually.

She stopped walking. "What about Phillip?"

"Phillip loves you. He's three, baby. He doesn't think in terms of sex, and I'm done pretending. I love you, and it's time you and I woke up in the same bed."

"Really?" She grabbed his side, afraid her wobbly knees would give out.

"Really, baby. If you want to."

Was he kidding? She wound her arms around his neck and went up on her toes, pressing a kiss to the center of his scruffy chin. "Can we live in the room with the bathtub so we don't have to run down the hall to get cleaned up?"

He laughed again, and he sounded so free, she wanted to hear it again and again. As she looked over her shoulder at the barn he'd brought to life, she had a feeling this was only the beginning of the freeing Nash would experience.

"I'll go one better. Once Phillip is in preschool and I sell my first sculpture, we'll make that nook into a real bathroom."

"You're going to do it? For real?"

"The bathroom?" he teased as they headed toward the house.

"Sculpt!"

"Yes. I texted Hattie and told her I'd have a piece ready by

Christmas. She hasn't answered the text because she's probably fast asleep, but—"

She squealed and leaped into his arms.

"I guess that's a yes to moving into the same room?"

"Yes! I love you, Nash. I love you and Phillip so much. Yes, yes, yes!"

He spun her around, and there beneath the predawn sky, a miracle happened. The stars finally aligned.

Chapter Twenty-One

"HONEY, ARE YOU sure Nash is okay?" Nash's mother, Sandy, asked Tempest as a round of applause sounded in the preschool auditorium. It was the week before Christmas, and Sandy and her husband, Bradley, were staying with them. Sandy and Bradley were both warm and lovely, and Sandy had come bearing so many handmade gifts she'd made over the last few years for Nash and Phillip, it was clear how much she'd missed them and how broken up she was about turning her back on them. Their reunion had been as devastatingly beautiful as it was heartbreaking. Sandy had obviously been drowning in grief for a very long time. Tempest was glad she'd finally found her way back up to the surface.

"He's more nervous than an expectant mother," Tempest's mother, sitting on Tempest's other side, chimed in.

Phillip had adjusted to preschool better than they could have hoped. His class's holiday concert was in full swing, and Tempest's entire family, along with Jilly and her siblings, had come to watch. Each of the children had a short singing solo, and Nash had been practicing with Phillip for weeks. He'd even offered to play the guitar to try to make Phillip more comfortable, but Tempest was pretty sure Phillip was already comfortable. His daddy, however, was another story altogether.

Nash sat on a chair on the side of the stage wringing his hands together. His guitar was perched between his legs. He looked so handsome in his white dress shirt and dark slacks, Tempest had dragged him into one of the classrooms for a quick make-out session while her family had gone into the auditorium.

"Stage fright, maybe?" Tempest whispered as Phillip stepped up to the front of the stage and Nash picked up his guitar. She was so proud of him. He had finished the sculpture of the boy looking up at the clouds, and he'd told her it had reminded him of PJ and his dreams of playing in the major leagues. They decided to keep those three pieces, and they now displayed them proudly. Nash was working on a new piece for Hattie, and he'd already begun talking about reaching out to Larry next fall.

Shannon tapped Tempest's shoulder.

She turned, taking in her sister's radiant smile and laced hands with her fiancé, Steve. Last weekend Shannon had helped with Tempest's music class. They'd spent a month preparing the barn, painting the inside, adding carpet, heat, and real lighting, and Nash had built her a wonderful, kid-friendly storage area, where the kids could reach the instruments. Shannon had been amazed and had said it looked better than any kids' classroom she'd ever seen. Phillip joined them on the days he wasn't in school. He'd been there when Shannon had helped, and Tempest had seen a longing look in her sister's eyes. It turned out Shannon and Steve hadn't actually *nailed down* the wedding date, but Tempest had a feeling it would happen soon. Maybe Cole and Leesa wouldn't be the only ones expanding their family in the near future.

Shannon leaned forward and pointed to Ty, standing off to

the side with his video camera. Then she pointed to the other side of the room, where their father was doing the same. "Dad insisted on getting every angle. I think he's more in love with Phillip than he was with us."

Tempest nodded in agreement. Phillip had taken to calling her parents Papa Ace and Granny Maisy.

"Phillip Morgan will now sing 'Jingle Bells,'" Miss Juliana announced, calling Tempest's attention back to the stage. "He'll be accompanied by his father, Nash, on the guitar."

Phillip looked out nervously over the crowd. His eyes found Tempest's father on the side of the room, and a smile lifted his cheeks. "Hi, Papa Ace!" He scanned the crowd, zeroing in on Tempest, and waved, calling out, "Hi, Tempe! Hi, Granny Sandy! Hi—" Miss Juliana hurried across the stage and whispered something to him. Phillip nodded, and she moved back to the rear of the stage.

Nash began playing "Jingle Bells," and Phillip sang so quietly at first, everyone leaned forward to try to hear him. His voice slowly rose.

"Tempe B,
Tempe B,
Tempe all the way,
Oh what fun
Life would be
If you say yes today!"

Tempest grabbed her mother's hand. Her heart leaped into her throat. Had she heard him right? There was a collective gasp as Nash rose to his feet, strumming the guitar as he walked toward Phillip, his eyes locked on Tempest.

"*Ohmygod*," she whispered.

Phillip drew in a long breath and belted out the next verse as they descended the steps from the stage.

"*Tempe B*
Tempe B
Tempe all the way
Oh what fun
Life would be
If you say yes today
Hey!"

They walked to where Tempest was sitting in the front row, and Nash handed the guitar to his mother and nodded to Phillip. They both got down on one knee. She could barely see through her tears.

"Tempe," Phillip said. "Me and Daddy want to marry you."

She opened her mouth to speak, but only a strangled noise escaped.

Nash took her hand in his, his eyes glistening, too. "Angel, you have given us more love than I knew existed. You've shared yourself, your time, your heart, and your family with us, and we hope—*I hope*—you'll share the rest of your life with us, too. Tempest, my sweet, wonderful angel, will you marry me?"

"And be my mom." Phillip cast an angry look at Nash. "Don't forget 'be my mom.' You said—"

Nash swept an arm around Phillip and hugged him, pressing a hard kiss to his cheek.

Everyone laughed, and Tempest cried harder, remembering last month, when Phillip had pasted pictures of them on the family tree they'd made out of construction paper for his family unit at preschool. He'd asked where to put Tempe's picture, and Nash had told him to put it anywhere he wanted. Phillip had glued it over the space for *mom*.

"Tempe, will you marry me and be Phillip's mom?" Nash asked.

Phillip nodded, his curls bouncing wildly around his face. He stepped out of Nash's embrace and pushed his whole body between Tempest's legs, blinking up at her with hopeful eyes. "Please marry us and be my mommy."

"Yes, sweetheart. Yes, I'll marry Daddy and be your mommy."

Everyone clapped, and Nash threw his arms around both of them, lifting her right out of her chair. "I love you so much, baby."

"I love you so much, baby," Phillip parroted, making everyone laugh again.

"The ring," Sandy reminded him.

"Oh, right." Nash took Tempest's trembling hand and slid a beautiful matching ring to the one he wore onto her left ring finger.

"It matches Daddy's," Phillip said. "He's gonna make me one when I'm bigger."

"I can make you something different," Nash offered her, "if you'd like."

Curling her fingers around Nash's, she said, "It's perfect. Just like the two of you."

Phillip threw his arms around her legs, and she lifted him up as Nash embraced them both and cheers sounded out around them. She'd watched all but one of her siblings find their happily-ever-afters. She'd witnessed perfect proposals, cried at beautiful weddings, but nothing—*nothing*—came anywhere close to this. To them. *To us.*

NASH HAD SPOKEN to every one of the parents from Phillip's class about his plans to surprise Tempest, and he'd arranged for Phillip's solo to come at the end of the program, so none of the other children missed out on their special moment. After a whirlwind of congratulatory hugs and more pictures than he'd ever had taken in his life, he finally had a chance to catch his breath. The women had gravitated across the room, talking in excited bursts interspersed with hushed laughter. Nash caught Tempest watching him and blew her a kiss. *Oh, my sweet angel. I love you more with every passing second.*

"Welcome to the family," Ty said. He'd come back from his photography assignment two weeks ago, and was due to leave for another one in a few weeks.

Nash was glad he'd had a chance to get to know him. Her brothers had brought Nash into the thick of their tight-knit group.

"For a minute there I thought you were going to chicken out," Nate said. "You looked like you were going to pass out on the stage."

"Not a chance in hell," Nash insisted. "I'd marry her tomorrow if she'd let me." The day after they'd decided to move into her room together, Nash had taken Tempest out to the barn and shown her what was in the trunk. They'd talked about every item, hung up every picture, along with the pictures Sandy had brought for them. When Phillip asked about the baseball mitt, Nash had told him that he'd once had an uncle, who was now in heaven. They'd talked for a few minutes about how much PJ had loved baseball, and Nash had let Phillip play with the mitt, which was too big for his little hands. That afternoon he'd taught Phillip how to catch a baseball. One day, he'd pass PJ's hat down to his son. And he hoped his son would wear it with pride.

Ace put an arm around Nash's shoulders. "I couldn't ask for a better son-in-law and little boy for Tempest. She's a lucky woman, Nash, and I just want to put my request in early for more grandbabies. We're having a hell of a good time with little Phillip."

He and Maisy had come to visit once a week since the trip to Oak River. The family unit at school had turned out to be quite extensive, sparking questions about grandparents and aunts and uncles. He'd gotten away with vague answers, telling Phillip he could think of Tempest's parents and siblings that way if he'd like. And his gut instincts had been right when it came to talking with Phillip about his mother. He'd told him that some mommies and daddies lived together and some didn't, and that although his mother didn't live with him, he was very, very loved. That seemed to satisfy him for now. One day he'd have to tell him the truth, but hopefully by then Phillip would have experienced so much unconditional love from him and Tempest and their close-knit families that it wouldn't turn his world upside down.

"He's having just as much fun with you," Nash said to Ace. "He's gone from a family of two to a family he'll never outgrow. Thank you, Ace. Not just for welcoming us into your family, but for raising Tempest to be the incredible woman she is."

"She's a good egg, all right," Cole said. "But, Dad, give the guy a break. You're going to be a grandfather again in a few months, and they're not even married yet."

"Right now they're all planning the big day." Ty pointed to the girls huddled together like they were scheming about something. "I give you a month, maybe two. Tops."

Sam nudged Ty. "You're the last single Braden in Peaceful Harbor. You know what that means?"

"That it's a good thing I'm going away on another assignment so you guys will stop pressuring me to settle down?"

Tempest broke away from the group, heading their way. She stopped to talk to Sandy, who was holding Phillip and tickling his tummy. Nash had thought that seeing his mother again would stir up all the anger he'd felt over the years, but when she'd stepped from the RV the week of Thanksgiving, all he'd felt was love and relief. She looked older, but she looked happier than he could ever remember seeing her. They'd both broken down in tears.

"I was going to say it means you had the pick of the town," Sam said, bringing Nash's thoughts back to the conversation.

"Been there, done that," Ty said. "Besides, I've got places to go, things to do. I don't have time to settle down."

"You realize you didn't say, 'women to do,' like you usually do." Nate pointed out. "I think we're getting to you after all."

As the guys gave Ty a hard time, Nash watched his fiancée walk toward him. He'd never been the type of guy to fall into a woman's bed, and it had surprised him how intensely he'd been drawn to her. Everything had changed the moment she'd stepped from her Prius in that floral skirt and set those gorgeous blue eyes on him. His sweet girl had come into their lives like a summer breeze, effortlessly breathing new life into their cracks and crevices, gently peeling back each scarred and chipped layer until she'd uncovered his heart and soul. And as he gathered her close, and she melted against him in the warm and wonderful way he'd come to expect and love, he knew he'd never stood a chance. She'd been right all along. There were forces bigger than either of them at play.

"We didn't overthink," she whispered in his ear.

"We did pretty well with being *carefully present*," he answered. "And I can't imagine anyplace more magnificent than where we ended up. I love you, sweet angel, and I always will."

Ready For More Bradens?

Fall in love with Ty and Aiyla in Thrill of Love

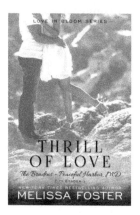

Fall in love with Ty Braden, a world-renowned mountain climber and nature photographer. He's about to take on his toughest assignment yet—winning the heart of the one that got away.

Buy **THRILL OF LOVE**

More Books By Melissa

LOVE IN BLOOM SERIES

SNOW SISTERS
Sisters in Love
Sisters in Bloom
Sisters in White

THE BRADENS at Weston
Lovers at Heart
Destined for Love
Friendship on Fire
Sea of Love
Bursting with Love
Hearts at Play

THE BRADENS at Trusty
Taken by Love
Fated for Love
Romancing My Love
Flirting with Love
Dreaming of Love
Crashing into Love

THE BRADENS at Peaceful Harbor
Healed by Love
Surrender My Love
River of Love
Crushing on Love
Whisper of Love
Thrill of Love

THE BRADEN NOVELLAS
Promise My Love
Our New Love
Daring Her Love
Story of Love

THE REMINGTONS

Game of Love
Stroke of Love
Flames of Love
Slope of Love
Read, Write, Love
Touched by Love

SEASIDE SUMMERS

Seaside Dreams
Seaside Hearts
Seaside Sunsets
Seaside Secrets
Seaside Nights
Seaside Embrace
Seaside Lovers
Seaside Whispers

BAYSIDE SUMMERS

Bayside Desires

<u>The RYDERS</u>

Seized by Love
Claimed by Love
Chased by Love
Rescued by Love
Thrill of Love

SEXY STANDALONE ROMANCE

Tru Blue
Truly, Madly, Whiskey

BILLIONAIRES AFTER DARK SERIES

WILD BOYS AFTER DARK
Logan
Heath
Jackson
Cooper

BAD BOYS AFTER DARK
Mick
Dylan
Carson
Brett

HARBORSIDE NIGHTS SERIES
Includes characters from the Love in Bloom series
Catching Cassidy
Discovering Delilah
Tempting Tristan
Chasing Charley
Breaking Brandon
Embracing Evan
Reaching Rusty
Loving Livi

More Books by Melissa
Chasing Amanda (mystery/suspense)
Come Back to Me (mystery/suspense)
Have No Shame (historical fiction/romance)
Love, Lies & Mystery (3-book bundle)
Megan's Way (literary fiction)
Traces of Kara (psychological thriller)
Where Petals Fall (suspense)

Acknowledgments

I hope you enjoyed Nash, Phillip, and Tempest's story and are looking forward to reading about Ty, the last of the Peaceful Harbor Braden siblings. I can't wait to get to the heart of that mysterious bad boy. If you haven't yet joined my Fan Club on Facebook, please do. We have a great time chatting about our hunky heroes and sassy heroines. Several Fan Club members have inspired stories, and you never know when you'll end up in one of my books, as several members of my Fan Club have already discovered.
www.Facebook.com/groups/MelissaFosterFans

If you don't yet follow me on Facebook, please do! I always try to keep fans abreast of what's going on in our fictional boyfriends' worlds.
www.Facebook.com/MelissaFosterAuthor

Remember to sign up for my newsletter to keep up to date with new releases and special promotions and events and to receive an exclusive short story featuring Jack Remington and Savannah Braden.
www.MelissaFoster.com/Newsletter

And don't forget your free reader goodies! For free family trees, publication schedules, series checklists, and more, please visit the special Reader Goodies page that I've set up for you!
www.MelissaFoster.com/Reader-Goodies

As always, heaps of gratitude to my amazing team of editors and proofreaders: Kristen Weber, Penina Lopez, Elaini Caruso, Juliette Hill, Marlene Engel, Lynn Mullan, and Justinn Harrison. And, of course, to my main heartthrob, Les.

~Meet Melissa~

www.MelissaFoster.com

Melissa Foster is a *New York Times* and *USA Today* bestselling and award-winning author. Her books have been recommended by *USA Today's* book blog, *Hagerstown* magazine, *The Patriot,* and several other print venues. She is the founder of the World Literary Café and Fostering Success. Melissa has painted and donated several murals to the Hospital for Sick Children in Washington, DC.

Visit Melissa on her website or chat with her on social media. Melissa enjoys discussing her books with book clubs and reader groups and welcomes an invitation to your event. Melissa's books are available through most online retailers in paperback and digital formats.

CPSIA information can be obtained
at www.ICGtesting.com
Printed in the USA
BVHW031834310819
557325BV00001B/178/P